Wrecked By You

A Contemporary Romantic Comedy
(Wilder Horizons Series, Book 1)

Kate Sweden

Wild Magnolias Press

ISBN-13: 979-8999002501 (Paperback)

For my husband,

Your faith in me, your not-funny-but-somehow-still-funny jokes, and your willingness to be my real-life alpha hero mean more than I could ever put into words. Thank you for holding space for my wild imagination and never making me feel silly for chasing this dream—even when it meant listening to me argue with imaginary people over dinner.

You're still here.

You still love me.

You still refill my wine glass without judgment.

That, baby, is the stuff romance novels are made of.

Contents

Chapter 1

Wilder Horizons, Wilder Baggage

"Rayann Wilder. My office. Now."

I swear, I tried to behave this time. But trouble finds me, especially when sisters are involved. I tucked a long strand of dark hair behind my ear, trying to look less like someone who just googled "how to fake innocence convincingly."

It's the full-name treatment. So yeah, I'm probably busted. Again.

I poked my head out of my door with a smile sweet enough to get me acquitted. "What's up, Summer?"

Behind me, the soft tones of my office—my sister Emme's doing—offered the kind of peace my brain rarely delivered on its own.

My older sister stood across the hallway, arms crossed and her best no-nonsense glare locked and loaded. Summer Wilder, Chief Operating Officer of Wilder Horizons and self-appointed dictator of my life, had clearly hit her limit.

Manicured, pressed, and terrifyingly efficient in heels that could double as weapons.

"What the hell were you thinking booking the McIveys with the McAlisters on the Isle of Skye? They despise each other!"

"It was their request, remember?" I said, reaching back for my oversized coffee mug. It read: *Don't Rush Me, I'm Waiting for the Drama.* Seemed fitting.

"The wedding? Fiona McIvey is marrying Collum McAlister. They want to celebrate the end of their feud. True love, clan unity, homeland vibes. All that crap."

Summer's brow arched so high I thought it might hit her hairline. "And you didn't think to flag this as a potential disaster waiting to happen?"

"Look," I said, taking a sip of coffee and leaning casually against the door frame. "They requested it, Summer. Fiona and Collum were very clear. They're in love, the feud is over, and this is about bringing their families together."

I flicked my fingers to make a point, the pale pink polish still glossy from yesterday's stress-manicure.

"They wanted something meaningful in Scotland, and I made it happen."

Summer didn't look convinced. "And you don't think there's even the slightest chance they'll drag each other back into a centuries-old grudge?"

I shrugged. "If they do, that's their legacy. I'm not here to fix their family therapy sessions. I'm here to deliver a perfect, once-in-a-lifetime experience, and Horizons is going to give it to them."

Her glare could cut steel. "Their families are among our top-tier clients."

Outside the floor-to-ceiling windows of our Maris Key office, the Gulf glittered beneath the late-morning sun, all sparkle and serenity. Around here, even the view knew how to impress—just like our clients expected.

"You're flying out early to make sure everything goes off without a hitch. And I'm sending Max with you."

Max Harrington. Head of Security. Former Navy SEAL. Full-time mood killer, part-time menace.

I choked. "Max? Not a chance. He's insufferable."

Always so damn calm and competent—engineered in a lab for maximum efficiency. A smug, gorgeous lab specimen. Showoff.

This morning, I couldn't even remember where I left my car keys. And that smirk? It's like he knows how much he annoys me—and enjoys every second of it. No.

"You owe me, Rayann. Don't act like I've forgotten about the mechanical bull incident at the Beaumont ranch gala. That client still thinks it was part of the itinerary."

"Exactly! It was on-theme. Western elegance meets wild instincts."

Summer sighed through her nose. "And don't think Brynn's off the hook either. She's handling the Costa Rica trip after that *additional* little cowboy prank you two pulled at the client dinner."

Damn it. How does she always find out about that stuff? We were so subtle this time.

"Max is the best insurance policy I've got against you charming your way straight into a civil war."

"Fine," I grumbled, twirling the mug in my hands a little too fast, sloshing the last few drops of coffee onto my wrist. "But I'm not bringing you home any presents this time. And I don't need a babysitter."

"Then stop acting like you need one," she shot back, her tone leaving no room for debate. "And you owe me some Scotch, too."

I slumped against the wall and stared after her. Her heels clicked down the hall, every step carrying divine purpose and zero patience.

This was how it worked. Summer issued orders, and the rest of us scrambled to make her vision sparkle.

Sometimes I hated how right she was. Most of the time, I just wanted to beat her to the glitter.

"Scotland, huh?" Brynn leaned against the doorframe, suntanned arms crossed, her grin as sly as ever. Her hazel eyes were my own. Same sun-kissed freckles, same wild grin. Though hers looked far less stressed.

"What did you do this time?"

I didn't even look up from the chaos on my bed: boots, chargers, and about half my closet scattered in what I liked to call my *packing system*.

The rest of my place didn't match the mess. Sunlight spilled through sheer linen curtains, brushing over white oak floors and beachy neutrals that felt more spa than sales director. Emme helped me design this too: clean lines, calming tones, zero clutter. At least, until I started packing. Now it resembled the aftermath of a boutique losing its mind mid-tantrum.

"Nothing!" I said, untangling a wad of cables. They'd somehow woven themselves into a knotted sculpture of doom, and working them loose was weirdly calming.

"I mean, technically nothing. Summer's just being her usual overbearing self."

Brynn arched a perfectly shaped brow, a mirror image of my own. "And this has *nothing* to do with us hot-wiring the client dinner playlist to 'Save a Horse, Ride a Cowboy' during that slow dance?"

I froze. "Wait... that's why she's sending you to Costa Rica?"

She gave a dramatic sigh. "Apparently, I need to 'practice restraint around high-profile guests.' So now I get to escort a group of millionaire man-babies who want to cosplay as Tarzan while comparing metaphorical penises on a jungle zipline."

I snorted. "Sounds like character-building."

"Yeah, well, at least she didn't saddle me with Max in a haunted castle." She pointed a flip-flop at me. "You're the one getting the raw deal."

"Punishment with bagpipes." I flopped back onto the bed. "Seriously, who settles a clan feud with a destination wedding? In a drafty Scottish fortress? With a guest list straight out of a Highland Hunger Games?"

"And you're the tribute."

"Exactly. And one wrong toast and someone's grandmother might challenge me to a duel."

She grinned. "I'm starting to think Summer just wants to keep us apart. Classic divide and conquer."

"Which is rude, considering we're both ruthlessly brilliant at our jobs. I'm the pretty little paperclip holding this whole damn operation together while Summer struts around like CEO Barbie."

I stepped around a pair of heels that cost more than I'd admit and flung a silk blouse across the bed, betrayal stitched into every thread.

"Okay, elitist energy." Brynn leaned back, propping herself up on her elbows. "If we're being serious for a hot second, which I hate, you might actually like Max if you'd quit using him as your personal chew toy. You might realize he's actually kinda decent. Annoying, sure. But decent. Oh, yeah, and hot as sin."

I snorted, shoving a pile of socks into the corner of my suitcase. "Max Harrington is not the kind of guy anyone likes. He's the guy who corrects grammar in text messages and irons his jeans. Who even irons jeans?"

Brynn laughed, tossing a pillow at me. "Okay, valid point. But maybe you need someone like Max to balance you out."

I froze mid-fold, one sock dangling from my hand. My brain scattered—just long enough for the silence to stretch. "What's that supposed to mean?"

"You're chaos, Rayann. Freaking brilliant chaos, sure, but chaos all the same. Max is order. Logic. Honestly? Maybe that's exactly why you'd be good for each other."

My fingers started tapping out some anxious Morse code against my thigh before I even realized it.

I opened my mouth to argue, but... damn it, she wasn't wrong. I was chaos—messy, impulsive, allergic to routine—and Max? Max was control in a dress shirt. Calm. Steady. Maddeningly perfect.

"Not happening," I said finally, slamming the suitcase shut with the finality of a debt collector collecting in full.

Brynn shrugged, grabbing a scarf from the bed. "Fine, but don't say I didn't warn you when you come back all heart-eyes over him."

"Get out." I threw the pillow back at her, laughing despite myself.

She stood, but before leaving, she paused in the doorway, her expression softer now. "Seriously, though, don't let Summer or Max get to you. Our clients adore you. You're the one they always ask for by name. You've got this, Ray."

Even after she left, her voice lingered, tangled up with my charging cables and self-doubt. I gathered the last of the chaos, but the knot in my chest pulled tighter with every folded shirt.

Maybe I need a Max in my life. I yanked the zipper shut with the aggression of someone who'd just lost an argument to her suitcase, then snorted. Or maybe I just need noise-canceling headphones and a Xanax.

My phone buzzed on the nightstand. I ignored it for thirty seconds—an eternity, really—before curiosity won.

Max. Of course. Because apparently the universe was feeling petty.

Chapter 2

How to Humiliate Yourself Before a Long-Haul Flight

SUBJECT: SCOTLAND ITINERARY REVIEW

Rayann, I've attached the finalized itinerary for the McIvey-McAlister wedding event. Please review and confirm alignment with their requests before we depart. Additionally, I've highlighted potential points of conflict and suggested mitigations for each.

Let's aim for zero surprises. Max Harrington

My eyes narrowed. *Zero surprises?* Was that a subtle dig at me, or was he just being his usual pain-in-the-ass, micromanaging self? Probably both.

I clicked the attachment, and sure enough, it was peak Max: everything neatly color-coded in a three-column spreadsheet with headings like *Security Risk Assessment, Emergency Response Protocols,* and *Client Comfort Ratings.* There was even a contingency plan for "Unforeseen Environmental Hazards," because apparently Max thought he could predict avalanches and schedule the fucking sunshine.

I snorted. He clearly thought the spreadsheet made him look competent. It didn't. It just made him look like someone who spent his Friday nights reorganizing his sock drawer.

I grabbed my phone and typed out a quick reply:

Subject: Re: Scotland Itinerary Review

Max, Got it. But FYI, I'm not a robot, so don't expect me to stick to your script. The McIveys hired us for a once-in-a-lifetime experience. A little wiggle room isn't always a bad thing. And "zero surprises"? Come on. Surprises are half the fun. You should try them sometime. Who knows—you might even like it. See you at the airport. Don't forget your color-coded passport. Rayann

I hit send and smirked, already picturing him rolling his eyes. A few minutes later, my phone buzzed again.

Subject: Re: Re: Scotland Itinerary Review

Rayann, Surprises might make life interesting for you, but for clients, they make life stressful and expensive. Let's stick to the plan. I've attached an additional checklist to help ensure we stay on schedule. Please review it so we're aligned.

For the record, the McIveys hired us to handle logistics and security so they could enjoy their once-in-a-lifetime experience—without unnecessary chaos.

See you at the airport. Don't forget your passport. Or your checklist. Max

My jaw dropped. A checklist? He had to be kidding.

I opened the attachment, and there it was.

Rayann's Pre-Departure Essentials.

- **Review itinerary (attached)**

- **Confirm hotel and transportation details**

- **Pack appropriately for weather conditions (see forecast in column E)**

- **Arrive at airport two hours early**

- **Avoid unnecessary deviations from itinerary**

The words blurred as a hot prickle of annoyance crept up my neck. My pre-departure essentials? Like I was some rookie who'd just stumbled into her first big-girl job?

"Oh, you're an ass," I muttered, clutching my phone tighter. My thumb hovered over the delete button. Tempting. But no—that would give him too much satisfaction.

Instead, I let my irritation drive my fingers across the screen.

Subject: Re: Re: Re: Scotland Itinerary Review

Appreciate the checklist, Boss. Super helpful. Really. Don't worry—I packed my big-girl pants and everything.

See you at the airport. Try not to stress too much. I hear chaos builds character. Rayann

I hit send with a jab at the screen. Summer ran my weekdays—Max didn't get to take the weekends.

The room fell quiet. Just the hum of the ceiling fan and the simmer of my frustration. I reached for the leather-bound travel journal on the nightstand. It had been Dad's, full of messy handwriting, doodles, and postcards from every corner of the world.

The first page always stopped me.

"The world is wide, and life is short. Don't waste it standing still."

I ran my fingers over the words, my chest tightening.

Dad had lived by that mantra, growing Wilder Horizons into a jet-setting empire built on one promise—flawless, unforgettable experiences for clients who refused to settle for anything less. But I sometimes wondered if he knew what he was asking when he tied our inheritance to the company.

Work together or walk away. That was the deal. And while I loved my sisters, working with them was a whole other beast. Six sisters. One empire. A miracle we hadn't killed each other yet.

I flipped to a random page—something about hiking through Patagonia, complete with a sketch of a mountain that looked more like a lopsided pyramid. I smiled despite myself.

"Don't waste it standing still," I murmured, closing the journal.

Late the next afternoon, I sprinted through the terminal, carry-on thumping against my thigh like it had a grudge. Boarding calls echoed overhead, but there was no way I was boarding a ten-hour flight without a caramel macchiato.

Sure, I was cutting it close. Max was probably already at the gate, checking his watch and mentally adding this to my list of professional failings. But flying internationally *and* dealing with Max's smug face without caffeine? Not happening.

Somewhere behind me, a barista was likely cursing me for stealing the last to-go sleeve before the lid clicked on properly. I took a sip anyway—and promptly dribbled caramel foam down my blouse.

Perfect. Max was going to love this.

He wasn't hard to spot.

Crisp button-down, perfectly pressed slacks, jacket folded just so. He looked like a damn business magazine cover—*not* someone escorting a feuding clan through the Highlands. He smelled like clean laundry and something sharp. Probably cedarwood. Or smug bastard cologne.

"You're late," he said as I skidded to a stop in front of him. His voice was low, clipped, and clearly engineered to get under my skin. He gave me the once-over, from the sweat-slick flyaways escaping my humidity-murdered bun to the sheen on my chest. His gaze lingered a half-second too long, but I let it slide.

I took a long, defiant sip of my coffee. "Good afternoon to you too, Max."

He cocked his head. Jaw tight. The look of a man counting to ten through gritted teeth. "You're holding us up," he said. "I told Summer I'd keep this trip on track. Didn't realize that included babysitting."

I nearly choked. "Babysitter? Please. You're here because Summer *thinks* I need one. I don't."

I yanked my bag upright for dramatic effect—which immediately tipped over, spilling everything across the floor.

Max sighed. Of course he knelt to help. Neatly stacked folders and guides with the quiet precision of a man mentally reorganizing my life choices.

"Your bag's unzipped," he said.

"Thanks, Captain Obvious," I muttered, diving for my toiletries bag before it rolled into someone's foot.

And then I saw it.

My vibrator.

Bright pink, bold as hell, and nestled right between my hairbrush and a travel guide to Scotland.

Max's hand hovered over it, frozen mid-reach. His eyes flicked to mine. Then back to it. "Is this...?" His voice trailed off as his lips twitched.

"Don't!" I hissed, snatching it and jamming it back in the bag. "Not a word, Harrington."

He stood and brushed invisible lint from his slacks, expression maddeningly calm. "I was just going to say… you're very thorough with your packing."

My cheeks went nuclear. "I hate you."

"That's fair," he said, grinning now. "But it's the wrong kind of batteries for the scanners. Might want to bury it deeper next time."

"It was a stylistic choice," I snapped, stuffing the rest of my things away.

His lips twitched again. "Stylistic or not, maybe aim for on time. The clients expect us to set the tone."

"The clients aren't even on this flight!" I flailed toward the boarding line and sloshed coffee on my sleeve.

Max gave me *the* look—part exasperation, part amusement, full-on maddening. "Let me guess," he said. "You stopped for coffee instead of checking the clock."

"No," I said too quickly.

He leaned in just enough to drop his voice. "Rayann, you have whipped cream on your nose."

Heat flared across my cheeks as I wiped my face and glared. He chuckled.

"You know what, Max? If you're going to spend this whole trip radiating self-importance, maybe you should fly solo."

"I'd love to," he said, grabbing his bag. "But someone has to make sure you don't burn down Scotland."

Before I could reply, he turned and walked off—composed, unbothered, and so pleased with himself I wanted to trip him.

I stared after him, clutching my coffee like it owed me emotional support. The faint scent of vanilla and steamed milk curled around me—warm, ridiculous, and entirely on brand for the morning I was having. Coffee-stained sleeves. Half-zipped bag. Hair doing its own thing. Not exactly the poised professional I usually presented to clients.

I hated him.

Except I didn't.

And that was the worst part.

Boarding Group 1—Now Boarding.

The alert lit up on my phone. I shoved it away and grabbed my bag. Time to get this over with.

I stepped onto the plane, praying for a peaceful, Max-free row to salvage the disaster of my morning.

Then I saw him.

Aisle seat. Calm. Already sipping something from a paper cup.

My row.

Of course it was.

Chapter 3

The Flight From Hell (Or Heaven, Depending on Who You Ask)

I STOPPED SHORT, MY carry-on smacking straight into the knee of the burly guy behind me.

"Excuse me," he grumbled, shoving past me.

"Seriously?" I muttered.

Max glanced up from his laptop, his expression neutral. "You're blocking traffic, Rayann."

Dread pooled in my gut as I looked down at my boarding pass. Then back at the only open seat in the row. Right next to him.

I blinked. Then looked again, as if the numbers would magically rearrange themselves.

"Oh, *hell* no. I'd rather sit in cargo."

Max released a long-suffering sigh and finally looked up. "What now?"

"I'm sitting *here*?" I gestured at the empty seat beside him, like it was a hazard the flight crew should be aware of.

"Afraid so. Perks of checking in early," he said, adjusting his tray table like he owned the airline.

"This can't be right," I mumbled, shifting my weight as I checked my boarding pass again. Maybe I'd read it wrong. Maybe there was another 14B. Maybe the universe wasn't actually plotting against me.

Nope. No such luck. I glanced around the rest of the business class section. Not a single open seat in sight.

Max arched a brow. "Need me to explain basic airline seating assignments to you?"

I blew out a breath and yanked open the overhead bin, shoving my suitcase inside with a little more force than necessary. "I don't need anything from you, Harrington."

He hummed, clearly unconvinced.

I dropped into the seat with a dramatic sigh and crossed my arms. "Fine." I yanked off my sweatshirt and shoved it into my bag, then tugged my tank top straight. Grumbling, I pulled out my favorite blanket. "But don't expect me to share the armrests."

Max smirked, stretching out with blatant precision to stake his claim on neutral territory. "Noted."

I narrowed my eyes. "Oh, bite me, Harrington."

"Tempting," he murmured, resuming his work like this was the most normal thing in the world.

Three hours in, I was regretting everything.

Max, of course, was the perfect seatmate. Quiet. Organized. Not even a hint of legroom encroachment. It was maddening.

Meanwhile, I had adjusted my blanket five times, flipped through every in-flight movie twice, and was currently staring at the ceiling wondering how many hours of my life I had left. I peeked at Max over the edge of my eye mask. He was reading now. Of course he was. "You don't even recline your seat, do you?" I asked, kicking at his foot lightly.

He didn't so much as flinch. "Reclining is inconsiderate to the person behind you," he replied, eyes still scanning the page, treating me as a mild disturbance in his perfectly curated travel experience.

I let out a slow, dramatic sigh. "Of course you'd say that. I bet you've never broken a rule in your life."

His lips quirked slightly. "I color outside the lines sometimes." He turned the page. "Just not where airplane etiquette is concerned."

I threw my hands up. "Oh, how thrilling," I drawled, tossing my blanket dramatically over my lap. "Remind me to alert the tabloids when we land. *Max Harrington, Rebel Without a Cause—Refuses to Recline Seat in Act of Daring Defiance.*"

That earned me a side glance. The kind that said *I'm not engaging with your nonsense*—which, naturally, only encouraged me further.

"You probably schedule your rebellious moments, don't you?" I pressed, tapping my chin. "Let me guess—*Tuesday, 6:15 p.m.: Eat dessert before dinner.*"

Max exhaled sharply—almost a laugh, but not quite. "Friday," he corrected. "And only if the dessert is worth it."

I blinked. "Oh my God. You *do* schedule them."

The ghost of a smile flickered across his lips. "I like structure."

"No, you like spreadsheets." I stretched, purposefully bumping my ankle into his. "It's fine. We all have our kinks."

His eyes lifted from the book then, just briefly, but the look alone sent a slow, unexpected shiver down my spine. That same woodsy scent hovered between us.

"Is that what you think?" he murmured, his voice as smooth and unreadable as ever.

My brain short-circuited for a split second before I scoffed. "Whatever, Harrington. Enjoy your rules."

I leaned back in my seat and yanked my eye mask down, pretending that single glance hadn't made me feel just a little bit warm.

Four hours in, things took a turn.

Or rather, Max's leg did.

I squinted down at the offending limb before nudging him with my elbow. "Your leg is in my space."

"No, it's not," he replied, not even looking up from his book.

At first, I thought I imagined it. But there it was—his giant, smug-ass foot, making itself at home with all the entitlement of a foreign dignitary. I leveled a glare and jabbed it with the toe of my shoe.

"Move."

He didn't even blink. Just flipped the page, unbothered as if I'd barely ruffled the air.

"I am moved."

"No, you're not. You're trespassing."

He turned a page, completely unfazed. "I don't think territorial disputes apply in business class."

I didn't bother hiding the sigh as I kicked his leg back where it belonged.

He sighed, long and suffering, but shifted. Barely. Just enough to make it clear this wasn't surrender. Fine. If he wanted to play this game, so could I. I stretched out my legs, letting my knee gently bump against his.

Max finally glanced at me over the top of his book. "Are you seriously doing this right now?"

I gave him my most innocent smile. "Doing what?"

His lips curved ever-so-slightly, but he didn't move. Neither did I.

We sat there, legs pressed together, neither of us blinking, locked in the pettiest game of in-flight dominance ever. Max exhaled through his nose, weighing whether I was worth the effort. Then, slowly, he leaned back in his seat and stretched farther, his thigh brushing mine in a casual claim of territory.

I sucked in a sharp breath. Was he *breaking his rule?*

Oh. Oh, it was on.

I dropped my foot deliberately against his, pretending to get comfortable. "Oops."

He arched a brow. "Oops?"

"Yeah, turbulence." I gestured vaguely at the completely smooth flight.

Max hummed quietly, amusement flickering across his face as he turned the page. That smirk? 100% intentional, and he damn well knew it.

Our legs pressed together, firm and defiant, neither of us willing to give an inch.

Legroom dominance became the battlefield—and the fight was on.

By hour five, we were both in survival mode.

I couldn't sleep. Max wouldn't stop reading. And every time the flight attendant walked by, she gave us that knowing look—the kind that screamed *oh, you two are so that couple.* Finally, I couldn't take it anymore. I shifted in my seat, angling toward him. "You're seriously committing to that book the entire flight?"

Max turned a page, completely unfazed. "Do you have a better suggestion?"

I tilted my head, pretending to consider. "Yeah." I leaned in slightly, lowering my voice like I was about to share a scandalous secret. "Try relaxing. You could at least *pretend* to be human."

He finally set the book down, his gaze lifting to mine for the first time in hours. The air between us shifted—heavy, electric. Unwelcome somersault in my stomach, party of one.

"This *is* me relaxing," he said, voice low and steady.

My eyes dropped to the title: *The Count of Monte Cristo*.

Of course. He's reading a thousand-page revenge saga with the intensity of a man planning a tactical op. Totally normal. Totally relaxing.

And damn it, that shouldn't have been hot. But my pulse betrayed me, picking up like it *knew* how close he was. Like it *knew* his stupidly steady breathing and unreadable expression were turning me inside out. I huffed, leaning back so fast I nearly smacked my head on the seat. I snatched up the in-flight magazine, flipping through it with unnecessary force. "Well, you're doing it wrong," I muttered, my voice tighter than I wanted it to be.

From the corner of my eye, I caught what might've been a flicker of gratification. Max Harrington, Mr. Uptight, Mr. Zero Surprises, was enjoying this.

And that was unacceptable.

I needed to win this round. I can be in control too.

I turned another page, feigning deep interest in an article about *The Top Ten Castle Destinations in Europe*. "Bet you haven't even napped once," I said, still watching him through my lashes. "Go on. Take a break. I'll keep an eye on things around here for a bit."

Max's head tilted, his smirk deepening just slightly. "Not a chance."

Damn him.

By the time we landed, I was exhausted, annoyed, and completely off-balance. Max, of course, looked completely unruffled as he retrieved his perfectly packed carry-on from the overhead bin. Not a wrinkle in his shirt, not a hair out of place, like the ten-hour flight had happened to everyone else but him. But that scruff? A five o'clock shadow sharp enough to rewrite a girl's moral compass. He slung the bag over his shoulder and glanced at me, his smirk subtle, but it lit my blood on fire anyway. "Welcome to Scotland. Try not to make me regret this."

"Give it a day. I'll have you in a kilt, smiling as if you were born here." I grabbed my bag and hauled it off the plane with the last scraps of energy I had.

My grin? Smug as hell.

My exit? Not so much. My carry-on caught on the seat, nearly launching me into the aisle.

Max's hand shot out, steadying me with one annoyingly steady grip on my arm.

"Careful," he said, calm and infuriating.

I yanked my arm back, heat crawling up my neck. "I'm fine. Thanks."

His hand lingered in the air for half a second before he dropped it, stepping back to let me pass. "Don't get too comfortable," he said as we walked off the plane, his voice low enough that only I could hear. "You're about to be way out of your depth."

I snorted, tightening my grip on my bag. "Please. I *invented* depth."

He hummed, his stride just a little too confident as we exited the terminal.

But as we reached customs, I couldn't shake the knot twisting in my stomach. It wasn't just the exhaustion, or the annoyance, or the fact that I'd been stuck in that seat for hours.

It was him.

I adjusted my grip and forced myself to breathe. Nearly ten hours of turbulence, both literal and Max-induced, and the trip hadn't even started.

If Max Harrington didn't kill me by the end of this trip, it'd be because he got distracted bending me over a security checkpoint.

Jesus. What is wrong with me?

Chapter 4

Welcome to Scotland: Would You Like a Disaster with That?

THE MOMENT WE STEPPED into the grand lobby of the castle-turned-luxury-resort, I nearly melted into the floor. Not from awe (though the vaulted ceilings, centuries-old chandeliers, and massive roaring fireplace were objectively impressive), but from sheer, bone-deep exhaustion. The air smelled like aged wood, hearth smoke, and something faintly floral—elegant and old-world, like the castle itself wore its own signature cologne.

Night flights were brutal.

The concierge, a handsome older gentleman in a perfectly pressed suit, beamed as I approached the counter. "Welcome to Castle Glenmara, Ms. Wilder. Mr. Harrington," he added with a polite but notably less enthusiastic nod in Max's direction.

I shot Max a smirk. See? People like me.

He didn't bite, just stood beside me scrolling through his phone with an air of practiced indifference.

"Two suites, just as arranged," I said smoothly, tapping the counter. "I triple-checked."

The concierge smiled, sliding our key cards across the polished surface. "Indeed, Ms. Wilder. You're in the East Wing, and Mr. Harrington is in the North."

I exhaled, already envisioning a steaming bath and at least an hour free of Max-induced tension. "Fabulous."

The concierge's gaze lingered on me with a friendly smile, maybe a little too friendly judging by the subtle clench of Max's jaw.

"If there's anything you need, Ms. Wilder," he said warmly, "our butler service is available 24/7."

I perked up. "That sounds dangerous."

The concierge chuckled. "Not at all. We're here to make your stay as seamless as possible."

I tapped the counter, considering. "Okay, be honest—what's the most outrageous request you've ever gotten?"

His smile widened. "We once arranged for a bagpipe player to wake a guest every morning."

I grinned, glancing at Max. "That is spectacular. I mean, who needs an alarm clock when you can have a full-on Scottish soundtrack to start your day?"

Max pinched the bridge of his nose. "For the sake of everyone staying here, please don't even think about it."

The concierge laughed, then slid me a discreet card. "If you change your mind, we have excellent local musicians."

Max made a strangled sound, but I tucked the card into my purse with a wink. "Duly noted."

"Ms. Wilder," the concierge added, tone softening, "we truly hope you enjoy your stay. Please don't hesitate to let us know if there's anything we can do to make your visit more special."

Max rolled his eyes, snatching his key like my superior customer service experience was a personal affront.

"See you at our meeting later this afternoon, Harrington," I said breezily, already turning toward the elevator. I barely heard his reply. I was too busy mentally checking into my future bathtub.

Late morning light streamed through the casement windows, pale gauzy curtains stirring with the breeze. I sank deeper into the oversized tub, letting the warm water coax out the last of the flight fatigue. I piled my long hair into a messy bun, a few wavy tendrils clinging to my skin as I let my head tip back against the tub's edge.

This. This was exactly what I needed.

I had just closed my eyes when a boom rattled the walls, immediately followed by a very concerning whooshing sound. I shot upright, eyes wide. A second later, water erupted from the vanity, spraying across the marble floor like a busted fire hydrant.

"You have got to be kidding me."

I scrambled out of the tub, barely grabbing a towel before the flood surged through the room. Dripping wet, I dashed into the next room and slammed the button for the front desk.

"This is Rayann Wilder in the East Wing," I said, towel-wrapped and breathless. "Either this suite comes with an indoor waterfall, or your plumbing is staging a rebellion."

The woman on the other end gasped. "Oh no! I'm terribly sorry, Ms. Wilder. We'll send maintenance immediately."

"Thank you, but I do need another room before I drown, please."

I dropped the towel, yanked on yoga pants, and grabbed the first thing I could reach—an oversized sweater that hit mid-thigh and clearly wasn't designed for emergencies.

The neckline slipped off one shoulder as I shoved my arms through the sleeves, the clingy fabric making it embarrassingly clear I'd forgotten a bra. "Please tell me you have another suite available.

Silence. Then: "I'm afraid we're at full capacity for the weekend. However... there is another suite."

"Okay. What's the catch?"

She hesitated. "It's already occupied."

My stomach dropped.

"By Mr. Harrington."

Shit.

By the time I reached Max's suite, I was running on irritation and wet hair. My sweater clung to me as if it had given up on dignity entirely.

Exhaustion pressed down, but frustration kept me upright. This was not how I'd pictured my first day in Scotland.

I knocked, bracing for whatever smug one-liner Max had locked and loaded. The door swung open almost instantly. There he was—sleeves rolled up, tablet in hand, eyebrows raised as his gaze flicked over me.

Bare shoulder. Yoga pants painted on. And oh shit.

No bra.

For a second, something unguarded flickered in his eyes. *And why, exactly, did my temperature just tick up a notch?*

I exhaled. "I know this isn't ideal, but... thank you for letting me crash here."

He didn't answer right away. His hand flexed on the doorframe with the tension of someone expecting punches, not peace. Then he stepped back. "Come in, Rayann."

I crossed the threshold, pulse beginning to settle. "I asked the hotel to move my bags. They should be here shortly."

Max studied me, then sighed and pushed his sleeves higher. His forearms flexed as he moved, stronger than I expected. "Rough morning?"

I let out a humorless laugh. "What gave it away? The near-drowning or the fact that I smell like luxury hand soap?"

He smiled, just barely, but it counted.

I pushed a hand through my damp waves and blew out a breath. "Anyway. I'll, uh, stay out of your way. Promise not to mess with your routine."

He shook his head. "Somehow, I don't believe that."

I smirked. "Smart man."

Max crossed to the desk, bracing one hand on the edge. His fingers dug into the polished wood as if it was the only thing anchoring him.

His stare held steady, just a little too steady, but something flickered beneath it. A hesitation. A quiet shift.

I turned toward the second bedroom, but his voice stopped me. "They said your bags will be here soon?"

I glanced back. His eyes swept over my face—no makeup, flushed cheeks, the kind of "natural glow" that only came from bathwater and panic—then lower, to the sweater clinging in all the wrong places. He didn't speak, but his jaw tightened, fingers flexing against the desk.

Like he noticed but was trying not to.

The air thickened. I swallowed. "Everything good?"

Max blinked, slow and deliberate, then dragged his eyes back to my face like it took effort. "Yeah," he said, his voice lower. "All good."

A twist tightened low in my stomach.

He sat down, opened his laptop, and the moment was gone. His fingers flew over the keyboard, business-mode re-engaged. "I need to make sure there aren't any surprises before the meeting. You can do... whatever it is you do to unwind."

I narrowed my eyes. "Max."

He didn't look up. "Rayann."

I huffed, snagged my tote, and headed for the other room. But as I reached the door, I swore I felt his eyes on me again.

The suite was, admittedly, as stunning as the other one. Floor-to-ceiling windows framed the misty Highlands, the air tinged with wood smoke and spring rain. From the bedroom, the view was breathtaking—rugged peaks, dark and brooding, set against a sky that couldn't decide whether to storm or shine.

I set my bag on the bed, pulled out my portable speaker, and queued up my favorite jazz playlist just as the concierge delivered my luggage. Warm, soulful notes spilled into the room, curling around me as though wrapping me in velvet. I let out a long breath, tension loosening with every smoky verse and slow brass line.

After about a half hour, a knock pulled me from my thoughts. I cracked the door. Max stood outside, sleeves still rolled, expression unreadable.

"Didn't peg you for a jazz fan."

I leaned on the frame. "I enjoy all kinds of music. Jazz is my favorite, though. Give me Ella or Miles any day. Helps me unwind."

He nodded slightly, tapping his fingers on the doorframe. "It suits you."

I blinked. "What does that mean?"

His gaze held mine. "Unexpected. But it fits."

My stomach dipped.

I turned away, grabbing a hanger and smoothing out the wrinkles in a blouse. "Do you have a preference? I can turn it down if it's bothering you."

Max shook his head. "It's fine. Keep it on."

The comment was so casual I almost missed it, but something in his tone sent a warm flush up my neck. He didn't move.

I glanced back. "Did you need something?"

He hesitated. "Have you eaten?"

I frowned. "Not since breakfast on the plane."

He nodded like that confirmed something. "There's a restaurant downstairs. We should get something before the meeting."

It wasn't a question, but it wasn't quite a demand either.

I raised a brow. "Are you inviting me to lunch?"

Max exhaled as if he'd heard that coming. "I'm saying it makes sense to eat now so we don't have to worry about it later."

I bit back a smile. "Sounds like an invitation."

He rolled his shoulders, ignoring that. "If you'd rather find something on your own—"

"No," I said quickly. "Lunch sounds good."

Max held my gaze another beat before nodding. "I'll meet you downstairs in ten."

Ten minutes? Shit.

I spun toward my suitcase, calculating fast. Behind me, his voice followed, low and amused, edged with smug satisfaction. "Try not to keep me waiting. And don't forget your notes."

I didn't dignify that with a response. I grabbed the first thing that wasn't wrinkled—a breezy ivory sundress that screamed unintentional distraction.

A swipe of lip gloss. A few loose waves clipped at the back of my head. Out the door in three minutes flat.

He'd get punctual. But he was damn well getting something else to fret about too.

Chapter 5

The Honeymooners' Special

MAX WAITED NEAR THE lobby entrance, scrolling through his phone. He didn't notice me at first but, when he did, his grip tightened for just a second before he slid the device into his pocket as though it burned him.

His face? Smooth, unreadable.

His eyes? Yeah, not so much.

I bit back a smirk and closed the distance. "Ready?"

His gaze swept over me, slow and intentional, before he exhaled. "Let's go."

And just like that, the game was on.

The castle's courtyard restaurant matched my vision perfectly: cozy, charming, and tucked against ivy-draped stone walls, with an open-air terrace overlooking the Highland moorlands. The scent of fresh-baked bread and slow-roasted lamb lingered in the air—buttery and rich, laced with rosemary and smoke—drifting through the low hum of conversation and bursts of laughter from nearby tables.

I exhaled slowly, taking it all in, already picturing how I'd sell this place to future clients. Romantic, intimate, effortlessly magical. Max, of course, scanned the place with all the suspicion of someone expecting a takedown. His gaze ticked over the kitchen, the terrace, the exits—grim and efficient, with the calm certainty of someone who'd already mapped the worst-case scenario.

I smiled as the hostess led us to our table. "You do realize we're not planning a heist, right?"

Max pulled out his chair but stayed standing, eyes still sweeping the room. "Give it time."

I rolled my eyes. "You live for worst-case scenarios, don't you?"

He finally slid into his seat, flipping open the leather-bound menu. "I plan for them."

"Right. And yet, has it ever occurred to you that sometimes things actually go smoothly?"

His lips flattened, a sigh hovering just behind them. "Optimism's nice. Right up until it gets you blindsided."

I frowned. "That's not—"

"You believe in best-case scenarios." His eyes met mine, flat and direct. "I prepare for everything else."

I opened my mouth to argue, but nothing came out. Because, annoyingly, he wasn't wrong. Max didn't just expect things to go sideways. He mapped it out in advance. Built a life around backup plans and lived in a world where failure wasn't an option. And me? I believed effort mattered. That if you wanted something bad enough, you made it work.

Neither of us broke the stare.

Before I could push the point, the waiter appeared as if dispatched by divine intervention, armed with a pressed vest. He was charming in a silver-fox, twinkle-in-his-eye kind of way, his smile landing on me and sticking. I reached for my water, pretending the sudden warmth in my chest was from the sun, not the stare. Max wasn't scanning the exits anymore. Or the guests. His attention had locked onto me and, this time, he wasn't pretending otherwise.

"Welcome, the two of ye sweethearts," the waiter said warmly, setting down two glasses of water.

Max froze as though someone had dropped a tartan-wrapped grenade in his lap.

I blinked. "Oh, we're not—"

But the waiter simply grinned. "Aye, no need to be shy. We get our fair share of honeymooners. What can I start ye off with?"

I could've let it go. Hell, I *should* have. But where's the fun in that?

Instead, I offered the waiter a smile but leaned into Max, skimming his forearm with a touch that was pure provocation. "What do you think, sweetheart? Champagne and oysters? Or are we saving indulgent for later?"

His fingers twitched as he shifted a breath closer. Barely, but enough to make my pulse spike.

The waiter beamed. "That's the spirit! Might I suggest the venison stew? A local favorite."

"Sounds perfect," I said, handing him my menu before turning back to Max, whose expression was so dry it could've distilled its own single malt.

"Lovely," the waiter said. "And for you, sir?"

Max's eyes didn't leave mine as he snapped his menu shut. "Same for me," he said tightly. "And two of your best house beers."

A flicker. A tiny hitch in his voice. Gone in a second, but not before I filed it away for later.

I barely withheld a grin. "Making drink decisions for me now? Careful, that's how rumors start."

As soon as the waiter walked away, Max leaned in, forearms steady and wearing the look of a man who'd just stepped into a game he didn't remember agreeing to. "Having fun?"

His voice was smooth, but his fingers tapped out a rhythm that screamed restraint.

I tilted my head. "Maybe a little. You?"

Whatever flickered behind his eyes, he buried it fast. Too fast. "Jury's still out."

I huffed a laugh, shaking my head. "You need a hobby, Harrington."

His brows ticked up, like I'd just suggested unicorn wrangling. "I have hobbies."

"Oh yeah?" I eased closer, propping my chin on my hand. "Name one."

A pause, so quick you'd miss it if you weren't looking.

Max sipped his water with the unbothered ease of someone operating on a different time zone. "I work." He took another sip, calm as ever. "And wrangle gators for stress relief. But only the mean ones."

I groaned and flopped back in the seat. "Okay, Florida Man. That still doesn't count."

"You should hear me scream in Excel," he said with a shrug.

"Oh, I bet your spreadsheets have spreadsheets."

Max leaned in, voice low. "Careful, Rayann. You're one smartass comment away from finding out exactly what I do for fun."

I raised a brow, matching his tone. "Is that a threat or an invitation?"

He didn't answer. He just stared me down, inviting every possible interpretation but offering none.

I grinned, shifting gears. "Alright, fine. Humor me for a second. If I asked what you actually do for fun on trips like this, something other than memorizing evacuation routes, what would you say?"

He studied me for half a beat too long, giving me absolutely nothing except for the subtle spark of mischief he couldn't quite hide.

Then, smooth as ever: "I'd say that's classified."

I let out a theatrical sigh. "God, you're exhausting. And a lost cause."

That tiny flicker of amusement returned, subtle but unmistakable. "So I've been told."

I tipped my glass toward him. "Called it."

The waiter reappeared just in time, setting down two pints with a knowing smile before disappearing again. The scent hit my nose with a trace of toffee and smoke—smooth, controlled, and a little too easy to underestimate. Just like him.

Max lifted his beer, took a measured sip, then set it down with that maddening, almost ritualistic calm of his. "It's not often I actually sit down for lunch."

I tilted my head, considering him. "Too busy saving the world?"

His lips twitched. "Something like that."

I smirked, swirling my beer. "And here I thought you at least treated yourself to a protein bar between disasters."

His mouth quirked, but his fingers tapped his glass, slow and thoughtful. "Eating at my desk gets the job done."

"Efficient, sure. Also kind of tragic."

His gaze flicked toward the terrace, lingering there for a moment before locking on me again. "Not everyone works for the perks, Rayann."

I lifted my beer. "You say that as if I don't get things done."

Max looked right at me, stone-cold poker face firmly in place. "Just an observation."

I was halfway to a comeback when I froze. Two tables away, one of the McIvey cousins was in full scowl mode, arguing with a venue coordinator, hands carving sharp lines through the air.

My stomach dipped, sharp and familiar.

Well, shit.

Chapter 6

Forecast: Stormy with a Chance of Drama

I STRAIGHTENED, SETTING MY drink down. "Back in a sec," I said, already pushing my seat back before Max could question it.

He shot a glance at the cousin, sharp and assessing. "Rayann."

I ignored him, weaving through the tables.

Lachlan McIvey looked up as I approached, his expression shifting from frustration to something warmer. The faint scent of aged leather and Highland whiskey clung to him—heritage and heat, with just enough bite to make you pay attention. "Ms. Wilder," he greeted, rising slightly in his seat.

"Rayann, please," I corrected with a smile, sliding into the empty chair across from him. "I hope you're enjoying your stay so far."

He hesitated. "Aye, it's—" His gaze flicked toward the coordinator beside him, who suddenly looked decidedly uncomfortable.

Something was definitely off.

I rested my arms on the table, keeping my voice even. "Lachlan, if there's a problem, I'd rather know now than be blindsided later."

The coordinator tensed, like he was waiting for permission to speak.

Finally, Lachlan sighed. "It's nothing against your team. Everything's been handled beautifully. It's just..." He dragged a hand down his stubble. "There've been a few murmurs. Some of my relatives aren't... thrilled about the location."

A flicker of unease curled in my stomach. "The venue? But this was Fiona and Collum's choice."

"Aye, but you have to understand that old grudges die hard." His mouth pressed into a tight line. "This land belonged to my family—until the McAlisters took it centuries ago. Some of the older family members aren't happy about celebrating here."

A slow, sinking feeling settled in my stomach. The history. The lingering tensions. The feud that hadn't fully settled, even after all this time. Summer's red flag was starting to look more like a full-blown warning siren.

I took a steadying breath. "I appreciate you telling me," I said, my tone even and smooth. "Let me do some checking on my end, see if there's anything we can do to make this easier."

Lachlan exhaled, nodding once. "Thank you."

I gave his hand a light squeeze before pushing up from the chair and heading back to my table.

Max was already watching me. Not casually—studying. His expression was unreadable, but his eyes were razor-sharp, cutting through the lively chatter of the restaurant like a blade.

I barely had time to sit before he spoke. "What's wrong?"

I lifted my beer, taking a slow, measured sip. "Nothing's wrong."

His brow arched in a silent call out.

I sighed, setting my glass down. "Yet."

Max put down his spoon. Deliberate and controlled. His full focus locked onto me like a heat-seeking missile. "Talk."

I considered playing it off, maybe letting him stew a little longer. But the heat in his eyes told me I wouldn't get far. I leaned in slightly, tone hushed and deliberate. "Some of the McIvey elders have reservations about the location."

His jaw flexed. "Meaning?"

"Meaning, this land used to belong to their family until the McAlisters ended up with it ages back. They're not exactly excited to celebrate a wedding here."

Max's fingers curled around his glass. His grip wasn't tight, but it was there. Like he was already bracing for impact. "That's more than 'not thrilled.' That's a problem."

"It's fine," I said lightly, picking up my spoon. "I told Lachlan I'd check in on my end and explore a few ways to ease the tension."

Max's features hardened. "And you were planning to tell me this when?"

I let the air out slowly, already bracing for the argument. "Max—"

"No. When?" His tone was low, calm in that deadly way that made my pulse pick up.

I threw up a hand. "I'm telling you now, aren't I?"

His gaze sharpened. "Should've told me the second you knew."

Oh, we were not having this argument in the middle of lunch. I stabbed a bite of stew, pretending not to notice the way his stare pinned me in place.

Max leaned in, forearms braced on the table. His words measured but unyielding. "We need to talk before the meeting."

I pushed my water aside, matching his stare. "Yeah. We do."

As soon as we stepped out of the restaurant, the shift was instant. Max's stride lengthened, features locked into unreadable efficiency. All business.

I, on the other hand, was still rolling every word of Lachlan's conversation around in my mind, trying to figure out if we had a problem or just a few cranky old men with long memories.

We barely made it five steps before Max spoke. "That wasn't a casual check-in. You confirmed resentment, and resentment this close to the wedding? That's a risk."

I let out a sharp breath, crossing my arms. "Oh, please. It's a sentimental issue, not a logistical one. A few grumbles from the old guard don't mean the wedding is about to implode."

Tension rippled across his face. "You don't know that."

"And you don't know that it will," I shot back, the volume kicking up before I meant it to.

A passing couple side-eyed us, but Max didn't even blink. He stepped closer instead. When he spoke, his words came lower, carrying even more weight.

"You're downplaying it," he said quietly. Firm. "Summer flagged this as a concern for a reason. If we don't get ahead of it, we'll be scrambling for a solution when it's too late."

Frustration surged, but I forced out a breath and reeled it back in. "Max, this is exactly why we work well together. You see every possible worst-case scenario, and I talk to actual human beings. It's a nice balance."

His brow lifted. "It's my job, Rayann. And I'm very good at what I do."

His nostrils flared, and for a split second, I thought he might actually growl at me. Instead, he held my gaze, unwavering. "You think flashing a smile and playing nice solves everything," he said, quieter now, but still coiled tight with intensity. "Some conflicts don't vanish because you charm your way through them."

Something about the way he said my name sent a shiver down my spine, but I refused to let it show. "I'm not naïve," I said, holding my tone level. "I know how to handle people. We don't need to go kicking hornets' nests when the wedding is three days away."

Max blew out a breath, raking a hand through his hair before stepping even closer. Too close. He didn't touch me. But I *felt* him.

His voice dropped. "This isn't about kicking hornets' nests. It's about having a plan before something escalates."

The air thickened. Neither of us moved. Max's jaw flexed, his eyes flicking over my face like he was searching for an opening. He finally breathed out. "Fine."

Oh, so controlled.

"We'll handle it your way. For now." It wasn't a surrender but a warning.

I lifted my chin. "Glad to hear it. *Sweetheart.*"

Chapter 7

The Art of Persuasion

THE CASTLE'S PRIVATE CONFERENCE room matched the rest of the estate with vaulted ceilings, an ornate fireplace, and a mahogany table that could've hosted centuries of noble debates. The room smelled faintly of aged paper, beeswax polish, and old smoke—like power and history had seeped into the stone itself. But today, the only thing being debated was whether this wedding was about to turn into a historical reenactment of the clan war.

I took a steadying breath, assessing the room before stepping inside.

The McIvey family sat to one side of the long table. The McAlisters to the other. Vendors and coordinators filling in the spaces between them. The tension in the air wasn't hostile, exactly, but it was taut, brimming with the kind of unease that could shift at any moment.

And then there was Max.

Standing at the head of the table, his presence effortless, controlled. He barely acknowledged me, already focused on the itinerary laid out before him, his phone next to it, probably with emergency contingency plans already queued up. I resisted the urge to smirk. He could run all the numbers he wanted, but people weren't spreadsheets.

This? This was my arena.

I set my folder down and offered the group my warmest, most effortless smile on the group. "I won't hold you long," I said with a practiced smile. I began smoothly, projecting the same calm confidence I used to close million-dollar deals. "But I wanted to bring everyone together to make sure we're all aligned before the celebrations begin."

A few polite nods. Some stiff postures.

Not quite engaged yet. Time to change that.

"Before anything else—I have to say, this venue?" I gestured around the room, letting just enough admiration seep into my voice. "Absolutely breathtaking. I don't know about you, but I can already see how stunning this wedding is going to be."

The younger members of the families smiled. Good. Start with the ones who are open to it.

Fiona McIvey visibly relaxed, her tension melting as she glanced at her fiancé.

Collum McAlister squeezed her hand. "Aye, she's right. It's going to be perfect."

Lachlan McIvey, the cousin I'd spoken with earlier, shifted slightly, expression neutral.

The older family members held their ground—arms crossed, brows drawn, expressions carved from stone.

Which meant I had work to do.

Max spoke next, his tone even, all business. "To keep things on track, we'll run through the final logistics, confirm any last-minute requests, and ensure that every vendor is aligned." He glanced up, sharp. "If there are any concerns, speak now."

That was my cue.

I folded my hands on the table, looking directly at Lachlan. "I understand there's been some *unease* about the venue."

A ripple went through the room. A shift.

Lachlan exchanged a glance with one of the older McIvey men before clearing his throat. "It's no secret that some members of the family feel conflicted about holding the wedding here."

One of the McAlisters scoffed, crossing his arms. "It's been centuries, man. Let it go."

Oh, *hell*.

I held up a hand before Lachlan could fire back.

"I completely understand," I said, my voice measured, warm but firm. "And I respect that history carries weight. This land is woven into your family's past. That's not something to brush aside."

Validate first. Make them feel heard.

A few of the older McIveys nodded slightly.

Now it was my move. I leaned in, lowering my voice just enough to make it feel like I was letting them in on a private moment. "Which is why I'd love to find a way to honor that history so this wedding isn't a reminder of conflict, but a celebration of both legacies coming together."

The air shifted. I could feel Max's focus settle on me like a weight.

I looked to Lachlan. "What's a meaningful gesture we could incorporate? A blessing, a toast, some small tribute to what this land meant to your family?"

"There's a Gaelic blessing—one my grandfather used to say," Lachlan exhaled slowly. "*Fad do latha agus oidhche mhath leat.* Long may your day last, and a good night to you."

His uncle perked up ever so slightly.

Oh, we were in.

I beamed. "That sounds beautiful. Let's do it right before the initial toast. A moment to recognize the past and step into the future."

Lachlan glanced over. No protest or visible resistance.

Max was studying me now, a weight I could almost name. Calculating. Reassessing.

I refocused on the group, flashing my best closer's smile. "And with that, let's go through the final logistics."

As the group dispersed, Fiona caught my arm, her voice low. "Thank you. That was so much smoother than I expected."

I squeezed her hand. "That's what I do."

By the time the room emptied, leaving only Max and me, I finally exhaled and shifted, catching him watching me, arms crossed, unreadable as ever. But under all that composure, heat simmered.

I tilted my head. "Got a thought you're dying to share, Harrington?"

His jaw flexed, but his expression shifted, thoughtful now, as it flickered over me. "You handled that well."

I smirked, reaching for my folder. "Did you just *compliment* me?"

He didn't blink, didn't flinch. "Don't push it."

I laughed, heading for the door. "Come on. You can tell me how impressed you are over another pint."

Max sighed but followed. And if I wasn't mistaken, his gaze lingered a little longer than usual.

Max and I had barely made it through the door before I was beelining for the bar. It was exactly what I needed after that meeting. Low lighting, old stone walls, and the rich scent of aged whiskey and oak lingered in the air—dark, smoky, and just sharp enough to cut through the day's tension. An old hound dozed beneath a worn barstool as the bartender tipped a well-loved bottle of GlenDronach into a waiting glass. Perfection.

"Two pints," I told the bartender, then glanced over my shoulder. "Or are we going straight to the hard stuff?"

Max stepped up beside me, scanning the bottles with the same intensity he used for mission briefings. "Dalmore 18. Neat."

I cocked a brow. "Feeling bold tonight, Harrington? That's not exactly the training-wheels version."

His fingers drummed against the bar, smooth and deliberate. "You're the one who dragged me in here. Might as well make it worth it."

Oh, that sounded like a dare wrapped in a threat and tied with a ribbon.

I braced an arm against the counter, letting my voice drop just enough. "In that case, make mine the same. Wouldn't want you thinking I can't handle the good stuff."

Max let out a low chuckle, dark and amused, as the bartender poured. "You sure you can keep up?"

I tipped my glass toward him, eyes dancing. "Guess we'll find out when one of us is under the table."

He glanced my way, sharp enough to slice. "Better hope it's not you. The floor's cold, and I'm not carrying you twice in one lifetime."

We clinked glasses, the scent of dried fruit and spice—warmth in a glass, seduction in disguise—filling the space between us before we brought them to our lips, savoring the first sip. The warmth spread through my chest, smooth and rich, settling just right. Max exhaled, setting his glass down with a satisfied nod. I leaned an elbow on the bar. "Alright, I'll say it. That meeting could've gone sideways, but it was damn near perfect because you had my back. So thanks for that."

Max glanced at me, brows lifting slightly as if he wasn't expecting that. "You giving me credit, Wilder?"

I smirked. "Don't let it go to your head. It doesn't happen often."

He took another sip, that nearly invisible twitch of a smile tugging at the corner of his mouth. "Noted."

I saluted him with my glass. "Still think you're insuffer-able, though."

"Good," he said dryly. "Wouldn't want to ruin your whole worldview."

I tilted my glass. "Didn't peg you for a scotch drinker."

Max swirled his snifter in his hand, watching the amber liquid catch the dim light. "There are a lot of things you don't peg me for."

I smirked. "Such as?"

He didn't answer. He just took a slow sip, like he enjoyed keeping me guessing. Then he looked at me, glass halfway raised, intent unmistakable. My pulse tripped over itself. Something in my chest stuttered hard enough to register as a system error.

Whatever was in that look, it wasn't about work. It wasn't about irritation, or logistics, or me driving him up a wall. It was something else. Something warmer. Something I prob-ably shouldn't be thinking about for too long.

I cleared my throat, leaning back in my chair. "Dangerous words, Harrington. Keep that up, and I might think you're actually an interesting person."

Max set his glass down, amused. "And that would be a tragedy, wouldn't it?"

I hummed. "I dunno. Maybe I appreciate a little mystery."

He swept his attention over me again, brief but deliberate.

The scotch burned warm and slow, but the look in Max's eyes burned hotter. God, I should not find this man attractive. I swallowed, gripping my glass a little tighter, about to steer the conversation somewhere safer. We pushed, we parried, we never let a moment settle too long. Then laughter erupted, smashing through the moment like it had no idea what it was interrupting.

Loud, drunk, and reckless.

Max's expression shut down.

I glanced up as a small group of wedding guests spilled inside, McIveys and McAlisters both, already looking for trouble. One of them, a McIvey cousin by the looks of him, spotted us and grinned.

"Harrington! Wouldn't have figured you for a drinking man."

And just like that, the moment was gone. The shift was instant.

Max straightened, his posture sharpening, his hand curling loosely around his glass. The easy buzz of scotch and warmth replaced with something else. Something colder.

Max exhaled, slow and steady. "I'm full of surprises."

The cousin turned to me, his grin widening. "And you must be the lovely Ms. Wilder. The one who smoothed over that nasty little family tension."

I lifted my glass. "That's me."

"Hell of a job. You know, for a minute there, I heard a rumor that someone was gonna start throwing fists." He laughed as if that was the best possible outcome.

Max rubbed a hand over his jaw. "Yeah, let's not encourage that."

"Barkeep! Glenfiddich, and none o' that weak pourin' either!" hollered another relative. "Tamnavulin, neat! And make it quick, aye? My cousin challenged me to arm wrestlin'."

I leaned toward Max, voice low. "Not even sunset," I muttered, "and already we're spiraling toward bagpipe karaoke and clan battle songs."

"Tell me, Ms. Wilder. How do you feel about a good old-fashioned drinking contest?"

I matched his grin, already feeling the reckless thrill curling through my stomach. "Oh, I'm gonna lose. Spectacularly. But I'll take you all down with me on the way."

Max exhaled, long and slow. "Rayann."

I leaned toward him, lowering my voice. "If I die, avenge me. Preferably with carbs."

His jaw ticked, the muscle twitching. And then, much to my absolute delight, he reached for the glass in front of him.

"Fine."

Oh, this was going to be fun.

Two drinks in, I felt the warmth of the scotch curl through my veins, loosening everything but my competitive streak.

Three drinks in, Max loosened his tie. I shouldn't have noticed it. The way his fingers brushed against his collar, the slow slide of fabric as he undid the knot. But I did.

Four drinks in, I caught myself watching his mouth when he spoke.

Bad idea.

I blinked, shaking it off, only to realize he was watching me, too. His gaze dipped, just briefly.

Warmth bloomed low, as the drink did exactly what it was made to do. But the way Max was looking at me? That screamed dangerous. And yet, I couldn't seem to look away. I licked my lips. "You doing okay there, Harrington?"

He glanced up, deadpan and dangerous. "Better than you."

Ohhh, a challenge. I tilted my head, drumming my fingers against the rim of my glass. "Prove it."

I couldn't say who leaned in first. One moment we were bickering, the next, just breath and heat and silence.

His face was entirely too close to mine. His breath, warm. Laced with scotch and temptation.

And for the one and only time all night, neither of us had a single witty thing to offer.

Chapter 8

The Morning After (Oh, Sh*t.)

M Y BRAIN WAS SLOSHING. That was the first sign the night had taken a nosedive. The second was that I wasn't entirely sure how I'd gotten into bed. I blinked up at the canopy above me, trying to make sense of the haze—whiskey, laughter, and the faint scent of woodsmoke still clinging to the sheets. Max's voice, low and too close, echoed in my head.

Oh, hell.

I sat up so fast my head protested violently, the room tilting just enough to make my stomach lurch. *Okay. Think, Rayann. Think.*

Last night. The bar. The scotch. Max in low light. That damn voice when he leaned in.

No. Nope. Not going there.

I patted the sheets beside me, my stomach twisting. Empty. That was good. I lifted the covers, glancing underneath. Fully clothed. Also good.

Still, what if I *had* changed? What if Max had seen me. Helped me.

"Oh my God."

I buried my face in my palms, my pulse hammering. Did we—?

No. No way. I would remember that. Wouldn't I?

Shit. Where is Max?!

I shoved the covers off and stumbled out of bed. A second wave of nausea hit, and I gritted my teeth through it as the room tilted hard left. Wincing, I braced myself against the nightstand and tried to piece together the gaping holes in my memory. That was when I saw it: a glass of water sitting neatly beside two aspirin.

Max.

I groaned, dragging a hand down my face. If that wasn't the most uptight, responsible thing he could've done, I didn't know what was.

Okay. So he got me back to my room. That was... oddly sweet. But it still didn't explain why my skin felt warm in places it shouldn't. Hesitantly, I lifted my wrist to my nose and sniffed. Scotch. And something else. Something clean, masculine, familiar.

Nope. Not thinking about that.

Then I saw it. Max's jacket hung neatly over the armchair, like it belonged there. Like he hadn't left in some kind of frantic escape. I stared at it, my stomach flipping. Why the hell is his jacket in here?

I snatched the lapels like they might hold answers, but all it did was confirm one thing: it smelled of him. That subtle, woodsy scent had no business being as distracting as it was.

Focus, Rayann. A memory flickered, sharp and clear. Max's arm around my waist, his words low and steady. *Come on, Ray. Let's get you to bed.* My own reply, slurred, stubborn. I can walk. A chuckle. A deep one. You're currently leaning against a wall.

Oh.

Oh no.

A firm knock made me yelp. I spun, heart racing, still clutching Max's damn jacket. Then came his voice. Low. Steady. Way too casual.

"Rayann."

Oh shit. *Oh shit oh shit.*

I flung the jacket across the room as though it had personally betrayed me and deserved exile, then cleared my throat.

"Yeah?"

Silence.

Then, dry as hell: "You okay in there, or do I need to file an incident report?"

I managed to cross the room in in a lurchy, vaguely vertical wobble and yanked open the door, instantly regretting it. There he was. Max Harrington looking freshly showered, sleeves rolled up, carrying two cups of coffee. As if he weren't the walking catastrophe currently unraveling my entire nervous system.

I squinted at him.

"You're suspiciously perky for someone who went full scotch-goblin less than twelve hours ago."

His lips twitched. "Some of us know our limits."

I scowled, snatching the coffee with zero gratitude. "Some of us don't care about limits," I muttered, rubbing my temples.

Max watched me over the rim of his cup, maddeningly calm. I hesitated, pulse hammering, then blurted it out with forced nonchalance, "Ummm... did we have sex?"

Max choked. Hard. Coffee nearly sloshed over his hand, and his control wavered just for a second, but I saw it. His entire body went unnaturally still, as if he were trying to compute the sheer absurdity of my question in a language he didn't speak. Even from a few feet away, I caught it again—that low-simmer scent of his cologne, all restraint and dry heat.

Not helping, Harrington.

His gaze snapped to mine.

"What?"

Oh no.

I held up a finger. "Wait." I pointed at him. Then me. Then the bed. "Are you sure we didn't?"

A muscle in his jaw twitched and then, slowly and deliberately, Max took a sip of coffee. In that impossibly steady, unreadable voice, he asked, "Would it make you feel better or worse if I said no?"

What kind of answer was that?!

Dammit.

I stared at him. Waiting. Chest pounding way too hard for someone who was definitely not about to have a panic attack.

Max, infuriatingly composed, took another slow sip the way someone might savor the final scene of a deliciously unhinged drama. Then he said, casually and without blinking, "If we had, you wouldn't be asking."

I gasped. My soul left my body.

"MAX."

His lips curved slightly, a smug little tilt that said he knew exactly what he was doing.

"You..." I sputtered, tightening my grip around the cup, willing it to anchor me. "You can't just say things like that!"

He took another sip, completely unaffected. "Seemed like a fair response to the question."

Oh no. No no no. That was not a confident man's answer.

I pointed an accusing finger at him. "You hesitated before answering."

Max arched a brow. "Did I?"

"Yes."

"No, I didn't."

I stared him down. "I think I'd remember sleeping with you."

His expression didn't change. "Would you?"

My brain short-circuited. I stood there, strong-holding my caffeine as though it were the final thread holding my unraveling sanity together as Max Harrington, my current nemesis and probable source of emotional scorch marks, walked away without an ounce of regret.

I needed a minute. Or maybe an exorcism.

He turned. "Rayann?"

I glared at him. "What?"

"Clan Games start in an hour."

I narrowed my eyes, sipping my liquid patience with all the menace I could muster. "Do I look like I care?"

Max's voice was maddeningly steady. "You will when Summer asks how things went today."

Dammit. Dammit. Dammit.

I ran a hand over my face. Right. The Clan Games. The McIvey family and McAlisters were spending the day engaging in traditional Highland competitions, which meant it was my job to ensure everything ran smoothly. Which also meant spending the entire day with Max. Again.

I exhaled slowly. *Professionalism, Rayann. You can do this.* "Fine," I called. "I'll be ready in twenty."

Silence.

Then, with pure, unfiltered smugness: "Make it fifteen."

My fingers curled into fists. I had two choices—comply, or make him regret rushing me. As I yanked open my closet, already formulating a new plan, one thought cemented itself in my mind. Max Harrington wanted a battle? Fine. Let the games begin.

He had no idea who he was playing with.

Chapter 9

The Tug-of-War Was Rigged & Other Lies I Tell Myself

T HE ESTATE GROUNDS LOOKED like they'd been ripped straight from a VisitScotland ad. The air smelled like fresh-cut grass and peat smoke, sweetened by the occasional waft of fried food from a nearby tent. Soft glens of heather and a mirror-still loch in the distance. And right now? A bunch of well-heeled people trying to hurl massive wooden logs like they'd trained for it their whole lives. I stood on the sidelines, arms crossed, watching two men in matching kilts grunt and flail as they tried to balance the long, tapered pole upright. The caber wobbled, the crowd roared, and the poor guy nearly took out a flower arrangement.

My job? Ensure the guests were having the time of their lives.

My real goal? One-up Max Harrington.

He stood a few feet away, looking entirely too composed in his tailored trousers and crisp shirt, as if he was auditing the financials of the Highland Games instead of attending one.

I tilted my head. "You going to stand there all day, Harrington, or are you going to try your hand at something?" Max's gaze slid to me, slow and deliberate, sending a faint prickle down my spine. I knew that look. The one that clocked my wild ponytail, sun-flushed cheeks, and casual attire and still managed to judge me as though I'd shown up to the Met Gala in Crocs.

"I'm here to make sure you don't cause any international incidents, not to participate."

"Oh, come on." I strode over, already spoiling for it. "You've got a competitive streak buried somewhere under all that stoicism. Afraid you'll lose?"

Max smirked, just slightly. "Afraid you'll embarrass yourself trying to win?"

The challenge sparked—sharp, electric, undeniable. And before I could think better of it, the words were already out. "Fine. Let's settle it. You and me. Tug-of-war."

Max's smirk deepened.

Dammit. I'd made a terrible mistake.

The coordinator, clearly enjoying the chaos, produced a thick, worn rope and handed each end off with the flair of a man kicking off a heavyweight title match. Before I could second-guess myself, Max and I were squaring off in the middle of the field with a crowd that had swelled to include every bored cousin and tipsy uncle within earshot.

"You sure about this?" Max asked, his voice low and entirely too amused as he wrapped his hands around the rope with the easy confidence of someone who made a habit of winning.

I was definitely *not* sure about this, but pride was a powerful motivator. "Positive," I said, planting my feet in the grass. "Try not to cry when I win."

Max chuckled.

Oh, that was infuriating.

As soon as the whistle pierced the air, I pulled with everything I had, digging my heels in like my reputation in this country hinged on it. To his credit, or maybe my utter frustration, Max barely budged. Not a fucking inch. His forearms flexed, and he gave a short, clean jerk of the rope.

I nearly face-planted.

"You alright over there?" he asked, still maddeningly calm.

"Is that all you've got?" I growled, gritting my teeth, gripping harder. "Because I'm just getting started."

The crowd whooped and hollered, some of them clearly betting on the outcome now.

For a second, just one beautiful second, I thought I was gaining ground. Max's shoulders shifted. The rope inched my way.

Then he planted his feet like a bloody oak tree and hauled.

I yelped and launched forward, limbs flailing in full rag-doll chaos. And landed flat on my back in the grass, right at his smug, perfectly polished shoes.

Dammit.

Max loomed over me, arms crossed and one brow cocked, looking like he'd just outbid everyone for the prize Highland cow. He held out a hand, barely containing the glee dripping off him. "Need a hand?"

I swatted him away and scrambled up, brushing damp grass and wounded pride off my jeans. "You cheated."

Max raised a brow, all innocent. "How exactly does one cheat at tug-of-war?"

"You just *did*, Hercules," I grumbled, scowling as laughter rippled through the crowd.

He leaned in, words pitched low, meant for me and me alone. "You're oddly graceful," he mused. "Even when you're flat on your back."

My jaw dropped. Steam might've poured from my ears.

Max simply turned and walked away. *Smug bastard.*

I stared after him, short-circuiting with comebacks that didn't make it past my tongue.

Blank. Nothing. Nada.

Which meant only one thing: playtime was *over*.

Max Harrington had no idea what was coming for him.

Just as I was mentally drafting the blueprint for Max Harrington's public downfall, the coordinator stepped forward, wearing the grin of a man about to stir the pot for sport. "Right then! Let's keep it going, folks. We need two teams for the Whisky Barrel Relay!" The crowd buzzed with a ripple of laughter, a few wary glances, and at least three McIvey men practically vibrating with the kind of anticipation you train your whole life for.

I perked up. "What's the Whisky Barrel Relay?"

"Dead simple! Each team rolls a full whisky barrel down the pitch and back again—"

"Oh, for Christ's sake," Max muttered under his breath.

"—without losing control. Fastest team wins."

I spun to Max, already grinning. "Oh, we're doing this."

"No," he said flatly.

"Yes."

Max exhaled sharply, glancing at the size of the barrels. "You do realize these weigh close to 120 pounds, right?"

I tilted my head. "Better hope you had a big breakfast, Harrington."

Before Max could so much as scowl in protest, we were split into teams, because naturally, the crowd wasn't about to pass up another round of Wilder vs. Harrington. Max was paired with two McIvey men who looked like they trained by deadlifting cattle. Meanwhile, I got Collum McAlister and a wiry wedding coordinator with the glint of chaos in his eye. Excellent. My people.

The field was marked, the barrels lined up in perfect formation, and the rules were as simple as they were brutal. I crouched, rolling my shoulders like I was preparing for the goddamn Olympics. My hair had half fallen down by this point, strands sticking to the sweat on my neck, but I didn't care. Let Max deal with the feral version of me. "You ready, Max?"

He flexed his fingers over the barrel and cast me a look that was pure deadpan. "Try not to fall on your face this time."

"Oh, I'm sorry. Are you *nervous*?"

His expression didn't shift. Stone cold. "Not even a little."

Then, because the universe likes to humble a girl, he unbuttoned his shirt.

Are. You. Fucking. Kidding. Me.

My breath caught. Fully short-circuited.

Then rolled the sleeves once—like it mattered—before sliding it off with the slow, practiced ease of a man who knew *exactly* what he was doing. He draped it casually over the nearest fence post with the casual grace of a man shedding responsibility.

And there he stood. White t-shirt, fitted just enough, the fabric clinging in a way that should've been illegal. I had never seen him without the armor of his crisp dress shirts.

Oh, fucking hell.

And then, because clearly I'd wronged some ancient god, I saw the tattoo. Just a hint of it peeking out from his sleeve. Nothing elaborate. No bold, attention-seeking ink. Just one single line of script, curling along his inner bicep.

Unfair. So deeply, criminally unfair.

Every neuron in my head misfired at once. I was going to expire in this exact spot, tragically and without closure. Because I needed to know what that damn tattoo said.

"Rayann?"

I snapped back to reality so hard I nearly gave myself whiplash. Max was watching me, head tilted slightly, smirking. Oh, he *knew*. Fucker.

I cleared my throat, which was somehow bone-dry. "I—I—what?"

His smirk deepened into something lethal. "You ready?"

The way he said it? *Indecent.*

Oh my God, does he know I'm mentally undressing him?

I yanked my gaze toward the field, scowling in the desperate hope it might save me. "More than ready."

The signal sounded. Gloves off.

By the time we rolled the last whisky barrel across the finish line, I was breathless, slightly sweaty, and still riding the high of beating Max's team by a fraction of a second. A very small but very satisfying fraction.

Max, of course, handled the loss like it was beneath him. One shrug, one saintly nod of acceptance, and the kind of polished restraint that only made me want to win again. Just to watch him pretend it didn't bother him.

Which was why I should've let it go. But where was the fun in that?

"You know, Harrington," I mused, brushing a speck of dirt off my sleeve as we stepped away from the field. "It must be frustrating, coming so close to victory, only to—" I made a dramatic gesture, wiggling my fingers in the air. "Lose."

Max didn't bite. He merely tilted his head slightly, blue eyes scanning me like I was a particularly interesting data set. "You do realize I let you win, right?"

I stopped dead in my tracks. "I beg your pardon?"

Max took a sip from a bottle of water, his Adam's apple bobbing with the motion. Unbothered and oh-so-goddamn-infuriating. "I mean, if it helps you sleep at night, Rayann, you can believe whatever you want."

I choked on pure indignation. "You did *not* just say that."

"Mm," he mused, swiping his thumb along his jawline, clearly calculating whether provoking me was worth the cost. "Pretty sure I did."

Oh. Hell. No.

That was it. That was the moment the gloves came off and the verbal grenades came out. I was ready to unleash something nuclear, possibly in Gaelic, when the coordinator's shout thundered across the field with all the subtlety of divine intervention.

"All right, lads and lasses, time for the final event of the day—the Kilted Dash!"

The crowd stirred—cheers from one side, groans from the other, tension thick enough to slice. Max exhaled, the sound of pure resignation wrapped in military-grade self-restraint. I, on the other hand, was practically bouncing out of my skin.

"What's the Kilted Dash?" I asked, already plotting how to win it before anyone answered.

"An 800-meter footrace. Kilts required. First to the finish wins."

Kilts. Running. Speed. *Oh, yes.*

I turned to Max, beaming. "Oh, we're doing this too."

Max's exasperation was instant. "Rayann."

"Max," I countered, bouncing on my toes like I'd downed three espressos. "Come on. Where's that competitive spirit?"

He glanced toward the open field, then back at me. "Did it occur to you that I'm here to ensure everything runs smoothly, not to—"

He gestured vaguely. "Frolic through the countryside?"

I gasped. "Did you just call this *frolicking*?"

Max sighed, already rubbing the tension from his forehead as if I was personally responsible for every ounce of it. "That's not what I—"

"LADIES AND GENTLEMEN!" The announcement exploded overhead, cutting off Max's protests. "STEP UP IF YOU WANT TO RACE!"

Then, out of nowhere, a tartan torpedo landed in Max's hands. A kilt. He stared at it like it was a ticking bomb, the color draining his face. "You've got to be kidding me."

Revenge? *Absolutely delicious.*

I nearly doubled over. "Oh, this is so happening."

Minutes later, we stood at the starting line, surrounded by a mix of wedding guests and locals all equally prepared for utter foolishness. Max, for his part, carried the air of a man being marched to his doom "I can't believe you talked me into this," he muttered, adjusting the waistband of his kilt like it might bite.

I grinned. "You look... sexy."

He shot me a look, all dry heat and warning. "If I see one single camera, I'm leaving you in Scotland."

I gasped. "Maxwell Harrington. Are you saying you don't want a commemorative photo of this moment?"

He exhaled. "This is a terrible idea."

"Terrible?" I scoffed. "Or an opportunity to redeem yourself after that devastating loss in the relay?"

His jaw ticked. "It wasn't devastating."

"Tell that to the scoreboard."

Max's nostrils flared, and I knew I had him. He stepped closer, voice low. "You should know by now, Rayann, I don't lose twice."

A shiver zinged straight through my core like it had something to prove.

And then the whistle blew.

I ran. Hard. My feet pounded the ground, the wind whipping my oversized kilt around me like a plaid parachute gone rogue. The field stretched wide and endless before me. At first, I held the lead for a glorious, cocky fifteen seconds. Then, like some impossibly controlled machine, Max lengthened his stride like a man on a mission. I glanced back for half a second and came this close to doing a full-body dive into the field.

Because *holy hell, he was fast.*

My breath came hard and fast, my pulse hammering as Max pulled even with me. And then, with infuriating ease, he surged ahead.

Oh, absolutely not. I dug deep, pushing harder, determined not to let him win—

Then, another defiant gust of wind hit the field, and suddenly kilts went flying like battle flags in a storm. A McIvey up ahead yelled as his kilt flipped dangerously high. I whipped my head away on pure survival instinct and nearly ate grass for my trouble.

Dignity? Barely hanging on.

Max cursed. Loudly. The kind of ex-military, not-safe-for-grandmothers cursing that said everything his expression didn't.

I grabbed my waistband, desperate to keep my own kilt in place, while Max, being the ever-prepared, too-perfect-for-his-own-good man that he was, barely even flinched.

"I'm fine," he muttered, barely breaking stride.

"Good for you," I gasped, trying to keep up.

The finish line loomed ahead. Fifty feet. Thirty. Twenty.

Max pushed forward.

I threw myself forward.

We both crossed the finish line.

And went down.

Hard.

Max's momentum crashed into mine, and suddenly, the world flipped. A full-body collision of limbs, kilts, and sheer competitive stubbornness hit the ground in a spectacular, undignified heap.

The crowd erupted.

Max groaned beneath me. "You are the most infuriating woman alive."

I grinned down at him, breathless. "Admit it. That was fun."

Panting, I leaned forward, hands braced on my knees. The grass smelled sharp and earthy beneath me, mixing with sweat and the lingering tang of competition in the air. Sweat clung to my skin, my lungs still trying to catch up. Beside me, Max stood with his hands on his hips, breathing hard, his chest rising and falling beneath that clingy, sinfully smug T-shirt. His kilt hadn't shifted an inch.

Of course it hadn't.

A beat of silence.

"I won," I managed, between gulps of air.

Max made a low, incredulous noise. "Delusional."

I turned to him, grinning despite myself. "Photo finish?"

"Whatever lets you hold onto that tiny shred of dignity, Rayann."

I narrowed my eyes. "That's the second time today you've been concerned about my well-being."

He stepped closer, just enough for his words to come out in a low, velvety drawl. "What can I say? You're fragile."

I blinked. "Excuse me?"

"You heard me." His lips twitched, eyes flicking over me. "Delicate. Breakable. Practically a damsel."

My jaw dropped. "I just outran you in a full-body tartan sail."

"And ate turf in front of everyone," he said, almost too calmly. "Graceful as a newborn deer."

I opened my mouth to argue, ready to launch the next volley—

Click.

A camera flash.

We both turned too late. A self-satisfied event coordinator stood nearby, holding up his phone as if he'd just hit the jackpot.

I gasped. "Oh no."

Max groaned, pinching the bridge of his nose. "You've got to be fucking kidding me."

I slapped a hand over my mouth and tried not to snort-laugh.

But it was too late. The damage was done. Our tangle of limbs, post-race sweat, and undeniable tension was immortalized.

Forever.

Chapter 10

Ceilidh Heat (Or Kay-Lee, Because Gaelic Is Hard... and So Is Max's Life Right Now)

B Y THE TIME THE last event wrapped up, my calves screamed with every step and my shoulders may as well have been carved from granite. I was still seeing flashes of wind-tossed tartan every time I blinked.

Max, of course, looked infuriatingly unaffected. Not a hair out of place and hardly winded. The man had competed in multiple events, outpaced half the wedding guests in a footrace, and still had the audacity to roll his sleeves back down, all nonchalance, as if he hadn't just been competing like a man possessed.

Damned robot. Not even a whiff of sweat. I hated him a little for it.

"You going to make it to dinner, or should I call in a stretcher?"

"Worried about me, Harrington?" I scoffed, adjusting my ponytail. "Easy there—you're giving off dangerously caring vibes."

Max hummed, not taking the bait. "You do realize the night isn't over yet, right?"

I stopped in my tracks. "What now?"

He turned, flicking his blue eyes over me with that maddening, lazy amusement. "Did you forget the ceilidh dance lesson? You didn't think you were off the hook, did you?"

I groaned. "Oh, wait. I think I really did sprain my ankle. Shame."

Max took a slow sip from his water bottle, eyes steady. "Pity. I had paramedics on standby." He started walking again. "Suck it up, Wilder. You can limp through it. I'll lead."

Heat curled low in my belly, sharp and uninvited. I passed it off as exhaustion, but even I wasn't buying it. Because dancing meant hands, heat, and proximity. And I was dangerously close to forgetting why that was a bad idea.

After a quick return to the castle to freshen up, the evening kicked off with a Highland feast set up on the castle grounds. Long wooden tables stretched across the open-air courtyard, each flanked by benches draped in tartan throws, their colors glowing in the firelight. The scent of roasted meats, fresh-baked bannocks, and rich scotch drifted on the crisp Highland air—smoky, spiced, and thick enough to taste. Somewhere near the far end, a fiddler tuned his strings, the soft hum of tradition threading through the rising laughter and clink of glasses as guests swapped stories beneath the twilight sky.

I found myself seated beside Max. Naturally. Because why the fuck wouldn't I be? The universe clearly had him bookmarked under *Buzzkill*.

"You look pleased with yourself," Max said, slicing into his lamb chop.

I leaned back in my chair, swirling my wine with lazy satisfaction. "Well, you know. Two out of three wins. Not bad for a 'fragile' woman."

He paused his fork midair, ticking his jaw ever so slightly. "You cheated in the Kilted Dash."

I arched a brow. "Oh? And how exactly did I do that?"

"You distracted me."

I gasped, pressing a hand to my chest. "Are you blaming *me* for your lack of focus?"

Max exhaled sharply, dragging a hand through his hair. "You did it on purpose."

"Did *what* on purpose?"

He narrowed his eyes, that quiet storm look that usually preceded a tactical takedown. "You *laughed*."

"You laugh all the time."

"Not *that* way," dipping his voice lower. He stabbed his lamb chop with the precision of someone settling a vendetta. "Not when you're running full speed. Not when you're already ahead."

A slow smile curved my lips. *Oh. Oh, yeah.* This was so much better than dessert. I leaned in, resting my elbow on the table. "So let me get this straight, you were so affected by the sound of my laughter that you lost?"

He gripped his fork with enough tension to bend metal. "It wasn't just the laughter."

I hummed, pretending to think. "Ohhh, wait. Do you mean when I *flipped my hair*?"

He blinked slowly, the picture of a man praying for patience.

I fought a grin. "Or when I *threw a wink over my shoulder*?"

His eyes darkened, and for a second, I could almost feel the growl vibrating beneath his words.

Across the table, Ian McAlister leaned in, grinning like a man who lived for chaos. Another cousin. Another lovable troublemaker in formal wear. He gave me a once-over, not subtle about it. "That dress should come with a warning label, lass." He lifted his glass. "To a day well spent and an even better night ahead!"

I clinked glasses with him, grinning back, pretending not to notice Max's eyes tracking every shared joke like he was logging evidence.

"You know what I love about freckles?" Ian said, loud and theatrical, because subtlety wasn't in his skillset. "They're like constellations. Sexy, misbehaving constellations."

I snorted into my glass. "I'm sorry, did you try to seduce me with astronomy?"

Max didn't look up. "It's not the freckles," he muttered. "It's the damn attitude under them."

"Careful, Harrington. You're starting to sound smitten."

Max let out a quiet exhale through his nose, fingers flexing against the smooth curve of the glass.

Oh yeah. Direct hit.

The meal stretched on—long shadows, full plates, and that golden hour glow that made everything feel enchanted. I laughed at a volume specifically calibrated to get under Max's skin, bumped Ian's shoulder once or twice, and basked in the glow of victory. Maybe I was laying it on too thick. Maybe I was being kind of a bitch about it. But dammit, Max had gotten under my skin. And if this was petty payback, it was also wildly satisfying.

Yet still, I felt Max watching.

Not sulking or stewing.

Just *watching*.

The occasional flicker of his gaze. The slow, lazy drag of one finger around his glass—measured, deliberate, calculated. The way his jaw tightened whenever I laughed just hard enough to piss him off at whatever nonsense Ian was spewing.

He wasn't brooding, not exactly. But there was a sharp edge to Max Harrington that looked an awful lot like a man who didn't enjoy losing.

And that?

That only made me want to win more.

As the last plates were cleared and the firelight flickered low, the celebration shifted indoors for the ceilidh dance. Guests had changed into dressier evening attire. Nothing overly formal, but a definite step up from the day's rugged wear. I smoothed my palms over my dress, an emerald green number that clung in all the right places and dipped low in the back, equal parts flirty and deliciously dangerous.

I glimpsed a flash of Max in the mirror. Charcoal-grey button-down, tailored within an inch of its life, the top button undone just enough to be rude. Dark navy trousers, soft wool blend, fitted so well it was clear they weren't bought off a rack. And way too much restraint wrapped in one annoyingly perfect package.

Not that I noticed.

Holy hell. What is wrong with me?

The dance instructor called for partners, and—boom—Max appeared beside me, all smug confidence and impeccable timing. My heels clicked across the hardwood, the open back of my dress sending a breeze up my spine I pretended wasn't his fault.

"This is going to be just magical," I said, syrupy sweet, already mapping out how to crush his foot without remorse.

"Define magical," he replied, his voice a low murmur that somehow still managed to trip every nerve on the way down.

"Now, take your partner's hands!" the instructor announced, far too cheerful for what was about to happen.

Before I could lift a hand, Ian McAlister appeared at my side like a damn magician, flashing an easy grin.

"Ah, Rayann, looks like ye need a partner." He held out a hand. "Fancy a wee twirl?"

Max's body went still. Not a twitch. Not a breath.

Oh-my, Mr. Cool short-circuited. How interesting. I tilted my head, fighting a smirk as I slid my hand into Ian's. "Why, Ian, how gallant of you."

Ian winked. "Can't have a lass like you left stranded, can we?"

But before I could so much as step into position, *my* hand was intercepted.

Strong fingers. Warm, unyielding. Commanding in that you-should-be-pissed-but-you're-actually-turned-on kind of way.

"Max," I said flatly, while internally melting into a puddle of emotional nonsense.

I didn't even have time to blink before he smoothly pulled me away, replacing Ian's grip with his own. "She's with me."

Ian arched a brow. "Taken, is she?"

Max's grip tightened slightly on my waist. "For now."

Ian chuckled, lifting his hands in mock surrender. "Ahh, well, can't blame a man for tryin'." He shot me a wink before retreating, leaving me face-to-face with the walking thundercloud formerly known as Max Harrington.

I exhaled through my nose, staring up at him. "Wow, cloak and dagger much?"

Max didn't even pretend to look guilty. "Effective."

I narrowed my eyes. "Possessive."

His thumb skimmed the side of my palm, featherlight and infuriatingly effective.

"Jealous?"

My heart did that stupid stutter thing again. Heat crawled up my spine, my stomach doing a traitorous little somersault.

Sweet bloody hell. That was not allowed.

I squared my shoulders, lifting my chin as if that could shield me. "You wish."

"He almost smiled, but didn't quite—something darker flickering in its place. "Good."

The instructor clapped. "Alright, partners! Let's get started!"

Oh, this was going to be *fun.*

Max extended his hands, palms up, his expression unreadable. I hesitated—long enough to make it awkward—then placed mine in his, doing my damnedest not to flinch at the heat that curled through my fingers, sharp and live and far too personal. He radiated warmth, steady and annoyingly solid, as if determined to prove a point. "Try not to step on my toes," I said, my tone light but my pulse anything but.

"Try not to trip over your own," he countered smoothly, his smirk sharpening as the music started.

The steps were simple—at least, they should have been. But every time his hand brushed mine, or his fingers grazed the bare skin of my back, my mind blanked so completely I nearly forgot which foot was left. He was too close, too composed, too... Max.

"You've done this before," I said as he guided me through a spin, his grip firm and unyielding.

"Once or twice," he admitted. "Precision and timing."

"Sure," I muttered. "You're some kind of dancing Zorro, aren't you? All broody, mysterious, probably secretly wearing a cape somewhere."

Smooth, Rayann. Bring up capes. That'll cool things down.

Max didn't miss a beat. "Would it make you feel better if I said I only wear the mask on special occasions?"

Oh no. That tone? That was flirting. Real, actual, melt-your-insides flirting.

I missed a step. He didn't. Of course he didn't. Show-offy, infuriating, rhythmically gifted bastard.

"Should've known," I said, trying to recover. "Let me guess, is the sword included?"

His lips twitched, eyes glinting with wicked intent.

"Careful, Rayann. You *really* don't want me to answer that."

Oh, I did. I absolutely *did.* Someone should really warn this man I'm not built for self-control.

And then, because fate's a sadist, the steps brought us chest to chest, so close the line between dance and foreplay didn't stand a chance—and I felt every damn second of it.

And then came the worst part.

The lift.

Max gripped my waist, lifting me effortlessly, his fingers pressing into bare skin above the curve of my hips as I locked my arms around his shoulders for balance. My breath hitched as my chest met his—no waistband, no barrier. Just me, in this dress, in his muscular arms. He was all heat and tension. Too much strength, too close, too Max. And suddenly, I wasn't teasing. I was toeing a line I hadn't realized I'd drawn.

He lowered me slowly, as if he wasn't in any hurry to let go, his hands leaving a trail of heat on my skin that lingered long after he stepped away.

The music surged, quick and bold, practically egging us on with every beat.

I misstepped. My heel skidded across the floor, and I wobbled—ready to go down hard. But Max was faster. His arm shot out, catching me around the waist, pulling me against him. He caught me like it was instinct, but held me like it was a mistake he wanted to make again. His chest pressed against mine. His hand splayed low on my back, possessive and unyielding.

My breath stuttered, lodged somewhere between my ribs and reason.

"Careful," he murmured, his voice a low rumble that vibrated through me. "I might start to think you enjoy being in my arms."

A jolt zipped through me—righteous indignation, sure, but it tangled with something molten and reckless that had no business being there.

"Don't flatter yourself," I managed, but the words lacked their usual bite.

Max's gaze locked onto mine and, for one dizzying second, I swore he was going to kiss me. There was hunger in his eyes, but it wasn't reckless. It was measured. Controlled. Like he wanted to devour me slowly and was still deciding if he should.

This was bad.

This was really bad.

Because for one terrifying second, I'd *wanted* him to kiss me. Worse—I wouldn't have stopped him. That was the moment it hit me—this wasn't a game anymore. Not for him. And maybe not for me either.

And that's when I saw her.

Of course she was here.

Annabelle Sinclair. A McIvey cousin, if I remembered right—though she carried herself like royalty on loan. Elegant. Effortless. The kind of woman who didn't need a spotlight because the room tilted toward her on instinct.

We'd crossed paths once before, at a McIvey event in Tuscany. Back when Max and I couldn't share a sentence without it devolving into sarcasm. She'd floated around the wine cellar in a silk slip and heels, brushing past Max like she had a right to him—as if the performance alone deserved his interest.

I hadn't cared. At least, that's what I told myself.

She stood at the refreshment table now—poised detachment, champagne flute, and the kind of practiced elegance that made sipping look strategic. Her gaze locked on us like we were part of her personal entertainment.

When Max finally saw her, his arm slackened. His posture shifted. Nothing dramatic—barely a flicker, but it landed anyway. The heat between us drained in a heartbeat, replaced by the chill of whatever the hell strutted in Valentino heels.

"I'll see you inside," he said. Too soft. Too fast.

He paused—barely—but it was there. A flicker.

Then he turned. Walked toward her without a single glance back.

My stomach flipped. I didn't follow.

If Max Harrington thought he could kiss me dizzy, then float off toward the first glimmer of silk and sin—

He had no idea who he was dealing with.

I don't chase.

I don't beg.

And I sure as hell don't get left behind.

Chapter 11

A Door Between Us

YOU DO NOT CARE, Rayann. You do not *care. Not even a little.* I spun on my heel and snatched a champagne flute off a waiter's tray because bubbly solves everything, right?

Don't care. Don't care. Not caring so hard it's practically a sport.

I downed half in one go. The bubbles fizzed, the burn flared, and absolutely none of it put out the fire in my chest. Max had spent the whole day watching me as though I didn't fit the algorithm. Some maddening puzzle with no clean answer.

And then? Poof. Vanished. As if it had all been a fever dream.

I set my glass down harder than necessary, the brittle clink lost in the crowd's buzz. I needed a distraction. Stat. Anything to drag me out of this ridiculous spiral.

Which is exactly when Ian found me again.

"Well now, Rayann, you put us all to shame out there."

I turned to find his easy grin waiting for me, his Scottish lilt teasing but warm. "You flatter me, Ian."

He leaned in slightly, voice laced with a charm that could probably unhook a bra from twenty paces. "Flatterin' would be sayin' every man in this room wished he'd been the one twirlin' you across the floor."

I laughed, playfully nudging his arm. "And here I thought you were supposed to be the respectable one."

"Oh, I am," he said with a wink. "But that doesn't mean I can't appreciate a little healthy competition."

I smirked. "Confident, are we? You really think you could've held your own against Mr. Harrington?"

Ian placed a hand over his heart, feigning offense. "Lass, please. I would've had you so light on your feet, you'd be beggin' for another dance."

I laughed, shaking my head. "Dangerous promise, Mr. McAlister."

"Ach, not even a wee clue," he teased, leaning in a fraction closer, his eyes twinkling with mischief.

And that's when I felt it. A flicker of static curled down my spine—a shift in the air, charged and electric, the atmosphere changing with his arrival. I didn't have to turn around to know. Didn't need to see him to feel the weight of his stare locking onto me like a freaking heat-seeking missile. But of course I turned. Because self-preservation has never been my strong suit.

And there he was.

Back in the room.

With Annabelle.

Jealousy licked up my spine, singeing and unwelcome. Naturally, while I'd been standing here, using lovely Ian as a distraction, Max had been off somewhere with *her*. Annabelle—glossy waves, graceful in that curated elegance that made you want to slap her and ask for skincare tips, all in the same breath. The kind of woman meant to be draped over his arm, not testing his blood pressure.

And there it was. Her hand. On him. Like she had a season pass to touch Max Harrington whenever the mood struck. One hand draped over his shoulder with the ease of a woman who'd never questioned her welcome, lingering long enough to make my eye twitch on principle. The tilt of her head said it all. She'd been wanted before, and she knew it—cocky little goddess.

I hate her.

And Max? He should've been monitoring the crowd. Watching the exits. Watching the guests. You know, doing his fucking job. Not vanishing with a woman who had no business draping herself over his bicep like a designer acces-sory.

My fingers clenched around my glass like it had answers. Why the hell was I spiraling over this?

I shouldn't be this hung up on the fact that he walked away.

I shouldn't flinch at the sight of him with her.

I shouldn't be comparing myself to her like a damn teenager.

But the worst part?

I shouldn't feel scorched by his gaze.

He wasn't looking at her.

Only me.

Max's stare didn't settle. It struck—jaw tight, eyes dark, a slow, brutal sear that branded every nerve.

And that slow curl of a dangerous thrill, reckless and ris-ing, winding through my chest as if someone had struck a match and walked away?

Let it burn.

Midnight crept closer, the ballroom energy fading with each beat of the clock. I made the rounds, checked in on clients and smiled at vendors, keeping my hands busy and my voice lighter than I felt. Anything to keep my thoughts off Max.

And poof—Houdini vanished again.

I gave the room one last sweep, sidestepping swaying guests and toppled champagne flutes while the music died a merciful death.

Not a single trace.

Maybe I imagined the whole damn thing. Probably for the best. Still, a bitter knot twisted in my gut, coiled and smug, like it had been waiting all evening to say I told you so. Showing up to a knife fight with a spoon, convinced I could win. And if he *had* come back? I might've made a choice impulsive enough to regret—and reckless enough to want twice.

I kicked off my heels without looking where they landed, pacing hard enough to leave scorch marks. The silence didn't soothe. It needled, poked, pricked at every raw edge I was trying to ignore. I'd spent the whole night pretending Max didn't exist, chasing anything shiny enough to keep Max out of my bloodstream—Ian's grin, pounding music, and flute after flute of champagne.

And now?

Now there was nothing. No laughter. No clinking glasses. No crowd to hide in.

Me and the noise inside my head, masquerading as silence.

You do not care, Rayann.

I repeated it on loop, clinging to it like a lifeline.

It wasn't working.

I needed sleep. I needed to shut my brain off. I needed to stop thinking about him.

You do not care, Rayann. You do not care that Max hasn't come back. You do not care that he's probably with Annabelle.

I climbed into bed, yanked the blanket up to my chin, and squeezed my eyes shut.

And that was when I heard it. A soft creak. The suite door opening. My pulse stuttered, every nerve flinching to attention.

Footsteps. Slow. Steady.

I slitted one eye open, catching the faint shift of light beneath the door.

He'd come back.

A long pause. Then—another step.

Closer.

Another step. Closer. The shadow shifted in the doorway, and I knew he was lingering just outside, checking on me.

My breath caught. *Speak, Rayann. Dammit. Open your mouth. Say* something.

But I didn't. I stayed perfectly still, eyes shut, breath shallow, as if staying motionless might erase me from the moment. My heart hammered so loud I was sure he could hear it through the walls. I didn't trust my voice. I didn't know what I'd say. Because if I acknowledged him, I'd have to admit I gave a shit. That it wasn't just irritation—I hurt. And wounded girls make terrible decisions.

The moment stretched. Then, softly, barely more than a whisper of movement, his shadow retreated. A quiet creak. The faint click of his door closing. And just like that, he was gone again.

I exhaled slowly, gaze fixed on the far wall as my stomach twisted into bundle of jagged, ugly nerves.

Max had come back.

He had checked on me.

And I'd played possum because sometimes the best power move is doing nothing with conviction.

The worst part?

I wasn't sure if that made me feel better or worse.

Sleep was a lost cause. I drifted in and out, trapped somewhere between exhaustion and unrest, twisting in the sheets, my mind caught in an endless loop of things I didn't want to think about.

Rough hands trailing heat across my skin, a whisper too close to sanity, and a kiss I had no business craving but couldn't stop replaying.

By the time the first pale streaks of sunlight bled through the curtains, dragging soft light across the floorboards, I was all frayed edges and emotional whiplash. Exhausted. Breathless. Yet still rooted in the same place, same ache, same fucking loop.

Max hadn't left.

I didn't need to check. Didn't need to look. I could *feel* him. That quiet, charged awareness that came with his presence, like leaning too close to something that could burn you if you weren't cautious. But I wasn't about to make the mistake of searching for him.

Nope. Play it cool, Rayann. You're totally unbothered. Pretend you didn't lie awake hoping the door would open again.

Instead, I did what I always do: keep moving. Showered, dressed, tied my hair back with hands that shook enough to piss me off. And by the time I stepped into the hallway, Max was already there. Boots on, hat in hand, patiently waiting. His gaze flicked to mine, unreadable as ever. I didn't stop. A curt nod but no words. Just walked past him like my heart wasn't still a tangled mess inside my chest. Like I hadn't spent the night thinking about the way his shadow had lingered outside my door. Like I wasn't still *feeling* him everywhere. Like I wasn't breaking my own fucking rules by wanting him anyway.

He let me go. A flicker of hesitation, a tiny beat of silence that hinted at unfinished business.

Too fucking bad.

I kept walking, spine straight, heart thrashing.

And he simply stood there calm, collected, cool as ever, as if my spiral hadn't registered on his radar.

Of course he didn't follow.

Of course he bought the act.

Max Harrington, with his perfect timing and maddening restraint, had no idea I was mentally setting him on fire with every step I took.

Chapter 12

Storms Don't Lie

THE MORNING WAS CRISP, the kind of damp that didn't just cling to your skin but sank in deep, settling in places no amount of warmth could touch. Tendrils of mist slid across the hills, cloaking the countryside in quiet magic. The scent of damp earth and wild heather clung to the air, sharp and grounding. I should have been excited. A trail ride through the Scottish Highlands? It was the kind of thing people put on bucket lists. But my stomach was still a knotted disaster. Tight. Restless. Impossible to untangle.

I dragged my feet through the garden, as if stalling could keep the inevitable at bay. Max was already at the stables, adjusting his saddle with that smug, Navy-SEAL-level efficiency that made me want to throw a saddle at his head. He acted like he hadn't been standing outside my door last night. Like I hadn't spent half the night tangled in sheets and picturing him somewhere else.

With her.

After a quick rundown of basic trail-riding procedure, I swung into the saddle in silence, spine stiff, gaze locked straight ahead. I ignored him.

Easy. Controlled. Borderline frosty.

I answered in syllables, not sentences. Didn't look his way. Didn't give him the satisfaction.

Like I hadn't spent the night awake, pulse racing, wondering where the hell he was and who he was with.

Like I wasn't still haunted by the sound of his footsteps in the hallway. The way they stopped. The way he didn't knock.

Like I wasn't one wrong word away from losing whatever grip I still had on this ridiculous façade.

Eight hours. That's how long I'd been pretending. But it was cracking now, and he had to know it.

One glance. One comment. One more second of silence, and I was going to fucking snap.

If the asshole had even a shred of awareness, he didn't show it.

The rest of the group drifted ahead, their laughter rising on the breeze, easy and unbothered. Everything I wasn't. I kept my eyes on the trail, knuckles tight on the reins, and ignored the heat of his stare like it didn't rattle me. And still, somehow, we fell behind. Maybe he slowed on purpose.

Maybe fate was being a jerk. Or maybe Max Harrington couldn't resist the slow torture of letting me stew in my silence. I wasn't handing him that victory.

I could feel his attention on me, steady and quiet, like he was waiting for a crack to show. My temper coiled tighter with every step. And of course, destiny wasn't done being a petty little menace. The mist curled low over the hills, soft and deceptive. Then the sky split wide, and the rain came down swinging.

"Fucking hell, that turned fast," Max muttered. "We need cover, Rayann. Now."

The wind ripped through the valley, rain slamming in sheets while the ground turned to slick mud beneath our horses' hooves. Through the storm-blurred landscape, I spotted it—a small stone structure sitting atop a rise.

A bothy. One of those old Highland shelters meant for hikers, sheep farmers... or apparently, very unprepared Americans. It would have to do.

We reached it just as the storm turned vicious, wind howling through the cracks, rain battering the worn stones. I swung off my horse, water dripping from head to toe, my dress a clingy, soaked mess plastered to every curve I normally pretended not to care about. Max's presence curled up behind me—hot, heavy, as if he was asking without asking if I'd finally stop running. His scent hit me harder than it should have. Clean skin, damp clothes, and a hint of whatever soap he used.

Inside, the air was thick. Rain. Silence. Or maybe something heavier—unspoken want, crawling between us. The space smelled of damp stone and lingering smoke, like a fire once burned here but gave up long ago.

I wrung water from my hair, pacing the small space, frustration rolling off me in waves. Max watched and waited, like he'd already heard the argument spinning through my head. And *that* was what finally broke me.

I turned on him, voice sharp. "Why do you do that?"

Max arched a brow. "Do what?"

"That! The watching. The hovering. The acting like—like this isn't—" I gestured wildly between us, my breathing shot to hell. "Whatever the hell this is!"

His jaw tightened. "You tell me, Rayann."

I exhaled sharply, hands curling into fists. "You infuriate me. You disappear all night, and I'm supposed to—what? Pretend I don't care? Pretend that what happened on that dance floor wasn't the hottest thing I've ever survived without combusting?"

I huffed, my voice snagging on a sharp knot in my throat. "And then you disappear. No text, no explanation. Simply vanish with the first perfectly polished goddess who who could've walked straight off a Bond film set right after you've had your hands all over me, holding me like you'd die if you let go."

Max stilled. Understanding clicked into place. A realization settling deep in his bones.

She noticed.

His fingers curled at his sides. His shoulders went rigid, as though his entire body had gone on high alert. *Did she know what she'd admitted? Did she hear herself?*

"You noticed," he said, his voice quieter now. Lower.

Everything inside me hit pause. *Oh, my God. Had I really said that out loud?*

His features held steady, but there was a new edge in his eyes.

"Did it matter, Rayann?"

I hated him for standing there like Zen fucking Buddha while I was one exhale away from igniting.

He knew exactly how deep I was in this mess, how far I'd sunk. And the bastard wasn't even flinching. His breathing was steady. His posture didn't shift, not even a twitch, like he was tracking every breath I took like it might detonate and knew I was two seconds from breaking. Every part of him was still, as if he was holding his breath... or bracing for impact. Just molten focus and that lethal calm that made my knees want to quit.

Or maybe he was better at hiding it. At staying stone still while I came undone.

My stomach twisted, my throat burned, everything behind my ribs tearing loose. I needed to hurt him back. Something. Anything.

"Go to hell, Max."

And then, without a word, he moved. One step. Two. I didn't even register the space closing before my back hit the wall, Max pressing in like he intended to stay.

His hands braced on either side of me, boxing me in, his body radiating heat despite the chill clinging to our soaked clothes. Rain-slick fabric hugged every one of my curves—thin, useless, obscene in how much it revealed. Drenched. Chilled. Every nerve lit and raw. And Max?

Max *noticed*.

His gaze zeroed in for half a second. Just long enough to betray him. Just long enough to give him away. His throat bobbed. His nostrils flared. His fingers curled into fists, fighting a losing war with himself.

I shivered, and it wasn't from the cold.

His jaw flexed. His breathing turned jagged, unsteady. He was losing control. Muscles coiled tight, his fingers twitched against the stone with white-knuckled restraint. His eyes dragged back up to mine, hungry and desperate. His gaze flicked to my lips. And then—

He snapped.

His mouth crashed against mine, a brutal, claiming kiss, hands gripping my hips, pinning me between the wall and every soaking inch of his being. It was everything I'd denied, buried, fought like hell not to crave. His hands tunneled into my hair, slid down, found my waist, then pulled me in—greed and need in every movement. The heat between us ignited, electric and consuming, a wildfire racing through my veins.

I gasped against him, and he took advantage, deepening the kiss, his grip tightening, his body pressing me harder against the wall. He closed every last inch between us. I could feel him.

All of him.

Solid muscle, searing heat, and the tension we'd barely kept in check now snapping free. Max let out a low, dangerous sound, all hunger and no hesitation. And God help me, I matched him. Everywhere he touched, I burned.

I should stop this. Pull away. Say anything other than the needy sound clawing its way up my throat. But I didn't. Couldn't. Wouldn't.

Because this was heat and hunger and way too much want. No logic or plan here. Just fire, and I wanted every damn second of it.

Max pulled back, barely. Forehead to mine, his breath warm and ragged on my lips. His knuckles brushed along my jaw, reverent and unhurried, as if he was memorizing me. Like he wanted to brand me into his bones.

Air surged through my lungs, my mind spinning in a million directions, lips tingling from the weight of his kiss.

"You are fucking beautiful. And it's driving me insane. You're in my head, in my blood. I see you, and everything else goes quiet. I can't stop thinking about you."

His forehead tipped to mine, breath shaking.

"When I finally have you, Rayann... it won't be because I lost control."

A sharp inhale. A muscle ticked in his jaw. His hands flexed, tension pulling at every muscle.

"It'll be because I let myself."

The heat of those words hit low, knocking the breath clean out of me.

Not a confession. A promise. A fucking warning.

Silence stretched. The kind of silence that challenges you to break it.

He inhaled slow and deep, as if reining himself in. His eyes dipped to my mouth. His restraint snapped again, only for a second. His thumb dragged across my bottom lip.

Slow. Deliberate. Devastating.

This is fine. Everything is fine. My soul is definitely not on fire.

His breath grazed my collarbone, hot and ragged. His voice dropped to a frustrated growl. "And when that happens, Rayann…" His hands clenched. "You won't have to wonder where I've been."

Oxygen hit like a slap—right. Annabelle. The whole sparkly Bond Girl thing I'd thrown in his face like a live grenade.

And he'd taken it. All of it. And stayed.

He was here. Saying this. Looking at me like I was the only thing that made sense to him. And now, he was making damn sure I knew where he stood. With me.

My lungs caught in the middle of *holy shit* and *get it together.* I didn't have a name for the way I felt—only that it was him.

For once, my mouth stayed shut, and not because I wanted it to.

Outside, the storm had slowed to a drizzle. Inside, I felt like a fuse—lit, frayed, one second from blowing everything to hell.

Chapter 13

Necessary, My Ass

I SWUNG ONTO MY horse first, desperate for distance. Movement. Anything but standing there, still simmering from the fire he left behind. Max swung into the saddle slower, like he was trying to shake something off. Guilt. Lust. Me.

He couldn't.

His jaw was tight. Too tight. I knew that look. He was off-kilter, simmering with frustration I could feel from here.

Frustrated at himself.

Oh. Ohh.

The storm. The timing. The fact that we got caught in it without warning. Max Harrington—logistics god, spreadsheet zealot, human embodiment of *I planned for everything*—missed one.

My lips twitched.

Oh, I was going to enjoy every glorious second of this.

I nudged my horse forward with the innocent grace of a woman who definitely wasn't planning verbal war. "So... do you need to add a weather column to your spreadsheet?"

Max exhaled through his nose, guiding his horse beside mine. "Funny. Drop it, Rayann."

Oh, absolutely not.

After the way he'd melted me into that stone wall like a walking fantasy with boundary issues, the least he could do was suffer some light teasing. I pressed a hand to my chest, all mock concern. "I mean, I just assumed you controlled the weather. You had it all timed so perfectly, after all."

His fingers flexed on the reins. His jaw ticked. But the corner of his mouth? Almost. *Almost.* Twitched.

I grinned. *Gotcha, big guy.*

"You're freezing," he said flatly, though his gaze flicked—low.

My stomach flipped. I shrugged, breezy. "Bit late for concern, Harrington. Pretty sure I was hypothermic by the time you pinned me to that wall."

A flicker of tension pulled through his fingers. "Pinned?" he echoed, voice rough. "Interesting phrasing." His jaw worked, his eyes dragging over my dress for one unforgiving second too long. If he felt guilty for losing control, he sure wasn't showing it. Not with that look.

I tilted my head, pretending to consider. "Right. Maybe *cornered* is more accurate. Or *pressed*. Against a wall."

My voice was casual. My pulse? Not so much. He was the one who caged me in like I was air and he couldn't breathe, and now he wanted to sit there pretending he hadn't short-circuited my brain? *Please*. Meanwhile, I was riding like this horse wasn't carrying the full weight of my unresolved sexual tension. I glanced at him, sharp, and couldn't decide if I wanted to kiss him again... or shove him off his saddle. "Call it what you want, Max. I remember where your hands were."

He exhaled slowly, something dark flickering in his eyes. Something still simmering. "*Necessary*," he said low, almost growling.

"Because if I didn't touch you, I was going to explode."

Ooh. So we're using more than two words now.
And sweet Jesus, someone get me a goddamn fan.

He looked at me like he was already mentally scheduling the sequel. So much for hypothermia. If he kept that up, I was going to do something extremely unprofessional. And possibly illegal. Hell, I'd help write the incident report.

I gave a low whistle, eyes locked on his. "So that was you trying not to touch me?" My lips curled. "You're gonna make one hell of a mess when you finally stop trying."

For half a second, I swore he might jump off his horse and grab me again, but the sound of distant voices carried on the wind—laughter and chatter signaling company had arrived. Max's head snapped toward the noise, and whatever softness had flickered in his eyes hardened into steel. The professional returned. Back to business. One minute, I was pinned like a heroine in a fever-dream fantasy. The next, I was left wet, pissed off, and wondering if I needed therapy or a taser. His words were still short-circuiting my brain by the time we reached the clearing.

The others weren't far. We slogged through the final stretch of muddy trail, our horses slipping with every step. Up ahead, cottage windows glowed with warm light, silhouettes moving inside, dry and laughing—completely oblivious to the mess of heat and havoc we'd just crawled out of.

I exhaled through my nose and braced for impact. Game face: engaged. Damage control mode: fully activated. I straightened in the saddle, ignoring the ache in my legs and the way my soaked dress clung like it had opinions. Beside me, Max seemed restored to factory settings like nothing ever happened.

*Go on, Max. Pretend we didn't almost set that bothy on fire. I'll be over here polishing your 'Best Bullsh*t Performance' trophy.*

We reached the clearing, Max riding in like the CEO of 'Nothing to See Here'. A few heads turned, and someone let out a low whistle. Cue the chorus of nosy Scots and the brutal, final death of my sexy fantasy.

"Well, well," Collum drawled, a twinkle in his eye as his gaze slid between us like someone was keeping score—and he'd just handed Max a point. "Thought the storm might've swallowed you up. We were about five minutes from sending out a search party."

I slapped on a grin that didn't quite reach my wind-slapped cheeks. "We're fine. We found... walls. Mostly vertical."

Max, damn him, didn't even blink. Of course not. The man could survive an avalanche without so much as adjusting his collar.

Collum crossed his arms, the corner of his mouth twitching with amusement. "And where exactly did the two of you find this refuge?"

I opened my mouth, ready to lie like a damn professional—but Max beat me to it. "We found a bothy." He didn't blink. Just dropped the word like it meant nothing.

Sure, Max. Play it cool, like that kiss wasn't a goddamn thunderclap.

Collum's grin widened. "Ah, a bothy, aye? Cozy little place, was it?"

"Fine. Damp. Holding together... barely."

I choked on my own breath. *Did he have to say it like that?*

I threw him a don't-you-dare glare, locking onto his face like a sniper. But before I could verbally light him up, one of the bridesmaids called out from the doorway, grinning like she'd just been handed the juiciest scoop of the night. "Some storm, aye?" the bridesmaid said, arching a brow. "Looks like you two found a way to pass the time." I wanted to hurl myself into the nearest puddle and let the mud swallow me whole.

Someone tossed me a blanket. "Ye alright there, lass?"

"Peachy," I said, teeth chattering. "Just living my soggy princess fantasy." I smiled so hard, I nearly sprained a cheekbone.

Ian tipped his head toward the door, voice smooth as sin. "So... did the bothy rise to your expectations?"

My stomach did a mortified back flip, then kept flipping just to be extra. *Oh, fantastic. They were picturing it. The wall. The hands. All of it.*

And then, naturally, came the worst part.

"You didn't have to sneak off, you know," the woman added, her voice lilting with amusement. "You've got the whole lot whisperin' like old aunties at a wedding after three drams and no shame."

My breath hitched before covering it with a smirk. "Let me know when they start placing bets. I want a cut."

"Nothing happening." Max's voice sliced through the warmth like a blade.

Oh. So that's *how we're playing it.*

Noted, Harrington.

I hadn't expected a declaration, but I sure as hell hadn't expected that quick of a dismissal either.

The sting spread fast, settling deep in my ribs. I should have let it go. Should have brushed it off with a careless wave.

But no. I wasn't built for silence, especially not the kind that burned. I forced out a light laugh and tilted my head toward Max like he was an unfortunate choice on a dating show. "Please. Like I'd pick him on purpose?"

The group chuckled. Collum snorted.

Max didn't blink, but something behind his eyes recoiled. Tight. Wounded. Not just annoyed. That one landed.

I pulled the blanket close, my smile sharp enough to slice concrete.

Fabulous. Public humiliation and hypothermia. What a day.

When we returned to the stables, the group peeled off toward the castle in loose pairs, chattering like the storm hadn't even happened. I dismounted without a word, fingers lingering on my horse's neck longer than necessary. *Lord, just give me one more second to get my shit together.* Just return the horse, nod politely, and escape. A few more steps and I'd be out. Done. Clear.

And then I saw him.

Max waited by the post—arms crossed, brim low, pretending not to watch me. I felt his stare from ten feet out. *Like hell he wasn't watching.*

He could've left. Could've gone back up to the castle with the others, pretending the bothy was just a weird detour in an otherwise ordinary day.

But he hadn't.

He waited.

Of course he did. Because God forbid I get a moment to untangle my dignity in private.

I bit back every petty word and took my sweet fucking time dismounting. Brushed off imaginary dirt. Adjusted the saddle like it had personally wronged me—then handed the reins over with the kind of casual precision that really screamed not-casual-at-all.

Do not engage. Do not combust. Just breathe.

Max was still parked like a statue probably betting on which vein in my forehead would pop first. I ignored the flare in my chest, the traitorous thump beneath my ribs. Ignored the way my skin still buzzed from the heat of his hands. The goddamn wall.

And that kiss—filthy, unhinged, and sexy as fuck.

Max Harrington was supposed to be emotionally constipated, not a walking fantasy with enough raw heat to blow every last assumption I had about him to hell.

You're fine, Rayann. You are completely fine.

Except I wasn't. I was furious. Flustered. Walking like my lips hadn't just betrayed me. I hadn't even looked back at him yet, and already my brain was two steps away from a blackout.

"Rayann."

My name, low and growly, landed like a match in dry brush. Pretty sure that man's voice could talk a nun into a tequila shot.

You've got two options, Wilder. You can make the smart choice. Or the hot one.

"If this is your attempt at damage control, I should warn you—I'm not exactly feeling diplomatic."

"It's not," he said quietly.

I paused. His voice wasn't sharp. Wasn't clipped or annoyed. Just steady. He took a step forward, exhaling slow and measured, his gaze flicking to the others still packing up in the distance. Then back to me.

"I put you in a difficult position," Max said, voice low and rough. "And I'm sorry."

I blinked, thrown by the sincerity.

But then he kept going.

"But don't stand there and act like you didn't feel it too," he said, quieter now. "Because I sure as hell did."

I stilled. "You're unbelievable," I snapped. "You spend the whole ride acting like nothing happened, and now I'm the one pretending?"

Max pushed off the post, stepping closer.

I deflected. Forced a smirk. Nudged his shoulder as I moved past him.

"You want honesty, Max?" I said, brushing by. "Fine. It meant something. But if you're gonna treat me like it didn't, then yeah. I'll pretend. Just like you did."

My voice came out lighter than it should have. Forced. Too polished to hide the sting underneath.

And when I walked away, every step felt heavier than the one before.

I didn't look back.

But I thought about it.

I had, I might have seen it—the way Max's jaw tensed. The flicker of something raw before he shoved it all down again.

Chapter 14

Playing With Fire

THE MOMENT I STEPPED through the castle doors, reality slammed back into place like a locked gate.

The bothy. The storm. The way Max had looked at me like he was one heartbeat away from forgetting every last unwritten rule between us. It still buzzed beneath my skin, but I buried it deep. Had to. The world didn't care what had happened between us.

The castle buzzed on, alive and unbothered. The scent of rain still lingered, soft as memory, sharp as regret. Candlelight flickered against the stone walls, casting the room in gold. Music floated from the far corner, laughter rising beneath it, bright and easy. Staff wove between tables, smooth and graceful, tying the last ribbons, pouring the last glasses.

Meanwhile, I was over here rocking the emotional stability of a wet paper bag—smiling just enough to hide the fact that

I'd nearly climbed their favorite broody security guy like a damn jungle gym against a stone wall.

No big deal.

Totally fine.

Oh yeah—and it was, obnoxiously fucking hot.

Business as usual, like I hadn't almost burned it all down.

I inhaled deep, steadying. My hair still smelled faintly like the lavender soap from the guest wing. At least we'd had time to rinse off the storm and swap our soaked clothes for something dry. I smoothed my dress and pasted on a smile like I wasn't one stray compliment away from either bursting into tears or making out with the next available bartender. Hot and bothered is a hell of a combo. Fifty-fifty, really.

Max walked in ahead of me but veered off without a word. Already back in work mode, already scanning the room like he was praying for a brawl to break out. Or a gas leak. Or maybe just a really aggressive floral arrangement he could neutralize. Anything but me.

Fine. If he wanted professional, I could out-professional his ass all night.

I turned on my heel and strutted off like I had zero interest in throwing him into the nearest coat closet. Bride. Vendors. People who didn't currently smell like pine, danger, and bad decisions. That was my lane now.

Max stationed himself at the far end of the room, stiff-backed and scowly, eyes sweeping the crowd, gripping the furniture like it was the only thing keeping him from violating at least three company policies. I kept my gaze trained on anything that wasn't six foot four and emotionally unavailable. I smiled. I laughed. I fluffed throw pillows and smiled through small talk like I wasn't secretly hosting an X-rated film festival on a loop in my head.

Everything looked picture-perfect.

Staged. Polite. Bullshit.

Okay—maybe not total bullshit. But let's just say I wasn't exactly feeling my most professional at the moment.

I mean... I'm not a monk.

Except that I couldn't stop watching him.
And he couldn't stop watching me.

I was giving one hell of a performance. Max just stood there radiating silent crisis like it was his full-time job.

But damn, it was killing me. I felt it every time our eyes met across the room—the way his gaze darkened, heavy, lingering like he was still memorizing the shape of me under his hands. Like he could still feel the way I'd come apart for him.

And when I laughed? When I tucked my hair behind my ear like I wasn't one bad choice away from crawling into his lap? Oh, I saw it. The crack in his composure. The sharp clench of his jaw. The way his eyes followed me like gravity—like he didn't even want to fight it.

God help me, I wasn't doing much better.

Dinner wound down in soft laughter and the clink of glass. Guests drifted toward the courtyard beneath the stars, easy and oblivious while my insides staged a full-blown rebellion. I stayed behind, handling the last few details. Smiles on autopilot, hands steady, voice smooth. My insides? A four-alarm dumpster fire.

And then—Max.

Close. Too close.

He didn't speak. Didn't touch me. Just stood there, radiating heat and purpose like it was its own goddamn gravitational pull. His gaze pinned me in place, steady. Certain. Like he'd already made the decision. When he finally leaned in, his breath skimmed the curve of my neck, low and deliberate. "Come with me."

There was no ragged edge in his voice. No crack. Just control. Full. Intentional. Absolute.

I should have walked away. Should have said no. But there was something in the way he said it—like the outcome had already been written and we were both just following the script.

I followed him out of the hall, my pulse hammering so hard I was surprised no one else could hear it. We barely made it inside the library before Max shut the door behind us—slow, measured, locking it with a soft click that felt louder than any slam.

He didn't lunge. Didn't rush. Just stepped into my space, bracing one hand against the wall beside my head, his body crowding mine without touching. His eyes steady on mine. Waiting. Watching. Choosing.

"Tell me to stop." His voice was quiet. Dangerous in how calm it was.

I met his gaze, breath caught somewhere between my chest and my throat, my head swimming. I didn't blink. Didn't look away.

I reached up, my thumb brushing over his lips—slow. Certain. "Don't you dare."

And that was all it took.

Max moved like a man with a plan—no hesitation, no second-guessing, no slip of control. His mouth landed on mine, his hands weaving into my hair, tilting my head back as he kissed me like he *meant* it. Like he'd meant to all along.

His hands dragged down my body, skimming over my breasts, over my hips, until he was gripping my thighs and lifting me against him.

I gasped against his lips, my legs wrapping around his waist before I could even think. My back hit the door with a soft thud.

"Max," I whispered, my voice shaky, desperate.

His answer was a low growl, the sound vibrating against my skin. His fingers flexed on my hips, his body pressing harder into mine as his mouth moved lower.

My jaw. My throat.

His teeth grazed the delicate spot at the base of my neck, his tongue flicking over it, soothing the burn. "You make me fucking crazy," he muttered against my skin, voice thick and edged with something dark. "Do you have any idea what you do to me?"

I was too far gone to answer. My nails scraped down his back, and he shuddered. He rolled his hips into me, and I felt him.

Every. Inch.

Hard and desperate. Ready to ruin us both.

My fingers fumbled between us, reaching for his belt. The leather slid free with a soft, sinful sound. His breath caught. He tangled his hands in the fabric of my dress, dragging it higher. I found the button of his slacks, popped it, slid the zipper down.

Max's head dropped against my shoulder, his whole body shaking. "Rayann." My name came out like a warning. Like a plea.

I kissed him instead. Hard. Hot. Wild. I wanted him. Desperately. I was seconds away from dropping to my knees.

Then—because of course—someone knocked. Sharp. Loud. Brutal.

I gasped.

Max froze.

"Rayann?"

Fiona.

My stomach dropped.

Shit.

Shit. Shit. Shit.

Another knock, sharper this time. "Are you in there?"

Max exhaled hard through his nose.

Fuck.

I scrambled, shoving at his chest, but he didn't move. Not right away. His forehead stayed pressed to mine, his breath hot and ragged, his hands still gripping my thighs like the knock was a minor inconvenience to be dealt with later.

The third knock snapped the tension.

With a harsh breath, Max finally pulled back, easing me down. I barely had time to yank my dress into place before the handle rattled.

Then again.

Then a sharper knock.

"One second!" I yelped, tripping over my own feet as I scrambled for the lock. My fingers fumbled with it—too hot, too shaky, too goddamn obvious.

When I finally wrenched the door open, Fiona stood there, one brow lifted, her gaze far too sharp for my liking. "You alright?"

Her eyes swept over me, lingering just long enough to make me sweat, then slid past my shoulder.

To Max.

Still standing there, looking every inch the model of composure, of course. Because obviously Max Harrington doesn't ruffle. Other people ruffle.

Well... except for the belt, sitting just off-center. And the faint smudge of red at the collar, right where a mouth might've been—if anyone around here were reckless enough to cross that particular line.

Hypothetically.

I fought for breath. Fought to claw my way back to something resembling composure, but every inch of me still burned. "Fine," I forced out, my voice way too bright. "Just... needed a breather."

Fiona's brows lifted. Uh-huh. But she didn't press.

"They're moving everyone to the lounge for a final toast," she said, her gaze ping-ponging between the two of us like she knew exactly how close we'd come to scandal.

I nodded. "Right. I'll be there in a sec."

She lingered for a beat, long enough to make my skin prickle, then finally turned and disappeared down the hall.

Silence.

I didn't turn. Didn't move. I didn't have to. I could feel him behind me. The weight of him. The charge still thick in the air between us.

And when I finally faced him—

Max wasn't unreadable this time. Frustration carved deep across his brow, breath still shaky, fists curled like he didn't know what to do with them now that they weren't on me. His eyes caught mine, flickering with something raw. A war of want and self-reproach.

My stomach twisted hard.

I should say something. Throw up my usual walls. Break the tension before it broke me.

But before I could—

Max lifted a hand. Not hesitant. Not unsure. Just deliberate. His knuckles skimmed my cheek, the barest touch—enough to tell me he wasn't really walking away.

Not from this.

Not from me.

Then he exhaled, rough and uneven, and let his hand drop.

"Christ," he muttered, pushing a hand through his hair like he was recalibrating—resetting the system, reining it all back in, piece by piece. And then he turned and walked out.

Not cold. Not shutting me out.

Just a man who knew that if he didn't leave right now, he wouldn't leave at all.

And the next time? There wouldn't be a damn door in this castle strong enough to stop him.

Chapter 15

The Illusion of Control

THE LOUNGE FLICKERED WITH golden candlelight, shadows stretching long over the stone walls. Laughter swirled through the room, glasses lifted, the final pre-wedding toast seconds from center stage.

I stood near the front, fingers poised on the stem of my glass, every inch the polished professional. Untouched. Unbothered.

Yeah, right.

Inside? I was shaking.

Across the room, Max stood like nothing had happened. Whiskey in hand. The way his fingers gripped that glass, white-knuckled, like it was the only thing keeping him grounded. His jaw worked like he was grinding the words between his teeth. Whatever he wanted to say, he swallowed it down instead.

No one would know.

No one would guess that less than thirty minutes ago, his hands were tangled in my hair, his mouth dragging fire down my throat, his body pinning me to the door like he meant to ruin us both. No one would have guessed that I'd been seconds away from taking *him* in that cozy castle library.

No one knew that Fiona had saved us both.

And still—I felt him. His heat. His presence. Even with half a room between us, even through firelight, music, and a dozen bodies, Max Harrington was still on my skin.

I waited for him to look at me. Just once. But he never did. His stare stayed locked on the far wall like it held the only safe place in the room.

Like if he met my eyes, we'd both come undone.

Except he had. With me. And if the tension rolling off him was any clue, it was killing him just as much as it was killing me.

I swallowed hard, forcing a polite smile as Fiona caught my eye. She lifted her glass, giving the signal. Showtime.

A hush fell. Collum cleared his throat, smiling wide. "We've had quite the journey to get here, haven't we?"

A ripple of laughter.

I barely heard it. My eyes kept drifting back to Max. He hadn't moved from that one spot by the wall. Half in shadow, half out. Like even his body couldn't decide whether to stay or run. Hell, maybe he was already halfway gone.

Collum lifted his glass higher. "To old grudges left in the past, to new beginnings, and to the love that brought us all together—may it burn brighter than any storm."

My breath caught before I could stop it.

Storm.

The word hit like a punch to the gut, dragging me back—back to the bothy, back to the fire in Max's eyes, back to the way his hands had actually trembled when he finally touched me.

Across the room, Max's arm froze mid-lift, whiskey glass hovering like even that had become too much. His grip tightened on the glass—just a fraction too hard. Enough to make me wonder if he might shatter it. But then he shifted, loosening his hold like he'd caught himself in the act.

Then his eyes locked on mine—hot, dark, and way too full of everything we weren't saying.

My fingers clenched around my glass. I lifted it slowly, and across the room, Max did the same.

He didn't look away. Not for a second. Like we were locked in some silent dare. A war. A secret confession we weren't brave enough to say out loud.

The toast ended. Laughter sparked again, little pockets of conversation blooming like nothing had just passed between us.

I kept moving. A smile here. A nod there. Staying busy. Polished. In control. Or close enough.

For half a second, I thought he might cross the room. But then his jaw locked, and he turned away, fast and sharp. Gone before I could even call him on it. Before I could call his bluff. Before I could corner him with a whispered *we need to talk.*

Of course he walked away. Of course he couldn't even look at me. Easier to pretend it meant nothing when you don't have to face it.

Me? I was done playing nice. And if Max Harrington wanted to run, he better be fast.

I found him just outside the main hall, posted up at the balcony, hands braced against the stone like he was trying not to jump. Or throw someone. Possibly me. His shoulders were so tight it was like they'd been screwed into place.

I didn't hesitate. My heels snapped against the stone like punctuation. I walked straight up to him, voice low, sharp, and fully out of patience. "You're being an ass, *Mr.* Harrington. Are you going to sulk all night, or are you actually going to say what's on your mind?"

Max's jaw clenched. His gaze stayed fixed on the garden below. "You don't want to have this conversation right now."

I blinked, caught off guard. "What the hell was that supposed to mean?"

Max stepped closer. "Fiona walked in on us."

I crossed my arms. "She didn't walk in. She knocked."

His jaw ticked. "Not the point."

Oh, this *insufferable* man.

"No, Max. What *is* the point, then?"

Silence.

But then I saw it—this wasn't just him being pissed. It was deeper. Messier. He wasn't stewing about the knock. He was mad at himself—furious, maybe—for letting go. For letting me in. He had already lost control once in the bothy. Then again in the library. And for the first time in who knows how long, I'd knocked something loose in him—and he hated it. Hated that his careful control hadn't stood a chance, that his well-ordered life didn't feel like his own.

"You're angry with me," I said, my voice a little softer. Just enough to be dangerous.

Max's chest rose, sharp. And for just a second, something raw flickered in his eyes—something I almost caught. And just like that, the wall slammed back into place.

"No."

He inhaled. Slow. Controlled. "I'm mad because it was a mistake." He didn't spit it. He didn't even sound angry. Just... gutted.

I didn't see that one coming. Not even a little. My chest pulled tight. Sharp. Like my lungs forgot how to work.

And then I laughed. Quiet. Disbelieving. The kind of laugh that hurt on the way out.

"A mistake."

Max didn't blink. "Yes."

I nodded once. Then again. Slow.

Then, I stepped forward. Closing the space between us. "Then why the hell are you still looking at me like you're starving?"

Silence.

His breath caught—just enough to tell me I'd hit the mark.

Ohh. I fucking had him.

His hands curled into fists like it was the only way to keep from reaching for me again.

I dropped my voice, low and dangerous. "Go ahead. Say it again. Look me in the eyes and tell me it was a mistake." I tipped my chin up, eyes locked on his. "See if I believe you."

His jaw clenched so hard I thought his teeth might shatter. His eyes burned into mine—but he didn't say a word. For one brutal second, I thought he might actually say it.

I saw it. Felt it. That crack wide open. But instead, he turned and walked away.

Well, fuck me sideways.

***

MAX

I, Max Harrington, who's supposed to have my shit together, just bailed like a coward with a hard-on and feelings.

Outstanding work. Ten out of ten. Real fucking smooth, you idiot.

I kept moving.

Down the hall. Past the castle walls. Into the dark and straight toward the only place I could sit with it and stew—the bar.

Warm enough. Crowded enough. But not enough to keep me from claiming this corner and staying the hell out of the way. Whiskey and smoke thick in the air. Damp still clinging to my jacket like it was holding a grudge.

The scotch burned steady on the way down. Not fast. Not slow. Just enough to feel it. Just enough to piss me off.

The bartender wandered over—older guy, sharp-eyed, more silver than red in the beard. The kind of look that said he'd seen enough bullshit to last a lifetime. "Ye keep scowlin' like that, laddie, and yer drink's gonna curdle."

I kept my eyes on the glass. "Long day."

He snorted. "Aye, and I'm the bloody Queen of England."

Didn't smile. Not really. But my mouth gave it a shot anyway.

"Name's Murdo," he added, dragging his rag across the bar with the kind of flourish that said I wasn't his first storm-drenched stray and wouldn't be his last.

The old bastard wiped a clean spot again, slower this time—like waiting me out was half the fun. "If ye came in here to brood and drink yerself blind, I suggest ye pick one and commit to it. Otherwise, yer just wastin' good whiskey."

I drew in air. Let it out slow through my teeth.

Should've gone upstairs and put the whole damn night behind me.

Should've.

But here I was.

Sitting in a bar.

Nursing a drink and stewing like the goddamn coward I didn't want to admit I was.

Hell, maybe that should've made it easier—put the night behind me. Lock it up. Move on. Simple. Clean.

The way I usually handled things.

She hadn't called me on it.

Hadn't chased after me.

Hadn't thrown one of those sharp little barbs my way.

And yeah—that should've made it easier.

It didn't.

Murdo didn't say a damn thing. Just watched me. Like he was weighing whether to kick my ass or pour me another.

"Trouble with a lass?"

I tightened my grip on the glass. "No."

"Aye, and the Pope's a Protestant."

I ground my teeth, trying not to say something I'd regret.

Murdo chuckled, pouring himself a glass and taking a sip. "Ye wouldn't be the first fool to sit at this bar thinkin' a dram or two would help him out of a self-inflicted mess."

I didn't argue. What the hell could I say to that?

Raised a brow. Didn't bother looking impressed. "You always this chatty with your customers?"

"Only the ones who look like they need to be smacked upside the head."

Dragged a hand down my face. "I'm fine."

Murdo gave me a look. "Lad, ye are sittin' in a pub alone, starin' into that glass like it's about to whisper the meanin' of life. Ye are not fine."

Kept my mouth shut. Bastard wasn't wrong.

"Ye keep checkin' that phone like it owes ye an apology."

No text. No call. Not even a missed one to throw me a bone.

Shouldn't give a damn.

But there it was anyway.

Murdo's sharp gaze flicked to my phone. "Ahh, now I see. Ye were hopin' she'd chase after ye, weren't ye?"

I snapped my head up, sharper than I meant to. "I wasn't—"

Murdo smirked. "Aye, ye were. Nothin' wounds a man's pride quite like a lass lettin' him walk away."

Didn't bother hiding the sigh. "You always this invested in strangers' lives?"

Murdo shrugged. "People are easy to read when ye've spent forty years watchin' men try to outdrink their regrets."

I didn't answer. Just kept spinning the glass against the wood, slow as hell. I knew better than to open my damn mouth.

Did it anyway.

"You ever seen anyone get it right?"

Murdo watched me for a long minute, then took a slow sip. "Aye. But only the ones who stop runnin' long enough to let themselves have it."

Didn't need the whiskey to burn. His words took care of that.

Yeah. That was the problem.

Right there.

Nailed it.

I'd spent years—hell, a lifetime—staying two steps ahead.

Always.

Planning, calculating, stacking the odds before I ever made a move.

Control was the point. The whole damn point.

Rayann?

She was all fire and trouble. Wrapped up so goddamn pretty it hurt to look at her. She made me reckless. Made me lose my grip. Made me *want*.

And that? That scared the hell out of me.

Murdo tapped his fingers against the bar.

Tap. Tap. Tap.

Could feel it coming before he even asked.

"So what's stoppin' ye?"

Didn't like the way that question sat. "Excuse me?"

"Ye like her. She likes ye. And yet, here ye are, alone in a pub, hopin' she'll do the chasin' for ye." Murdo leaned forward, bracing his elbows on the bar. "What's stoppin' ye, lad?"

Felt that one hit, square and ugly. "It's complicated."

Murdo let out a low chuckle. "Aye, love usually is. But in my experience, when a man says it's complicated, what he really means is he's too stubborn—or too scared—to own up to what he wants."

Wanted to call bullshit.

But he wasn't wrong.

Too stubborn. Too afraid. Maybe both.

It wasn't just that I wanted her. It was what she did to me.

The way she wrecked my focus.

Pulled me in.

Unraveled every thread I'd spent years tying down.

She made me feel alive. And Christ—didn't know what to do with that. Not even close.

Murdo exhaled through his nose, shaking his head. "Whatever it is ye're runnin' from, lad... sooner or later, it'll catch up."

Didn't need Murdo to spell it out. Already felt it breathing down my neck.

Murdo didn't look away. Didn't need to. Already had me pinned wide open.

Knocked back another sip, slow as hell. Like maybe the whiskey could shut him up for me.

Murdo snorted. "Aye, that's what I thought."

Didn't look at him. "And what's that?"

The bartender leaned back, giving me a long, assessing look. "Ye're not just afraid of wantin' the lass."

Murdo's gaze held steady. "Ye're afraid of what happens if ye let yerself have her."

Gripped the glass hard enough my knuckles burned.

Murdo nodded, like he'd just confirmed something I already knew. "Aye. That's it, isn't it?"

I stayed quiet. Harder to lie that way.

Murdo wiped down the counter with slow, steady movements. "Men like ye, lad... ye don't fear love. Ye fear what happens when it's gone." He tilted his head. "And I'd bet every last bottle in this place that it's not the first time ye've lost somethin' that mattered."

Could feel that one hit low. Right where I kept the things I didn't talk about.

Couldn't breathe right.

Gripped the glass until my knuckles turned white.

Murdo didn't press. He just poured another dram of whiskey and slid it across the bar like it was a goddamn confessional.

"Go on, then. Tell me."

I wasn't going to say a damn thing. But the words came anyway.

Chapter 16

The Reckoning of Max Harrington

"IT WAS SUPPOSED TO be a simple extraction."

The words scraped out rough, like they didn't want to leave my mouth.

Murdo didn't say a damn thing. Just stood there, waiting me out.

I let my breath out slow, chest too damn tight to pull another one in. "We had a man trapped. Intel was shit. We thought we had time."

My jaw clenched hard enough I could feel it grind. "We didn't."

I forced another breath. "I made the call to go in."

Murdo stayed quiet. Just let it hang there. He gave the smallest nod, slow and steady. "And?"

The scotch didn't help. My throat still burned. "And I was wrong."

That was the truth of it. The ugliest piece.

I didn't move. Didn't breathe.

"We lost two men that night," I said, choking on the words. "Because I thought I could control the situation. Because I fucking knew better."

The memory hit like a goddamn hammer. Chaos. Gunfire. Their voices over comms—desperate, still holding the line even as it all went sideways.

And me?

Trapped. Pinned down. Forced to listen. Forced to wait.

I could still hear it—the moment I knew they weren't getting out. And worse? The moment I knew it was my fault.

Murdo's face didn't give me a damn thing. "Ye were the one who called it?"

I nodded. Tight. Like my neck might snap if I moved any more than that.

Murdo let out a low hum. "Aye. That'd do it."

"They pulled me from field ops after that. PTSD, they called it." I swirled my glass slow. "Stayed a few more years, but it wasn't the same. I came back different. Got out. Took a job where I could control the risks."

Ground my teeth. The words came out flat. Empty.

Murdo didn't say a word. Just took another sip, eyes still on me.

Might've laughed if there'd been anything left in me. "Spreadsheets. Risk assessments. High-profile security work. Predictable. I know the variables. Nothing left to chance."

Murdo lifted one brow, slow as hell. "Except ye do, don't ye?"

Felt that one land like a stone drop. Heavy. Right in the gut.

Murdo leaned in, elbows braced on the bar like he had all night. "Ye see, lad, the problem isn't that ye lost control back then."

He tapped the wood between us, slow and deliberate. "The problem is ye think it was yer fault."

Locked up so tight my teeth ached. Swallowed hard. Let the scotch sting like it was supposed to. "It was."

"Ye were trained for war, lad. Trained to make the best call when the whole bloody world was burnin' to hell around ye. Sometimes that call's made on piss-poor intel, sometimes it's gut instinct. Either way, it's a choice—and choosin' wrong doesn't make ye a failure. It makes ye human."

Didn't want to hear it. Bastard wasn't wrong.

I knew exactly what Murdo was doing. Knew it was working—because that night came barreling back, full force, like it always did.

There were six of us.

Pinned down in a crumbling building, RPGs lighting up the sky, comms screaming static and panic into my ear.

We'd been pushing forward. Securing the extraction point.

One decision. One second. One call—mine.

I thought I was right. Swore to God I was. Didn't even blink.

But I wasn't.

Saw the blast before I heard it. Took the shockwave before the impact. Watched a man I was supposed to protect disappear in the fire.

I was trained for that. Trained to make the call. To act without hesitation. To adapt.

But now?

Now I second-guessed every goddamn thing.

Every instinct. Every move.

Every breath.

Because what if my gut wasn't just wrong that night?

What if it's broken?

Murdo leaned back against the bar, arms crossed, eyes steady. Watched me the way only an old bartender could—like he'd seen this play out a hundred times and knew exactly how long it'd take for me to crack.

I wasn't cracking. Not yet.

Not until he opened his damn mouth. "Ye don't trust yerself, do ye, lad?"

His words hit low. Right where I didn't want them.

I let the breath out slow through my nose, fighting the urge to bite back. "I trust myself fine."

Murdo snorted. Didn't even try to hide it. "Aye? *That* why ye need yer plans? Yer spreadsheets? So ye don't have to rely on instinct anymore?"

I froze. Just long enough for him to know he'd hit the mark.

He leaned forward, elbows braced on the bar. "What's worse, lad? Trustin' yer gut and bein' wrong once in a while? Or never trustin' it again and losin' every single thing worth havin'?"

Felt that one land, square and solid.

Couldn't stop the flinch. No way to hide it.

Murdo saw it. Knew exactly what he was doing—hitting dead center.

He leaned in, voice dropping low. Not soft. Just sharp enough to hit where it hurt. "Ye think yer protectin' her by holdin' back. But what if ye're just protectin' yerself?"

Didn't answer. Hell, I didn't know anymore.

His gaze flicked to my glass, then back to me. "Tell me somethin', lad. Ye really think those men would want ye carryin' that weight forever?"

My whole body went rigid. Felt the words coil tight in my chest. Because no—I hadn't really thought about it. Not like that. Not in a way that let the air in.

If I wasn't to blame, then what the hell had I been punishing myself for all these years?

Murdo leaned back, patient as hell, studying me like a man piecing together a puzzle. Then he dropped the hammer. "Ye keep tellin' yerself that control keeps ye safe. But all I see is a man afraid of livin' his own damn life."

My pulse thundered. He was right, and I knew it.

Rayann made me feel alive. Pulled me out of my own head. Made me forget. Made me reckless.

And that? That scared the hell out of me.

I stared down at the glass. Swallowed hard.

Murdo's smirk faded. His voice went soft. "Careful, lad. Die with your guard up, and no one's there to notice."

He took a long sip of his whiskey. Let the words settle. Then, quieter still—

"That the life ye want?"

The ache in my chest kicked harder. My fingers clenched the glass, knuckles burning white.

Because maybe for the first time in years, I wasn't just thinking about the past.

I was thinking about what came next.

***

Rayann

I didn't call after Max. Didn't chase. Just stood there and watched the crack split wider than I wanted to admit.

Nice move, Rayann. Next time, maybe offer to hold the door open while he stomps all over your soul.

I barely made it back to the suite before the breath punched out of me—sharp, ragged, ugly. My chest pulled so tight I might snap clean in two.

I knew he'd fight it. Knew the second I pushed too hard, Max Harrington would slam the brakes and run like hell.

But knowing didn't soften the hit.

Because that's the thing about wanting too much—you learn exactly how fast people can run.

I kicked off my heels. Poured a scotch—heavy-handed, zero patience. Yanked the nearest blanket off the couch and wrapped it tight, armor against the goddamn freefall.

Then I dropped straight to the floor by the fire.

The flames crackled, steady and solid. Warm. Real. The only thing in the room that wasn't falling apart.

I curled up at the base of the couch, knees tucked, fists clenched hard in the blanket, holding still like it might keep the ache from breaking loose.

Which, let's be honest, was a total long shot—but desperate times.

No idea how long I stayed like that—and honestly? Didn't care.

Max walked away.

And that? Worst part.

But the part that really bothered me?

I wasn't even sure I wanted him to come back.

Okay, that's a lie. I wanted him back so bad it hurt.

But he'd come back. He always did.

...Right?

The fire had burned low by the time I heard the door open. Shadows flickered long across the stone, stretching wider as the flames faded. I felt him there. Lingering. Watching.

I was still there.

Still curled on the floor, blanket wrapped tight like it was the only thing holding me together. The scotch glass dangled loose in my hand, half-forgotten. My legs were numb beneath me, but I couldn't make myself move.

Couldn't make myself stop waiting.

The latch clicked softly behind me.

I didn't look right away. Didn't breathe.

But then—I felt him.

Max crossed the room slow. Careful. Silent.

He knelt beside me, steady as ever, and reached for my hand.

My fingers tightened, threading into his like I'd been waiting for that exact touch. Maybe I had.

When I finally looked up, his eyes met mine.

Soft.

Wrecked.

Wide open in a way that made my throat burn.

I'd spent so long bracing for the fight, I never once stopped to think what it might look like if he stopped fighting me back.

He didn't speak. Didn't explain. Just took my hand and pulled me to my feet.

And then—he kissed me.

Not hard.

Not desperate.

Slow. Steady. A surrender I could feel all the way down to my bones.

I exhaled against him, fingers fisting into his shirt like I couldn't hold on tight enough.

Max deepened the kiss, pulling me closer until there wasn't a single inch left between us. Then, without a word, he lifted me into his arms.

He carried me straight to his bedroom.

Because tonight?

Tonight he didn't look like a man about to fight it.

And God help me—neither was I.

Chapter 17

The Only Easy Day Was Yesterday

Max lowered me onto the edge of the bed, his grip lingering like he wasn't ready to let go. His fingers dug into my waist—tight, desperate—like he needed the anchor just as badly as I did.

I opened my mouth. Nothing came out.

Max kissed my forehead, his voice rough as gravel. "Don't. Just stay with me."

Okay. Sure. Just casually drop the sexiest demand in existence and expect me to function like a fully formed human.

God, this man. All that strength, all that control—and he was handing it over, one breath at a time, like I was the only thing holding him together.

His hands slid down, tracing every inch of me like he had all the time in the world. One hand lifted to cup my jaw, tipping my face toward his.

His mouth hovered—so close, so goddamn close—but he didn't kiss me again.

He just stayed there, breath mingling with mine, dragging out the ache until I was two seconds from losing my goddamn mind.

Holding back. Drawing me in. Daring me to break first.

"Tease," I whispered, fingers curling into his shirt, hauling him closer until his breath skimmed my lips—hot and shaky, just like mine.

His mouth curved in a slow smirk, all cocky control and wrecked edges.

"You have no idea," he murmured, his voice a low vibration against my skin.

And just like that, Max Harrington—the most dangerously organized man alive—decided he wanted to play dirty.

Well shit.

Playful Max? That's new. And stupid hot.

That was lethal. And God help me, I wanted more. I wanted every raw, unguarded inch of him.

I let out a breath, slow and shaky, way more dramatic sigh than I meant it to be. Full-on *woe is me* levels of sigh. But he didn't let go.

I tipped my head back, eyes locking on his.

Oh, those fucking beautiful eyes.

Not dark and stormy—Max didn't do brooding poet vibes—but sharp. Blue steel. Locked on target. Focused. Fierce enough to ruin me.

Honestly, I'd file that look under *"all of the above" and yes, please.*

And then, just to make things worse?

I liked him.

Like... *actually* liked him.

This was supposed to be flirting, not the prelude to a mental breakdown.

Way to stick to the plan, Rayann.

And I was pretty sure that was going to be a problem. The kind that doesn't just blow over. The kind that sticks.

I opened my mouth to make some snarky comment.

Say something. Anything. Give him a reason to laugh. To pull back. To not see how hard you're falling.

Couldn't do it.

Couldn't say a goddamn word.

I breathed his name—"Max"—like it was the only thing keeping me upright.

His mouth claimed mine like we'd just skipped four bases and gone straight to stealing home.

His grip in my hair? Possessive. Unhinged. Like Max Harrington had just gone rogue, and I was about to love every reckless second of it.

And holy hell, I let him.

Fucking threw the door wide open and handed him the keys, actually.

Might have even offered to drive.

This wasn't the library kiss—the one that fried my nervous system before he pulled the fire alarm and bailed, leaving me confused, stunned, and maybe just a little heartbroken.

It wasn't even the hot-as-fuck bothy kiss—and that one nearly did me in.

No, this wasn't stolen.

It wasn't rushed.

This was deliberate. Calculated.

Like Max Harrington had put in a formal request, filed it in triplicate, and now he was here to collect.

And damn if I wasn't ready to sign in blood.

Hell, I'd notarize it myself. Gold-foil seal and everything.

I felt it in his hands, tight and steady, like he wasn't convinced I wouldn't Houdini my way out of this the second he blinked.

Nope. Consider me officially pinned and purring.

His lips moved over mine like foreplay with a vengeance—slow, dirty, and so goddamn good it should've come with a safe word.

Not just the heat. Not just the tension.

Cool, cool. Brain's gone. Thought process: dead. That's where we're at.

But him.

The real him. The one he keeps locked up tight, buried so deep no one ever gets close enough to touch it.

Tonight, I didn't give a single damn.

I kissed him back—

Hard. Thorough. Handsy.

If Max Harrington was going to lose control tonight, I sure as hell wasn't letting him go down alone.

And I'm pretty sure this counted as a team building exercise, right?

He slowed just enough to make sure I felt every sinful second. His mouth stayed on mine, deepening the kiss like he was taking inventory—every sigh, every shift, every secret my body gave away.

Somewhere deep inside, I must've been saving space for this. For him. For this exact moment.

My sweater rode up as Max's hands moved—palming my waist, skimming my thighs, pushing fabric aside like it was a mild inconvenience on his way to a very good time.

Ten points for determination, Mr. Harrington.

Then—*sweet Jesus*—this beautiful man dropped to his knees.

His fingers skimmed slow up my thighs, bare skin lighting up beneath every pass.

His lips followed, trailing heat like it was his job description.

A kiss, soft and deliberate, at the inside of my knee.

Another.

Then higher.

I shuddered, my fingers diving into his hair, fisting at the back of his head like I was holding on for dear life.

Honestly? If he'd asked me for a kidney in that moment, I would give it to him gift-wrapped.

His breath ghosted over my skin, every move slow and surgical in its precision—designed to drive me certifiably out of my fucking mind.

This man wasn't in a hurry.

Not even a little.

He was savoring.

Every shiver. Every breath. Every inch he claimed like he was writing his name on my fucking soul.

My heartbeat hammered so hard I was one good thump away from needing medical attention.

Unraveling didn't even begin to cover it.

I was flat-out coming apart—for the man who never let me get too comfortable.

So rude. Outrageously, sinfully rude.

His hands slid higher, slow and cocky and absolutely infuriating—the kind of pace that said *I've got all night, sweetheart.* His mouth hovered just out of reach, lips skimming the edge of where I wanted him most before pulling back again, teasing the ever-loving hell out of me.

*If this is foreplay, I'm not surviving the main even*t.

And God help me, if he didn't touch me properly soon, I was going to fucking cry.

My body buzzed with need. My skin ached for more. My mouth knew one word:

"Max."

His name tumbled out, gasping and messy, like my body didn't even bother asking permission.

My fingers tugged at his hair, like maybe I could speed this up.

Spoiler alert: it didn't.

His grip locked tight on my thighs, keeping me right where he wanted while that wicked chuckle rumbled through me—slow, smug, and sinful as hell.

Oh, he was enjoying every fucking second.

His gaze flicked up, pinning me in place with *that* look—the one that hit like a slow drag of fire through my chest. Dark. Devastating. Just a little too pleased with himself.

And then his lips started moving higher.

Slow. Purposeful. Because apparently torture was step one on the Max Harrington seduction plan.

"Max," I warned.

"Hmm?" He nipped the sensitive spot where my thigh met my hip.

Breathing? Yeah, forgot how to do that.

"Holy hell," I whispered—and yep, my voice was wobblier than my self-control.

He lifted his head, silent.

Didn't need to speak.

That look, hungry and unholy, hit me like a lit match tossed on gasoline.

Starving. For me.

Maybe it was real.

Maybe it was just what I needed to believe.

Either way... I was already on fire.

And sweet hell, I wanted him just as fucking badly.

Every inch. Every second. Every goddamn thing he was finally letting me have.

My fingers trembled as I reached for the buttons of his shirt, fumbling, of course, because I was in way too much of a hurry.

I huffed out a breath, caught somewhere between flustered and feral, and couldn't help the grin when he tensed beneath my hands.

Already starting to come apart—just from a little heat and my wandering fingers.

Good. Let him feel it.

I pushed the fabric off his shoulders, my palms skating over solid muscle, the heat of his skin bleeding straight into my hands.

I stilled, breath catching as my fingers brushed ink.

That tattoo.

The same one that nearly short-circuited my panties back at the Games—

now under my palms, real and unfairly sexy up close.

Dark, sharp lettering inked clean against the cut of his upper arm.

Striking. Strong. Just like him.

Honestly? If I licked it right now, would that be weird?

Asking for a friend.

A horny one.

I reached for it, my fingers tracing the Latin phrase, slow and deliberate, reverent.

His body shifted beneath my touch, tense and twitchy, like he didn't know whether to lean in or bolt.

Like no one had ever touched him like this before.

Not with care. Not with curiosity. Not like I saw all of it.

I read it aloud.

"Unica dies facilis fuit heri."

Max locked up solid beneath my hands, like I'd just hit the kill switch.

I looked up, searching his face, heat curling low in my belly at the sharp hitch of his breath—the way his eyes darkened like I'd just knocked the air clean out of his lungs.

Yeah. I got it.

I felt it.

Still, I took my time—tracing each letter slow and deliberate, letting the weight of it settle between us before I finally whispered,

"The only easy day was yesterday."

Max exhaled hard, tension cracking off him like a live wire—sharp and sparking.

"You read Latin?"

His voice came rough, hoarse—frayed around the edges.

I smiled, still tracing the ink.

"What can I say? Brains, beauty, and poor impulse control—I'm the whole damn package."

He didn't move. Didn't even breathe.

And yeah—I was pretty sure he hadn't meant for me to see this much of him.

Definitely not like this.

But I had.

And I wasn't about to look away.

I leaned in and kissed the ink, my breath soft against his skin—like maybe my mouth could soothe whatever that tattoo still carried.

Max swore, low and guttural, like the sound had been ripped out of him.

Just when I thought he might say something, just when the air started to tilt toward something heavier, my fingers moved.

Lower.

Around.

And brushed over what felt like scars, rough and raised.

The air didn't just shift—it braced. Like it knew I'd just stumbled into something that wasn't mine to touch unless I was certain.

I froze, breath snagging mid-chest, sharp and tight.

When I looked up, Max wasn't just watching. He was holding still.

Waiting.

For what, I wasn't sure.

A question? A reason to stop?

Permission to keep going?

I didn't ask. Didn't push.

Just turned him enough and kissed them.

Soft. Slow. One scar, then the next.

Not a question. Not a demand.

Just a quiet promise:

I'll learn the stories someday.

But not tonight.

Max's breath hitched, sharp and ragged.

His grip tightened at my hips, like he couldn't decide whether to pull me closer or push me away.

Like standing there and being seen, without the armor, was too much.

Yeah, not happening. I wasn't about to let him hide behind that.

I turned him again, hands gliding up his chest.

Then lower—slower.

I flicked my tongue over the tight peak of his nipple, felt the shudder ripple through him as his body jerked beneath my mouth.

Sweet Jesus.

That sound he made. Rough. Wrecked. Like I'd just knocked the last bit of fight right out of him.

Then his hands were in my hair, hard and sure, and his mouth crashed into mine.

And whatever grip he had left on his restraint?

Yeah. That was gone.

His hands dropped to my hips—firm, greedy, possessive—guiding me back until my knees hit the edge of the bed.

I sank down.

He followed, wrapped me up, pressed me into the mattress, and made damn sure I stayed exactly where he wanted me.

His mouth found mine again, deeper now, rougher, desperate.

His tongue swept against mine, not asking. Claiming.

A declaration, clear as hell.

The man was done holding back.

I moaned into his mouth, my nails dragging down the hard lines of his back, yanking him closer, pulling him deeper—needing every inch of him like I needed his mouth everywhere and his hands everywhere else.

He broke away, breath rough and uneven against my skin.

He kissed a path from my jaw to my throat, then lower, his mouth taking its time like he wanted to memorize every inch of me.

Lower.

Max didn't pause. Didn't even blink.

Just kept going. Kept taking.

He paused at the swell of my breast, breathing heat across my skin before closing his mouth over my nipple.

My breath shattered on impact.

Holy hell. I'm gonna need someone to explain to my ances-tors why I just gave up heaven for this man's mouth.

The first sweep of his tongue was slow, teasing, and smug as hell.

The next? All business. All hunger.

Then he sucked, hard enough to make my head spin.

I arched, gasping, fingers digging into his shoulders like I needed something to hold me to earth. Heat unraveled inside me, sharp and blinding, pooling so deep I could barely stay in my own skin.

A guttural sound rumbled against my skin before he dragged his mouth to my other breast.

Tracing. Tasting. Taking. Like he had all goddamn night.

His hands drifted lower, slow and certain, possessive as hell, leaving nothing but fire in their wake. Then he moved down my stomach, fingers trailing heat behind them.

I barely had time to breathe. To beg. To do anything but feel—

before his hand slid between my legs like he already knew what I was desperate for.

His fingers found me.

Wet. Needy. And nowhere near done.

A sharp inhale—mine.

Oh, hell.

Oh, fucking hell.

Then—

his voice.

Deep. Rough. Raked raw with approval, possession...
pure, unholy fucking hunger.

All for me.

"*Rayann,*" he growled.

I grinned. "That's my name. Don't wear it out."

His eyes darkened. "You're *insufferable.*"

"And yet here you are, rock hard and still pretending
you're the reasonable one."

My body shattered. No permission. No patience. Just raw
fucking need and his name tearing off my lips.

"Max," I breathed. Wrecked. Wide open. My hips rose to
meet him, not just begging—but trusting.

His eyes never left me. Not for a second.

*Okay. Sure. Just torch me from the inside out with that stare.
Casual.*

His fingers kept moving, slow and torturous and deliberate.

Every pass stole my breath.

Every stroke left me aching and undone beneath the
weight of that stare.

He moved his thumb in slow, sinful circles. I gasped like I'd forgotten how to breathe. Every pass dragged me closer, slick and trembling, nerves shot, skin buzzing.

But he didn't give me what I needed.

Not yet. He held it just out of reach, like he wanted to watch me fall apart first.

If he didn't finish me soon, I was going to climb on top and fuck us both into oblivion—then maybe smother him with a pillow for making me wait.

Max leaned in, his lips brushing my ear, his breath rough and ragged, laced with something dark and satisfied.

"You're so goddamn beautiful like this," he murmured, voice raw like it cost him everything to hold himself together.

He eased one finger inside me, every inch unhurried and exact.

I cried out. My head dropped back. My hands scrabbled for his shoulders like I was seconds from spontaneous combustion. My body clenched tight around him, heat pulsing deep as Max swore, breath hissing through his teeth like I'd just branded him.

He kept going, slow and unrelenting, like this was his personal mission from hell.

He added another finger, hitting the spot with such deliberate care that pleasure bloomed sharp and fast, leaving me gasping. My breath tore out in sharp, ragged gasps, my thighs trembling as his name slipped past my lips.

Pretty sure I could come on those fingers alone and still write him a thank-you note after.

His eyes gave it away, that last thread of control barely holding. His lips brushed over my hipbone, then the sensitive skin of my inner thigh. When he finally spoke, his voice came low and dark, the kind that could talk a girl into climax and then politely ask if she wanted dessert.

Jesus. Who taught this man manners and murder in the same breath?

"Let go for me, Rayann."

Like I had a choice. The man said it like a fucking commandment.

I tightened around him again, slick and pulsing with desperation, and Max swore low like I'd just knocked the last brick from his wall.

He doubled down. Harder. Rougher. No mercy in sight.

I was tight, trembling, wrecked—and Max?

He was just getting started.

"Still sarcastic?" he murmured, his thumb circling my clit in a rhythm that made my toes curl.

I choked out a laugh. "Fuck you."

"Oh," he said, voice rough with promise, "I plan to."

Sweet Jesus, marry me.

The loss of him hit like a jolt, sharp and instant, and a broken whimper tore from my throat.

He didn't soothe. Didn't stall.

Just moved lower. Down, down, down—

He groaned, low and filthy, like I was already undoing him. "Christ, woman."

"Less talking," I panted. "More—"

His mouth closed over me through my panties. Words gone. Brain gone. Everything gone.

Well, well, Harrington. Turns out you're a filthy little menace.

Max pulled back just enough to smirk. "More *what*, exactly?"

I kicked him in the shoulder.

He caught my ankle, kissed the arch of my foot like it earned him loyalty points, and dragged my panties down with his teeth, grinning like a man who knew exactly what kind of chaos he was about to unleash.

Yeah, cool, like that's not going straight into the spank bank for the rest of my natural life.

I was going to murder him.

Or kiss him.

Probably both.

Then his tongue hit that perfect spot, and every brain cell I had went up in smoke.

I arched, breath snagging as pleasure ripped through me, fierce and burning and impossible to outrun.

His tongue flicked over my clit, slow and devastating. His hands locked on my hips, holding me down as I tried to move, tried to breathe, tried to chase the high he refused to let me catch.

Max didn't let me.

Didn't let me run.

Didn't let me do a goddamn thing but take what he gave, one filthy flick at a time.

He licked and sucked like he'd just discovered his favorite flavor, and I cried out, my brain completely peacing the hell out while I came apart on his tongue.

God help me, he fucking tongued me into an orgasm—and now he looked fully prepared to fuck me into the afterlife.

I tried to gasp his name but only managed a noise that sounded like a dying squirrel and an exorcism had a baby.

"Max—"

My voice didn't even qualify as a voice.

Just gasps. Shaky, raw, embarrassingly desperate.

He hummed against me, working me without mercy. The vibration shot straight through my core like a detonation, tightening everything, coiling me with need.

Closer. Closer. Fuck, closer.

I shattered again—harder this time. Violent. My pulse pounded like it was trying to crack me open from the inside out. My body clenched around nothing, chasing it, riding it, breaking apart as the orgasm slammed into me like it had a fucking vendetta.

Wave after wave. Unrelenting. Blistering. Like my body didn't know when to quit.

Max didn't stop.

Didn't ease up.

Just kept stroking.

Kept licking.

Kept dragging it out like I was his favorite way to commit a felony.

Too good.

Too fucking everything.

He lifted his head at last, lips slick, eyes dark with hunger, thick with need, heavy with satisfaction.

Then his mouth claimed mine.

Deep. Slow. Possessive.

His mouth stayed on mine as he reached between us, lining himself up with where I was already soaked and aching for him.

We were safe. I was covered. All I wanted was him.

One slow push, deep and steady, until all that remained was heat, breath, and the breaking point we both chased down together.

Yep. There went my last coherent thought. Just tapped out with a "you got this, babe."

I gasped, fingers digging into his shoulders as heat poured off him, my breath tangling with his skin.

He stilled, buried deep, forehead resting on mine, his body shaking like I was the only thing tethering him to earth.

I moved first. A slow roll of my hips, soft and steady, more prayer than plea.

And that was it. Max snapped, unraveling in the best fucking way.

He started slow, thrusting deep like he meant to memorize every inch of me, every sigh, every gasp.

But it wasn't enough. I needed more.

He locked his grip on my hips, snapped the last thread of control, and slammed into me harder, faster—chasing the kind of pleasure that didn't leave survivors.

I clung to him, breath ragged, my body meeting every thrust like it was built to match him. His hips rolled with purpose, slow and lethal, every thrust deeper, sharper—pulling me closer to the edge like he knew damn well he'd be the one to send me flying.

Oh god. I'm gonna break. I can't—I can't—I'm already—

When I came again, I clenched so tight around him I half expected to black out. His name tumbled out of me, slurred and needy, like I forgot how words worked.

That did it. Max's control snapped, his final thrust brutal and deep, his release ripping through him like I'd just rewritten his entire fucking DNA.

Jesus. I just broke him. I broke Max Harrington.

Minutes passed.

Or maybe an entire fiscal quarter.

Neither of us moved. We stayed wrapped up in each other, limbs tangled, hearts fried, too far gone to care.

Our heartbeats slowed, syncing like two idiots who'd just had sex so good we might've unlocked a new dimension.

Max exhaled and pulled me against him, his arm locked tight around my waist like I might try to escape.

Spoiler: I was going *nowhere*.

His fingers traced circles on my back. Real ones. Not metaphorical, emotional spirals—though those were probably coming later.

He pressed a kiss into my hair. Soft. Lingering. Possibly illegal in several states.

I yawned. "So. That happened."

He huffed a laugh. "Eloquent."

"Shut up. I had an out-of-body experience."

His chest shook. "Glad you came back."

"Jury's still out. My soul's hovering above the bed trying to file a Yelp review."

Max chuckled low, kissing me again. "Five stars?"

"Oh, Harrington. I'm gonna need more stars."

: Chapter 18

Heat of the Moment

I WOKE TO WARMTH and the slow, steady rhythm of breath ghosting across my skin. Max's arm lay heavy around me, warm and possessive. Familiar. Infuriating. Like he had the right to uproot my whole damn life just by existing.

Last night hit me in slow, shivery waves: the flicker of firelight on his skin, the way I fell apart beneath his hands, his mouth. And the way he came undone right along with me.

And now, I was still here, tangled in his sheets, wrapped around him like I had every right to be.

He's warm. He's naked. He smells like sin. This is a trap. And holy hell, I didn't have this on my bingo card.

He shifted against me, fingers flexing at the small of my back. His touch was too warm. Branded.

I should've pulled back. Put distance between us before this turned into something even more dangerous than it already was.

But instead I stretched, a lazy sigh slipping out as I curled closer—chasing the heat of him like a girl who hadn't learned a single goddamn lesson. My fingers skimmed his ribs, barely there, but enough to shift the air between us. Charged. Aware. Every inch of us humming like we'd been rewired.

"I feel you staring," I murmured, voice thick with sleep.

He exhaled slowly, lips twitching like he was debating a grin. "I'm appreciating."

My eyes blinked open, sleep still fogging the edges of the morning light.

I looked up and met his gaze, cool and unreadable, like he was giving me room to run but already knew I wouldn't.

Nope. Not running. And if he kept looking at me like I mattered, I was going to need a minute.

I shifted slightly, pulling the sheet higher like it might protect something more than just skin.

Max's hand moved slowly, fingers brushing mine as he tugged the sheet back down, just enough to undo my retreat.

His voice was low. Gentle.

"I like seeing you like this."

Wait—this is real? Like, real real?

If this is some kind of magical sorcery, hex me now. I'm all the way in.

I reached up without thinking, brushing my fingers across his lips. Just once. Just to feel him soften under my touch.

Then my gaze drifted lower, slow and shameless, tracing the carved lines of his chest, the strength in his arms.

I let my gaze wander across his chest, tracing the carved lines of his arms. My fingers followed, gliding lower across firm muscle and the familiar scars I'd traced the night before. My fingers drifted lower, gliding over the curve of his torso—and paused.

There was ink beneath my touch. A shape I recognized.

Sharp angles. Long limbs. Still.

The bone frog.

He exhaled hard, but it wasn't playful. It wasn't arousal.

It was something deeper. Sharper.

Like the breath had been pulled from somewhere he didn't want me to find.

The tease caught in my throat before it could land.

This wasn't just a tattoo.

It was sacred.

A symbol carved in silence. Grief in black ink.

My fingers stilled. "This one's not for show, is it."

He didn't answer right away. Just kept his eyes on the ceiling like he was somewhere else entirely.

When he finally spoke, his voice was quiet. Rough.

"No. It's not."

Oh, Max. Who did you lose?

I didn't say anything.

Didn't ask. Didn't push.

Just leaned in and pressed a kiss beside it. Soft. Careful. Let my hand rest there a moment longer, like maybe I could hold some of it for him.

My fingers slid lower, tracing the curve of his calf. My fingers caught the dark, sharp lines of another tattoo: a trident. Bold. Unyielding. The mark of a warrior.

I brushed my thumb over the stunning design, following every clean angle and jagged edge. A symbol forged in salt and shadow. Built to survive. To fight. To win.

Well hell. He's not just hot—he's haunted. And it's doing things to me.

Max tensed beneath me, every muscle pulled taut like a bowstring ready to snap.

I smiled slow. "You really were built for war, weren't you?"

He swallowed hard, like the words lodged in his throat weren't safe to say.

I kissed his trident. Slow. Reverent. My breath swept over the hard lines of his thigh and another story marking his skin.

He jolted beneath me as every last thread of control snapped.

His fingers speared into my hair, tugging me back to his mouth. The kiss that followed? All heat. All hunger.

All Max.

We were seconds from forgetting the world entirely.

Then came the knock.

No. A fucking *bang*. Loud. Sharp. Criminal.

I groaned so loud it echoed off the stone. Flopped back, face in my hands. "No. No, no, no. Tell me that's not someone at the damn door."

Max exhaled through his nose. "It's someone at the door. And they sound... eager."

I shoved at his chest. "Go answer it."

"I'm still naked," he said, like that was my problem.

"Oh, I'm very intimately aware." I raised a brow. "And?"

Sweet merciful Jesus.

Max grumbled something that sounded like a death threat, grabbed the nearest thing—his sweatpants—and stalked for the door. No doubt in my mind—if they didn't have a damn good reason, Max was ready to launch them off the nearest castle turret.

The second he cracked the door open, a breathless staffer blurted, "Mr. Harrington! Miss Wilder! You need to evacuate—now!"

Max was through the door before the last word even landed, yanking it open the rest of the way. The hallway behind the staffer was chaos. Guests and employees rushed toward the exits, voices overlapping, the air tight with panic.

"There's a fire. It's contained," the guy said quickly. "Started in the kitchen. Electrical. Spread faster than expected. No one's hurt."

Fire.

I shot into the main room, heart hammering, breath caught halfway up my throat. The blanket tangled around my legs, slipping down as I scrambled. "Wait—what?"

The guy's face pinched with urgency. "The reception hall took smoke damage. Kitchen's down."

Max didn't flinch. "Who's in charge?"

The staffer hesitated. "Uh—I'm not sure. I think someone from facilities? Maybe the manager on duty—"

Max was already moving. "Get a head count started. Direct all guests through the east exit. Pavilion is the rally point, right?"

The staffer blinked. "Yes, sir."

"Good. Find whoever's supposed to be running point and tell them I want a status update in five."

He spun, crossed the room in three strides, and pulled a sweater from the back of a chair, tossing it toward me as I yanked on my clothes. Then shoes. Then his own sweatshirt.

"Fiona," I said, breathless. "I need to find her."

Max's jaw clenched. "We need to evacuate."

"I will. But not until I make sure this wedding isn't completely screwed. Fiona's family is practically Scottish royalty, Max. If this day goes down in flames, so does Wilder Horizons—and probably half of our international reputation."

He crossed the room again, already pulling his shoes on, eyes locked on mine.

"Go," he said. Not a question. A command.

So I did.

And five seconds later, so did he.

Fiona was near the garden, barefoot in the grass, her satin robe clinging to one shoulder like she'd barely made it out in time. She looked seconds away from collapse.

Out of the corner of my eye, I spotted Max in the distance, already speaking into his phone, posture locked beside the fire chief like he'd been born to run the damn place.

Okay. I should not be halfway to an orgasm just watching him take charge.

Nope. Absolutely not. That's inappropriate. And unhelpful. And—Jesus, look at him.

"Rayann, the reception hall. There's smoke everywhere. They think the kitchen's out. I don't even... what the hell do we do?"

My pulse kicked into gear. "The tent," I said. "From last night. Please tell me it's still standing."

"I... I think so?"

"Okay. Good." I reached for her arm. "Fiona, where's Collum? And your parents? Are they somewhere safe?"

She nodded, a little too fast. "Yeah. The parents are fine. Someone took them out through the side garden. Collum went to check on the rest of the family, I think. I haven't seen him since."

"Alright. The tent's our move. We'll shift the decor, redirect guests through the garden, check the power and lighting, and get catering to confirm what's salvageable."

Fiona blinked. "Okay. Okay... that'll work."

I squeezed Fiona's arm. "Find your wedding coordinator—now. Tell them we're shifting everything to the tent. They'll need to redirect the floral team, move the table settings, and reroute guests through the garden entrance."

Fiona blinked like she was still spinning.

"Got it?" I asked, voice steady.

She nodded. "Yes. On it."

She darted off, robe fluttering behind her as I turned into the crowd, scanning faces for someone in a chef's coat.

I found two members of the kitchen crew near the stone path, clustered together, one of them rubbing flour on his pants like it might calm his nerves.

"You're with catering?" I asked.

The taller one nodded.

"Good. I need a quick assessment. What's usable? What's ruined? When the outside caterers arrive, I want a list of what we can still serve and where we'll need reinforcements."

He blinked. "I—I think the back freezer was untouched. Some of the cold apps might be okay."

"Start there. Move fast. We've got maybe three hours."

As he turned to relay the order, I was already flagging down one of the castle staff in a navy vest and radio.

"Who's the manager on duty?"

"I—uh—think Ms. Keane, but she was helping with the evacuation—"

"Get her. I need approval to relocate the reception dinner to the tent. We'll need backup lighting, power access, and a team to sweep the area for safety."

He nodded and took off without another word.

Well, shit. I had one shot to hold the line. And apparently, fire and floral emergencies now counted as "other duties as assigned."

I turned just as Max strode back across the lawn, all calm command and lethal focus. He was assessing everything. Including me.

His presence cut through the chaos like a war drum.

"You good?" he asked, his gaze sweeping me from head to toe.

"Last night's makeup, hair like I lost a bar fight, and this sweater? Full goblin mode."

His eyes didn't budge. "You're running point out here like a general." Then, with a wink, "And you look sexy as hell doing it. Goblin mode's kinda working for me."

Wait. What?

How the hell was he even noticing me in the middle of his own crisis?

I stared at him a beat too long, brain buffering. He couldn't be serious. The man was still stupidly sexy in sweatpants, and yet—he looked at me like I was the only person on this field he trusted to win the damn war.

"Um. Thank you?"

"The grounds are secure. Everyone's safe." He stepped in, close enough for my pulse to notice. "What do you need? How can I help?"

"You're kind of hot when you go full commando," I muttered.

He smirked. "Back at you."

Chapter 19

Six and a Half Minutes

W E SAVED IT.

The fire didn't take down the wedding. Just a few floral arrangements, some scorch marks, and half a tray of bougie little pastries that probably cost more per puff than my entire dress.

One exploded cream puff even hit a linen napkin like a crime scene. May it rest in sticky, overpriced peace.

The emergency crews packed up fast, voices low and efficient. Cleanup teams swept through right behind them with rubber gloves and the energy of people paid very well not to panic.

Fiona stood barefoot in the grass, veil crooked, mascara smudged just enough to look romantic instead of wrecked. Champagne in one hand, her other clutched the event timeline like she might slap someone with it. She smiled at me, wild-eyed and buzzing.

"This is... better, actually," she whispered, like we were sharing a secret. "More romantic."

I nodded and smiled like I hadn't just handled a five-alarm crisis in yesterday's underwear with someone else's radio clipped to my ass.

The marquee sparkled like it knew it had something to prove. Candles glowed on every table, flickering in tall glass cylinders we salvaged from the original setup. The music started again—low and lush and exactly what the guests needed to start pretending none of this ever happened.

My heels sank slightly into the soft ground, but I didn't move. Just stood still for a moment, letting it land.

We pulled it off.

Somehow, we actually fucking pulled it off.

Though somewhere, Summer probably felt a disturbance in the force and started mentally chewing my ass. Yay, me.

My dress still hugged in all the right places. My curls were hanging on by sheer willpower and a travel-sized can of hairspray. And even after everything, my lipstick hadn't totally abandoned me.

I didn't need to turn around to know Max was watching. I felt it. Low and warm, like static across my skin.

"You always this good at pretending you're not about to pass out?"

The voice hit low and smooth behind me, curling down my spine like it had a map.

I turned.

Max stood just outside the tent, jacket off, sleeves rolled, dress shirt open at the collar. The man looked like he'd just been carved out of *calm under pressure* and dragged through a cologne ad on the way.

I blinked at him. "Define 'pass out.'"

He stepped in closer. Not touching, not crowding—just near enough to remind me what it felt like to want something with no good sense of timing.

His gaze slid from my hair to my shoulders, taking in the stress I hadn't let myself feel until right then.

"You held it together," he said. "That wasn't luck."

I scoffed. "It also wasn't in my job description."

"Doesn't mean it wasn't impressive."

His voice dropped half a register on the last word. And my pulse did *that thing* it does when he talks like that.

I swallowed hard. "You checking on me?"

He shrugged, lazy and lethal. "Someone's gotta."

He tilted his head, watching me like he was still deciding something.

Then he leaned in, low and quiet. "We need to go over a few things."

I blinked. "Now?"

His voice was barely audible. "Urgent timeline review."

Before I could ask what the hell he was talking about, he turned and walked off like a man on a mission—calm, composed, and entirely too confident. Like this wasn't wildly suspicious behavior and I wasn't about to follow him like a woman with absolutely no regard for public appearances or professional boundaries.

But I did.

Because of course I did.

He led us around the side of the marquee, past a curtained staff entrance, and down a hallway I was pretty sure only servers were supposed to use. Then he stopped in front of an unmarked door, opened it, pulled me inside, and shut it behind us.

Click.

Storage closet.

Shelves of wine glasses. A pile of linens. Some banquet chairs stacked in the corner.

And Max.

Blocking the door. Eyes dark enough to make my knees forget how to function.

"Max—"

"Six and a half minutes." His voice was low. Rough. Dangerous in the best way. "That's how long I missed you before I started losing my goddamn mind."

I opened my mouth. Closed it. My pulse was somewhere near orbital.

"We're supposed to be working," I whispered.

"I am." He stepped closer. "Actively managing a situation." His eyes flicked to my lips. "And right now, the situation is that you gave a speech that made me imagine exactly what you'd sound like with your mouth otherwise occupied."

Air? Who needed it.

"That sounds like an HR violation."

He smirked. "Good thing I'm not technically on the clock."

He backed me into the linens so fast the shelves rattled behind me. Then he kissed me—hard. Like the whole damn day had been building to this. Like *we* had been building to this.

His hands were everywhere. My dress was halfway up my thighs. And I had completely forgotten how to breathe.

One of my heels slipped on a rogue mop bucket.

I yelped.

Max caught me with one arm and shoved the bucket away with the other like it had insulted my honor.

"Focus, Wilder."

"You pulled me into a broom closet. How focused do you expect me to be?"

His voice dropped.

"Oh, I'll help."

"Max—"

His hands were on me again before I finished the word, gripping my hips, walking me back until my spine hit the wall. His mouth crushed mine—hungry, demanding, *filthy*—and I melted into it like my body had been waiting all day for this exact pressure.

I gasped against his lips, and he used it, licking into me with the kind of focus that should've been illegal. His tongue swept against mine, slow and devastating, and when I whimpered, he groaned low in his throat and grabbed my ass like he needed a firmer hold on reality.

"You wore that dress on purpose," he rasped against my jaw, already dragging the hem up my thighs. "Knowing damn well I'd be in this state all fucking day."

I—okay. Wow. Fucking holy hot crisis manager, you've been thinking about this all day? Like, while giving security briefings? Were you mentally undressing me mid-head count?

Head. Ohhh.

Fuck no. Jesus. Get it together, Rayann.

"I wore it because I look good in it."

"Exactly."

He kissed me again, then dropped his mouth to my neck, teeth grazing the sensitive spot below my ear. I arched into him. My dress hitched higher.

Then his hand slid between my thighs, fingers bold and unrelenting, finding me already soaked through my panties.

"Fuck," he growled. "Wet for me already?"

I nodded—barely.

He slipped his hand under the fabric, fingertips dragging through slick heat, then circled my clit with a pressure that made my knees buckle.

"I don't have time to be gentle, Rayann."

"Good," I panted. "Don't."

He yanked my panties aside and pushed two fingers into me, deep and fast.

My head slammed back against the wall. "Jesus—Max—"

He pumped his fingers, curling them until I was shaking, desperate, clutching his shoulders like he was the only thing holding me upright.

"Let me hear it," he whispered. "I want to know what it sounds like when you come around my hand."

It didn't take long.

A few more strokes and I was there, moaning into his shoulder, hips grinding down, body clenching tight as everything else dropped away.

He kissed me through it, slow now. Awed. Like he needed to claim every piece of it.

Then he dropped to his knees.

Just looked up at me from between my thighs like he was about to ruin me on purpose.

"You said I pulled you into a broom closet. You didn't ask what for."

He hooked one of my legs over his shoulder, pushed my dress up past my hips, and licked me with one long, possessive stroke that stole the breath from my lungs.

Then again.

And again.

Tongue circling, teasing, building—until he sealed his mouth around my clit and sucked.

Hard.

Like he was trying to summon a damn genie.

My hands flew to his hair. "Max—fuck—oh my god—"

He didn't stop. Not when I gasped. Not when I came again, shaking against his face. Not when my leg nearly gave out and he growled something filthy into me like he *wanted* to be drowned in it.

He stood slowly, lips wet, pupils dark enough to swallow the room, and every big, hard, God-help-me inch of him was threatening to rip through his slacks like it planned to fold me in half and bless the structural integrity of this folding table.

"Turn around."

"What?"

He spun me, bent me over the table, pushed my dress up, and slid his cock between my thighs in one long, perfect thrust that stole the air from the room.

"Holy sweet merciful fuck—"

He laughed low, soft and wrecked. "Jesus, I love when you fall apart for me." His voice dropped, a whisper. "But if you keep sounding like that, I'm gonna need a better cover story."

He drove into me, hard and deep, his hands gripping my hips like he couldn't bear to let go. My cheek hit the table. His pace was brutal. Beautiful. Unapologetic.

"Been wanting this all day," he growled. "Since I saw you take fucking charge all morning. All confident. All fucking mine."

Wait. Did he just growl-claim me? Is that legal?

"Then take it," I gasped. "Take all of it."

He pulled me up by the shoulders and fucked me harder. And I let him.

Because in that moment, there was no timeline. No wedding. No world beyond this heat, this pressure, this man breaking me in half with nothing but hunger and sweat and need.

"Max—I'm—"

"I know."

His hand slid between my legs and finished me off, just as he came with a growl in my ear and my name on his lips.

He held me there for a second, both of us panting like we'd survived something catastrophic. His hand still splayed across my stomach. His mouth pressed to my neck.

"Timeline reviewed," he muttered, voice still rough.

"Yeah. My favorite kind of oral report."

Chapter 20

The Evening Briefing

W E DIDN'T TALK ON the walk back to the reception. Too winded. Too smug. Too sore in places I couldn't exactly ice in public.

My legs wobbled like they'd forgotten their job, and my underwear was somewhere in a storage closet, probably traumatized.

The garden glowed under candlelight, champagne catching the flicker, music drifting through the air with practiced elegance and a price tag to match. Guests laughed and lingered in small clusters, raising glasses like a kitchen fire hadn't nearly torched the event off the itinerary.

We slipped in quiet and casual, blending into the crowd like we hadn't just desecrated perfectly innocent banquet table.

But that bartender. Murdo?

Murdo spotted us the moment we crossed the threshold, like he'd been waiting just to pounce.

He stood behind the bar in a full tux, straightening wine glasses with the elegance of a man who'd smuggled champagne through a war zone and made it look classy. His gloves gleamed. His smirk didn't.

He lifted a single brow the second we got close, then leaned in with all the grace of a man about to narrate a scandal in detail.

"Well now," Murdo said, his accent thick and far too knowing. "Glad to see the two of ye've come back up for air."

I swallowed wrong and nearly choked on what was left of my dignity.

Max didn't even blink. "Timeline reviewed."

Murdo slowly polished a glass, eyes twinkling. "Ah. That what we're callin' it these days?"

Nope. Not blushing. Just recalling the exact decibel I hit when he sucked on my—yeah, that's enough.

Murdo passed Max a tumbler of scotch, me a glass of champagne, then hit us with that ancient Scottish oracle stare. Like a man who'd hosted a bachelor party, an exorcism, and a royal orgy in the same weekend.

"Congratulations," he said, bone-dry. "You've got that freshly debauched glow."

Max took a sip like scandal couldn't touch him. "Appreciate your discretion."

Murdo blinked. "Discretion? Please. I've already taken bets at the bar. You owe me twenty quid and a mop bucket."

Champagne went up my nose. Dignity gone. Again.

Murdo gave me a little bow, all old-school charm and tuxedoed menace. The kind of move that probably made women abandon their morals in 1974.

"Miss Wilder, pleasure to finally make your acquaintance. Murdo Campbell—bartender, confidant, chaos tracker, and unofficial therapist to emotionally unstable grooms and at least one runaway stripper."

I blinked. "Wait—you actually know who I am?"

He tilted his head like I'd just asked if scotch came from grapes. "Lass, you're the reason this wedding didn't end with kilts on fire and guests fleeing into the woods. Of course I know who you are."

Murdo tipped his glass toward us with absolutely zero ceremony.

"Well then," he declared, voice carrying like a scandal cannon, "a toast to the lass who tamed the flames, rescued the reception, and still found time to get thoroughly, gloriously wrecked in a linen closet."

I spit my champagne straight into my hand. Sexy.

Max, deadpan as ever: "It was storage."

Murdo raised a brow. "I stand corrected. Linen closets are for amateurs."

A few guests clapped.

Clapped.

I considered diving headfirst into Murdo's ice bucket and pulling the lid shut behind me.

Max, infuriatingly calm, leaned against the bar and muttered just loud enough for *me* to hear but *not* quiet enough for it to be safe: "Pretty sure I'd go to confession if it didn't mean lying about what I'd do to you again."

My face went thermonuclear.

Murdo nodded like a man who'd personally sinned, survived, and brought snacks to purgatory. "Aye. Best not risk damnation without backup.

Preferably liquid."

I was actively reconsidering every choice I'd ever made in life—up to and including the one that led me to a Scottish castle, a storage closet, and this tuxedoed menace behind the bar.

Without so much as blinking, Murdo reached under the bar and retrieved a polished silver flask like he'd just been *waiting* for this moment.

He slid it across to Max like a seasoned dealer with the last ace in the deck. "For you. You'll need it if you've got any plans of surviving this one."

Max accepted it with one hand and pure sin in his smile. "Oh, I'm not surviving her. I'm going down happy."

Max. Fucking. Harrington. One-lining me into orgasm #7 without even touching me.

Murdo arched one perfectly judgmental brow. "Spoken like a man who just met his match."

Max looked at me like I was both the match and the wildfire. "She's the beautiful kind of chaos. I'm just the lucky bastard trying to keep the flames pointed in the right direction."

I was seconds from melting straight into the lawn. Just a little puddle of overheated girl goo fossilized beneath a whiskey-soaked sky.

Murdo turned toward me with a devil's grin and an angel's delivery. "You're dangerous, Miss Wilder. I respect that. Just promise if you kill him, you make it look like an accident. I hate paperwork."

My mouth opened. Nothing came out. Not a goddamn thing.

Some random woman lifted her glass. "What's going on over there?" she called, far too eager for someone not standing in the splash zone.

Murdo didn't miss a beat. "Just your average romantic success story. Girl meets boy. Girl seduces boy in a crisis closet. Boy begs for more."

I died. I *died*.

Max? Max just downed the rest of his scotch and said, "Timeline updated."

Murdo poured him another. "And thoroughly reviewed."

Murdo hummed to himself as he updated the chalkboard. Casual. Professional.

Like he wasn't about to set my entire dignity on fire with flair.

He spun it around with a flourish.

Tonight's Signature Cocktail: The Evening Briefing
— Scotch. Champagne. Slow-building burn.
— Goes down smooth. Bold finish.
— Best served as a double.

Max read it. Sipped his drink. Looked directly at me.

"It's missing something," he said.

Murdo raised an eyebrow. "Oh?"

"Needs more... bite," Max murmured, far too casual. "Just a touch of danger. Maybe a line about making someone forget their own name."

I full-body *wheezed* like someone who just got caught reading smut in church.

That's when a guest—mid-thirties, probably named Bob—wandered up and tapped the menu. "Evening Briefing? That sounds safe. I'll take one."

Murdo didn't even blink. "You sure, lad? It's a bit... spirited."

"I like bold," Bob said.

Murdo made the drink. Slid it across. "Just don't let it knock you on your ass."

Bob took a sip. Made a face. "Wow. That's strong."

Murdo smiled like a man with secrets. "So was she."

Max coughed into his fist.

I turned thirty shades of crimson and whispered, "We have to leave. Immediately."

Murdo polished a glass. "Too late. You're a legend now."

I was still trying to regain control of my face—and dignity—when Fiona and Collum made their way through the crowd toward us, looking unfairly radiant for two people who'd survived both a castle fire and a storage closet scandal on their wedding day.

"Rayann," Fiona said, grabbing both my hands like I'd personally kept her veil from going up in flames. "I know I've said this a hundred times already, but thank you. *Thank you.*"

"Seriously," Collum added, shaking Max's hand like he was bestowing an honorary clan title. "You both saved the day. And gave us one hell of a story to tell our grandchildren."

I let out a wobbly laugh. "Hopefully just the fire part. Not the closet."

Fiona's eyes sparkled. "Oh no, the closet part *makes* the retelling. You're full-on legend now."

Murdo, right on cue, raised his flask like he'd choreographed the moment.

"Listen," Fiona said, tightening her grip on my hands, "I know you're probably heading back to the States soon, but Collum and I want to offer you something. A thank-you."

My stomach pinched. "That's really not necessary—"

"Oh, it's not a thank-you," Fiona said with a grin. "It's a bribe. We want you to stay a few more days. Take a proper break."

"We've got a family cottage on the northern tip of Skye," Collum said. "Right on the beach. Remote. Quiet. Just you two, the sea, and a few judgmental sheep."

Max raised a brow, clearly intrigued. "Is there a lock on the door?"

Fiona laughed. "Barely. It's rustic. Romantic. And stocked with enough whiskey to survive a mild apocalypse."

"You're offering us a beach cottage?" I blinked. "That's criminally generous."

Cool cool cool, just casually accelerating through all the relationship milestones today.

Wait—did I just say relationship?

"Technically, it's more of a charming shack," Collum said. "'Driftwood chic', as the ladies might say. Plumbing that *mostly* works."

Max looked at me.

I looked at him.

And just like that, we both knew.

My brain said fly home. Get back to work. Responsibilities. Structure. Definitely no Scottish beaches or SEALs in borrowed beds.

But my mouth said, "That sounds perfect."

Max grinned. "Guess we're revising the timeline again."

Murdo's voice drifted over from the bar. "Just don't set the thatch on fire this time."

Fiona clinked her glass to mine. "To legends, linen closets, and the best goddamn wedding day ever."

And just like that, we weren't heading home.

Not yet.

Chapter 21

Just Leave Me for the Bagpipers

B Y THE TIME WE got back to the room, I was running on fumes, caffeine, and the last stubborn endorphins from a very satisfying afternoon.

The fireplace glowed low. Both beds were turned down. Our bags had magically relocated. And someone—probably an enchanted woodland creature moonlighting as housekeeping—had left two shortbread cookies on the nightstand like this was a totally normal Saturday.

Max stepped in behind me and clicked the door shut. I stared at the domestic tableau like I'd wandered into a fairy tale written by someone with extremely specific kinks.

"We should be dead," I muttered.

"Agreed," Max said. "From exhaustion or public humiliation. Pick your poison."

I collapsed onto the couch, heels still on, like a woman staging one last rebellion against adulthood and responsible decisions.

"I should probably check in with Brynn," I groaned. "Last I saw, she'd sent four texts, two fire emojis, a burning vibrator GIF, and one voice memo of her screaming, 'ARE YOU DEAD OR GETTING LAID?' So, you know. Totally calm."

Max coughed like air had turned on him. "And she doesn't even know it was me?"

I blinked. "Max. You're six-plus feet of tactical-grade brooding hotness with a voice that could melt titanium. Every woman in our company has you listed under '*Fantasy HR Violation.*'"

He stared like I'd just spoken in tongues.

"You stomp around like an emotional thunderstorm and expect no one to notice? Please. You're basically a walking 'Do Not Disturb' sign in tailored pants."

Max actually looked scandalized. "I thought they were afraid of me."

"Oh, honey," I snorted. "They are. That's half the appeal."

Max scrubbed a hand over his face like he was buffering.

"Great. I'm a fantasy and a cautionary tale."

He walked to the sideboard, grabbed the Blue Label, and poured two fingers with the calm precision of a man prepping for a boardroom ambush, then handed it to me like I was the one who needed fortifying.

"You're not wrong," I said, taking the glass. "But HR's still in the dark. Mostly because you terrify the interns."

He poured one for himself, brow furrowed. "I don't even talk to the interns."

"Exactly," I said, sipping. "You're the stuff of whispered lunch break legends. There's a spreadsheet ranking the odds of what's under that suit. Shirtless field photos? Absolutely analyzed."

Max blinked hard. "Analyzed?"

"With zoom. Annotations. One girl even color-coded your abs."

He took a slow sip. "Can't decide if I should feel flattered or mildly violated."

"Oh, it's absolutely both," I said, all sunshine. "But mostly a public service."

He looked at me like I'd detonated a glitter bomb inside his brain and walked away whistling.

I grinned and melted back into the couch. "I should probably text Brynn before she launches a full-scale rescue op."

Max didn't even blink. "She's already named the mission, hasn't she?"

"Operation Rayann Has Fallen," I said, nodding solemnly.

"You talk to Summer yet?"

I nodded. "Earlier. Gave her the fire scoop, the damage rundown, and the full wedding save play-by-play. She was... professionally chill."

Max dropped into the couch beside me. "Professional's code for unimpressed."

"I didn't say that," I hedged.

"Didn't have to." He tapped his glass to mine. "You saved the wedding. The client. The whole damn brand. I'll make sure she knows it."

I sipped, letting the warmth unfurl through me. "You think she'll believe it if it's coming from you?"

"I'm extremely persuasive when I'm right." He smirked. "Which is basically always."

I smiled into my drink and tapped out a quick message to Brynn: *Alive. Mostly intact. Wedding saved. Call you in the morning.*

"Short message," Max observed.

"She'll read between the lines. Then build a whole conspiracy theory where I'm being held hostage by the world's sexiest security consultant."

He lifted a brow. "Am I armed in this scenario?"

"Are we talking physically or emotionally?"

He gave me a long, deliberate once-over. "Sounds like she gets it."

I rolled my eyes. "This is the same woman who once stuffed my suitcase with glitter and condoms before a work trip."

Max choked mid-sip. "Please tell me that's a joke."

"Absolutely not. The condoms were color-coded. The glitter? Tiny, penis-shaped confetti. And she rhinestoned 'Go Get 'Em, Slut' across my toiletry bag like she was designing for Dior."

He blinked. "And you're supposed to be the calm twin?"

"She's chaos in lip gloss. I'm chaos in heels and an expense report."

Max tipped his glass like he'd solved the mystery of me. "Explains a lot."

I sipped my scotch and sank deeper into the couch. "If today were a meme, it'd be 'How it started vs. How it's going.'

First frame: smug post-sex glow, smooth hair, not a care in the world.

Second frame: hair like I've been electrocuted, lipstick somewhere on my forehead, gripping a smoke-stained clipboard and muttering battle plans to a catering team.

Max blinked slowly. "Sorry. You lost me at post-sex glow."

I smacked his arm. "Focus."

"I am," he said, entirely unbothered. "What?"

I rolled my eyes. "You're impossible."

He drank, slow and deliberate, and nodded toward the fireplace like he was debriefing a mission. "You barked orders at a fire chief and he actually listened. Guy had thirty years of experience and nodded like he was back in boot camp."

I grinned. "What can I say? I'm very motivational when need be."

Max raised his glass. "Terrifying, actually. That poor busboy nearly fainted when you sent him for ice. Poor kid. He ran like it was a live grenade. And you didn't even say please."

I swirled my scotch. "It's been a week stuffed into three days."

Max took a long sip, maddeningly calm. "You've been in crisis mode since wheels down. Honestly, I thought you'd combust somewhere between baggage claim and espresso number two."

I gave him a slow, filthy smirk. The kind that promised danger. "Oh, I combusted."

His eyes cut to mine.

"Multiple times," I added, tracing my glass rim like I had secrets to spare. "With enthusiasm. Against a wall. In a storage closet. Ringing any bells?"

Max choked. On air. On life. On everything.

I grinned, fully unapologetic. "Next time, try a better evacuation plan."

He dragged a hand down his face, half laughing, half wrecked. "Jesus. You're gonna kill me."

"You're a good man, Max Harrington," I murmured, tucking my feet under and leaning into his side.

"And you," he said, voice a low rumble near my ear, "are finally sitting still."

I let out a soft laugh and let my head tip against his shoulder. "Be honest. Did Murdo really know about the closet?"

Max didn't flinch. "I might've mentioned you needed a quiet place to decompress."

I tilted my head, eyeing him. "Decompress?"

"Mentally. Emotionally. Maybe... physically. Possibly with a hug."

"Jesus," I groaned, throwing a hand over my face. "So he absolutely knew."

"He might've seen us walking that direction."

I peeked through my fingers. "And Fiona? How does she know?"

"Murdo told her."

My jaw dropped. "He *told* her?"

Max took a slow swallow, completely unbothered. "They've been orchestrating this since breakfast."

I blinked. "You mean... matchmaking?"

"They call it 'strategic guest placement.' But yeah."

I stared at him. "Wait. They *wanted* this to happen?"

Max gave the world's slowest nod. "There was a bet."

I narrowed my eyes. "What kind of bet?"

He glanced at me with a perfectly straight face. "Closet or coatroom."

I full-body groaned and dropped my head to his chest. "This is it. I'm dying right here. Just leave me for the bagpipers and tell them I went out a legend."

His hand skimmed down my arm, slow and steady. "Nope. You're not dying on my watch. I like breathing, and your sister would murder me with a smile."

I yawned again, melting deeper into the firelight—and the ridiculously solid shoulder I'd claimed like it came with a lease. "You're alarmingly calm about being the victim of romantic espionage."

"Not a victim," Max said, voice low. "Just a man smart enough to stop fighting a good thing."

"You're impossible," I mumbled, already slipping beneath the surface.

"And you're beautiful," he murmured, voice low. "You walk into a room and everything else just... dims."

The silence wrapped around us, warm and heavy.

"Max?" I whispered, barely conscious. "What changed your mind?"

He let out a soft laugh. "Let's just say a Scottish Yoda handed me my ass. Called it perspective."

My eyelids dropped. The fire crackled. His warmth pressed in—quiet, steady, and dangerously easy to get used to.

Right before sleep took me, I could've sworn he shifted—just enough to pull me closer. Maybe... to hold on.

Not sure what tomorrow held, but tonight? I was exactly where I wanted to be.

Chapter 22

I Should've Been an Only Child

THE SCENT OF COFFEE hit me before I opened my eyes.

Bold. Rich. Sinful enough to qualify as foreplay.

I blinked, stretched, and processed two things in rapid succession—one, I'd slept on the couch, and two, someone had tucked a blanket around me like I was a literal princess in a coma.

Max.

The fireplace crackled low across the room, and Max crouched in front of it, poking at the embers with one hand and holding a mug in the other. He was dressed in joggers and a fitted black tee, faintly damp from what I could only assume was a morning run.

Because of course he went for a run.

Because he's a machine. A disgustingly disciplined, smugly hot machine with abs that have their own fan club.

"Morning," he said, still facing the fire. "You're officially the last guest standing."

I groaned and sat up, blinking at the soft light and clutching the blanket tighter around me. "What time is it?"

"Little after ten," he said, rising to his full, annoyingly tall height. "I asked for a late check-out so you could sleep."

I blinked at him. "You did?"

He handed me the mug with zero ceremony. "You've earned it. And the staff love you. They'd probably let you move in if you asked."

I took a sip and nearly moaned. "God, marry me."

"Tempting," he said, deadpan. "But you're still technically unconscious. I don't want to be accused of emotional entrapment."

I narrowed my eyes at him. "You're enjoying this."

"A little."

I stretched again, letting the fire's warmth and the coffee's magic work their way down my spine.

"Cottage check-in?"

"Technically whenever. Fiona said the keys are under the gnome."

"Of course there's a gnome." I shook my head. "This is the Highlands. Nothing shocks me anymore."

He ran a hand through his damp hair and gestured toward the bathroom. "Shower's yours unless you want me to go first."

I froze mid-sip. "Wait—Brynn. I promised I'd call her this morning."

Max paused, eyes ticking toward my phone like it might bite. "Then you'd better prep accordingly.

I raised a brow. "Why?"

"Because she's your twin. Which means she's had twelve hours to spiral and at least eight to create memes."

I winced. "Valid."

"Mmhmm." He pointed at the screen. "You have fun explaining things without perjuring yourself."

"You're ridiculous," I muttered, thumbing my phone open.

Then he disappeared into the bathroom, peeling off his shirt as he went.

I stared down at my phone like it was a bomb.

Five minutes later, mid-sip of coffee and seriously considering a splash of morning scotch for emotional support, my phone buzzed.

I squinted at the screen.

Brynn.

Shit. The bitch beat me to it. Oh no. Oh hell.

Video message.

Because of course she skipped straight to the nuclear option.

"Not now," I whispered like my phone could hear me. "Not today. Not ever. I'm already dead."

It buzzed again. Longer this time. Definitely possessed.

Max strolled out of the bathroom right on cue, towel slung dangerously low, hair damp and disheveled like he'd just stepped off the cover of a smutty romance novel. One of mine, probably.

I groaned. "Max. *Hide.*"

He arched a brow. "Excuse me?"

I held up the phone like it might burst into flames. "Brynn. Video call. She knows. I'm toast."

He didn't move. Just poured another cup of coffee, each motion slower and smugger than the last. Like the towel-wrapped incarnation of audacity.

"You could just tell her the truth," he said, calm as a monk. A devastatingly hot, insufferably *serene* monk.

"What truth?" I hissed. "That I've spent the past two days stress-banging the guy I called a walking spreadsheet with a superiority complex?"

His grin tugged lazy and lethal. "That's one version."

Buzz. Buzz. BUZZZZZ.

"Jesus. She's relentless."

I swiped to answer and angled the camera like I was shooting a hostage video. "Heyyy, Brynn!"

Her face popped into frame—bedhead in full bloom, eyes narrowed like a hawk mid-hunt. "You look... weird."

"Weird how?"

"Glowy. Suspiciously calm. Like you meditated or murdered someone."

Then it happened.

A blur. A flash of abs. Towel.

Max. Casually prowling behind me like that damn towel wasn't enough to make me pulse with the memory of his mouth.

Brynn gasped. "Wait—was that a *man*? Ray, are you—did you—OH MY GOD, WAS THAT MAX HARRINGTON?"

I flinched. "No! That was...a towel ghost. Super rare. Only appears to the morally conflicted."

Max passed through again, slower this time, like a walking orgasm with zero shame and calves carved from stone.

"Hi, Brynn," he said without looking up, like this was all perfectly normal.

I slapped a hand over my face. "I hate everything."

Brynn screamed loud enough to rattle the phone. "YOU HOOKED UP WITH MAX FREAKING HARRINGTON?!"

And just like that, I dropped the phone like it was radioactive.

My stomach bottomed out.

Oh God. She knew.

She was probably already designing a group chat intervention. There'd be memes, for sure.

"I should've been an only child," I muttered to the floor.

Max didn't even blink. Just sipped his coffee like my emotional meltdown was background noise. His brow lifted in that slow, amused way that made me want to throttle him. And kiss him. And then throttle him again.

"I need to shower. And pack. And maybe fake my death before Brynn assembles a task force."

"You could always scream into this towel," he offered, tugging at the edge like a menace.

I blinked. "Was that a joke? Did you just make a *sex joke*?"

He sipped his coffee. "Little of both."

"I'm spiraling and you're flirting," I groaned, pacing in frantic little circles like a Roomba with anxiety.

"Do you have any idea what happens now? She's going to demand answers. Definitions. Labels. She's going to update my relationship status before I even figure out what this *is*."

"And?" he asked, completely unfazed.

I stared at him. "And?! Max, we've been living in some weird little castle bubble. A sexy, highland-themed fever dream. And now we're going to a beach cottage. Alone. With no distractions. Just...us. What if this was all just vacation brain and castle hormones and—God—I don't even know what I'm saying."

Max crossed the room in three long, unhurried strides, stopping just close enough to hijack my oxygen supply. His voice dropped—low, calm, serious.

"Rayann," he said, steady as stone. "I'm not confused."

My breath caught.

He reached up, slow and steady, and tucked a loose strand of hair behind my ear like he'd done it a hundred times before. "I like you. All of it. The fire, the chaos, the way you talk with your hands when you're mad. I want to see where this thing goes. And I don't care if your sister knows. Hell, I don't care if the whole damn travel team livestreams it."

"But what if we mess it up?"

"Then we'll mess it up together."

I stood there—frozen, spiraling, blushing, wanting.

He didn't break eye contact—not once—as he nodded toward my suitcase like we weren't both silently contemplating staying exactly where we were.

His voice dropped, low and steady. "As much as I'd love to throw you over my shoulder and cancel checkout..."

He stepped in just close enough to send my nervous system into a tailspin.

"I'm intentional," he said quietly, like a vow. "And when we're alone... I'm going to take my time showing you exactly what that means."

I didn't move.

Couldn't breathe.

Pretty sure I forgot how legs worked.

Chapter 23

Climbing the Tree

THE SKY BLUSHED LAVENDER and gold as Max eased the car to a stop. The private cottage sat tucked between ancient trees and a stretch of untouched shoreline. It looked like something out of a travel ad—only better. Not polished. Not filtered. Just perfect.

Rustic, my ass. Collum forgot to mention jaw-dropping and vaguely magical.

It was real. Quiet. Remote.

And there were no fire alarms.

No wedding guests.

No bartenders giving us the side-eye like we were the reason the linen closet needed hazard pay.

Just us.

And maybe it freaked me out a little that it felt like peace—and not the fake kind you get from bath bombs and denial.

I stepped out first, the breeze catching my hair as I lifted my face to the fading sky, letting the moment wash over me.

Salt air. Sunset light. The kind of silence that felt thick with promise.

Max didn't move behind me, so I glanced over my shoulder.

He was still gripping the steering wheel, eyes locked on me like I'd just walked out of one of his fantasies and he hadn't quite caught up yet.

Oh no. Nope. I was not equipped for that level of smolder today.

"Are you seriously giving me heart-eyes right now?" I quirked a brow. "You're not that subtle, Harrington."

He finally stepped out of the car, gaze still pinned to me. "Can you blame me?"

I snorted. "That's your line?"

He closed the distance in a few long strides, pulled me flush against him, and kissed me like the world had finally shut up and he didn't want to waste a second of the quiet.

Heat unfurled low in my belly as I melted into him.

I fisted my hands in his shirt and pulled him closer, anchoring us to the quiet, to the moment, to everything waiting behind that door.

By the time we came up for air, my heart was racing and I was already smiling. "You going to carry me over the threshold, Harrington?"

His brow arched. "You want me to?"

"I want you to try," I teased, backing toward the cottage like I hadn't just dared a Greek god with something to prove. "Might pull a muscle in that old man back of yours."

I didn't even get the satisfaction of watching him react. One second I was upright. The next, I was in the air.

"Max!" I yelped, laughing as he scooped me up and used one foot to shove the door open—like this was the part of the movie where the music swells and the lingerie budget pays off.

The cottage was cozy and warm, scented with something fresh and clean, linens maybe. Wildflowers. The kind of smell that whispered stay awhile, kick off your shoes, and forget the rest of the world.

A stone fireplace stood at the far end, already stacked with wood. On the table, a welcome basket waited with local chocolates, fruit, and a bottle of champagne chilling like it had been expecting us.

"Wow," I whispered, eyes sweeping the room. "Okay, this is... yeah. Perfect."

He set me down slowly, like he wasn't quite ready to let go, and pressed one last kiss to the top of my shoulder before stepping back.

I clocked the champagne chilling in the basket and lifted a brow. "Is that for drinking or mood-setting?"

Max stepped behind me, his breath warm near my ear. "Depends. You want it in a glass... or dripped down your stomach?"

Dripped. Down. My—okay. Yep. I'd beg.

I turned to him, hair tangled from the wind, still catching my breath and probably looking more emotionally exposed than I meant to. "I want a lot of things right now," I said with a half-laugh. "But I'll start with a glass."

Max didn't say a word. Just uncorked the champagne with a quiet pop and handed me the bottle like he actually trusted me not to make a mess of it.

I poured us both a glass and tapped mine lightly against his. "To surviving," I said.

"To you wrecking me every chance you get," he said, gaze locked on mine.

A grin tugged at my lips. "You like it."

"I really fucking do."

I leaned against the table, letting the rim of the glass hover at my lips as my voice dipped low. "And just so we're clear, Harrington? I have some intentions of my own for you tonight."

His smile turned slow. Dangerous.

"I'm intrigued," he said.

I sank into the oversized sofa, kicked off my shoes, and tucked my legs beneath me. The champagne glass shimmered in the cozy glow of the room, cool against my fingertips and kissed with condensation.

Across the room, Max knelt at the hearth, stacking kindling like the man who'd conquered actual battlefields but still couldn't resist doing things the hard way.

"You know there's a starter log in the basket, right?" I called, swirling the champagne like I had nowhere else to be.

"I know," he grunted. "I'm ignoring it to maintain my rugged and capable illusion."

I grinned. "You carried me over the threshold, you've got twelve hours of rugged points banked."

He glanced over his shoulder, one brow arching. "Only twelve?"

I sipped slow, my smile curling behind the rim. "We'll renegotiate depending on your flame skills."

He chuckled and struck the match anyway. The flames caught fast, curling over the logs with a low roar.

When he stood, barefoot, sleeves rolled, heat on his cheekbones, he looked so stupidly good it felt personally unfair.

Then he disappeared into the bedroom, leaving the fire and me to quietly lose our minds.

The flames crackled. The silence stretched.

And then—

He returned.

Jeans slung low on his hips. Black T-shirt clinging to his chest like it had been sewn on by someone with a very specific fantasy in mind. My champagne glass froze mid-air.

Do not stare, Rayann.

I stared.

He dropped onto the couch beside me with a low sigh and reached for his glass. "I'm never wearing dress shoes again."

"Did they cramp your brooding?" I asked, trying very hard to sound normal.

"They offended my soul."

I snorted. "Your soul's tougher than that."

We sipped in silence for a while, letting the fire do the talking. The air had shifted, less chaos, more charge. Like the part of a movie where everyone knows what's coming, but no one dares say it yet.

"So," I said eventually, tipping my head toward the welcome basket. "You gonna offer me chocolate, or do I have to seduce it out of you?"

Max raised a brow. "That was seduction?"

"It was a preview."

He stood, crossed to the table, and picked up a square of dark chocolate wrapped in gold. "This one's infused with Highland honey and sea salt."

I held out my hand.

Max paused. "Or I could just feed it to you."

I narrowed my eyes. "Are you trying to be romantic, or are you just horny right now?"

He didn't even blink. "Yes."

I plucked the chocolate from his fingers, let it melt on my tongue, then winked. "Points for honesty."

He grabbed another square for himself and poured a finger of whiskey—the bottle beside the champagne like it had been waiting for permission. Then he sank into the couch with a groan that made my stomach clench and my brain reboot.

I stretched, slow and unbothered, the fabric of my dress sliding over my skin with the kind of lazy grace that would've made me self-conscious if I weren't riding the high of champagne, firelight, and a man who looked one breath away from combusting.

"I need to get out of this dress," I murmured.

Max choked on air. "I need a priest."

I bit back a grin and stood, strolling toward the hallway like I had all the time in the world and zero shame. The hem of my dress swished behind me like it had its own agenda—and it wasn't subtle. I didn't look back. Didn't need to. I could feel him watching. Practically hear the prayers.

I disappeared around the corner, pulse steady, breath not so much. My heart was full-on "what the hell are you doing," but my body? It was riding a whole other wave. One that really liked the idea of Max Harrington coming undone.

I slipped out of the dress and tossed it aside, then pulled on the shirt he'd worn earlier, the white collared one, soft and still warm from his body. It hung just long enough to count as clothing, and buttoned just far enough to avoid arrest. Barefoot and emboldened, I padded back toward the living room.

Max looked like he'd forgotten how time worked.

Perched on the edge of the couch, glass dangling in one hand, mouth parted, he looked like his brain had just blue-screened, hard.

"Jesus," he rasped.

I raised my glass, slow and innocent. "What?"

His eyes dragged over me like it hurt. "You. In that shirt. Looking like every fantasy I didn't know I had."

I sauntered to the armchair across from him and curled up slowly, deliberately. The firelight kissed my legs as I tucked them beneath me.

Then I reached out, clinked my glass against his.

"To upgraded fantasies," I said.

His voice was thick. Rough. "To delayed gratification."

I smirked. Wicked. Unbothered. "Oh, baby—don't act like you're suffering."

He groaned, dropping his head back. "I am. But I've never been more willing to suffer."

"You're so dramatic."

Max lifted his glass, pointed it at me. "You say that now, but in ten minutes, you're gonna be climbing me like a tree."

I tilted my head, slow and smug. "Only if the tree begs real nice."

He choked on his drink. Hard.

The silence wasn't awkward, it was electric.

I swirled the last sip of champagne in my glass, catching Max watching me out of the corner of my eye. His gaze kept flicking from my legs to the fire to me again, like he thought I wouldn't notice.

He was not subtle.

Not at all.

"I can feel you looking at me," I murmured, voice lazy, lips curving into a smile.

"I'm not looking," he lied.

Still stared like he didn't want to blink and miss a second of me.

I cocked my head. "Then why are your pupils the size of dinner plates, hmm?"

He set his glass down slowly, the sound too deliberate to be casual. "Because you're torturing me."

I stretched, slow and smug, letting the hem of his shirt inch higher up my thighs. "Poor baby."

"You know what the worst part is?" he asked, leaning forward, elbows braced on his knees, eyes locked on mine. "I think I'm developing a kink for suffering."

That earned him a smirk.

I stood and crossed the room barefoot, every step slow and fluid. The hem of his shirt whispered against my thighs.

I didn't rush. Didn't need to.

The tension was already stretched so tight I could hear it hum.

I stopped in front of him, let the last sip of champagne slide down my throat, then set the glass aside with a soft clink.

He didn't move.

Didn't breathe.

Just watched me like a man standing on the edge of something and looked real damn ready to swan dive straight into it.

I climbed into his lap without hesitation, one knee on either side of his thighs.

His hands found my hips instantly, big, warm, sure, like his body knew exactly what I needed before his brain had a chance to catch up.

"Still suffering?" I whispered, close enough for him to taste it.

His breath hitched. "I'm hanging on by a fucking thread."

I slid my hands up his chest, slow and teasing, my fingertips grazing the base of his throat. "Then let go."

His jaw flexed. Grip tightened. But still, he didn't move.

So I leaned in, lips grazing his ear. "Or are you afraid I'll wreck *you* this time?"

The groan he let out was low and feral, his restraint unraveling in real time.

His hands slipped beneath the shirt, rough palms gliding up my thighs, over my hips, along my spine, agonizingly slow. I braced my hands on his shoulders, heart pounding loud enough to drown out thought. My skin buzzed.

"I'm not afraid of you," he murmured against my throat. "I crave you."

His lips trailed along my collarbone, slow and reverent, like he wasn't sure if he was allowed but couldn't stop. "You make me feel... everything."

My fingers tangled in his hair, tugging just enough to make him groan. "Then feel me."

He kissed me.

Deep. Consuming. Like I was something sacred and dangerous all at once.

His hands slid higher, drawing me closer as his mouth moved like he knew exactly what he was doing—and planned to take his damn time doing it. I ground down, slow, deliberate, and his head dropped back with a curse.

"Sadist," he rasped.

I grinned. "You're the one who said delayed gratification."

"Fuck delayed," Max growled.

In one fluid, lethal move, he wrapped an arm around my waist, lifted me clean off his lap, and lowered me onto my back in front of the fire.

I landed breathless and laughing, hair fanned out across the rug.

"Oh, so we're playing now," I gasped, my breath hitching as he hovered above me, one hand planted beside my head.

"I'm always playing," he said, voice like rough silk. "You just keep raising the stakes."

I curled my legs around his waist, hips lifting just enough to close the distance.

"Then let's raise them again."

Chapter 24

A Full-Body Amen

I DIDN'T GIVE HIM a chance to reply.

I pushed against his shoulders, rolling him onto his back in one clean move. Max let me. Eyes dark. Lips parted. Already halfway gone as I slid back onto his hips. The heat of him pressed against me, hard and thick beneath his jeans, and holy hell if that didn't make my whole body clench.

My fingers found the button at his waistband.

Slow. Deliberate. Torture on purpose.

"Fuck," he breathed, hands fisting into the rug like he didn't trust himself not to flip me right back over.

I smirked. "Patience."

His thighs flexed. Jesus. Focus, Rayann.

I eased his jeans down and palmed the thick line of him straining beneath soft cotton. God help me. His boxers weren't hiding anything.

Because boxers. Of course. Like he hadn't caught me eye-fucking him all day and built a whole goddamn strategy around it.

But I wasn't done teasing yet.

I leaned down and kissed the inside of his thigh, soft and slow, right against the tense muscle.

Max hissed. His hips jerked.

"Rayann—"

"Shh. You're mine now." I licked the same path, slow and hot, savoring the way his breath stuttered. Then I hooked my fingers into the waistband of his boxers and dragged them down, freeing him completely.

He groaned, head thumping back against the rug as I wrapped my hand around him, firm and sure, stroking once. Twice. Just enough to make every muscle go tight beneath me, like his body wanted to take over but he was letting me drive.

"Still hanging on by a thread?" I murmured, letting my thumb circle his tip and smear the bead of pre-cum.

He didn't answer—just cursed.

I smiled, then lowered my mouth to him.

The first lick was slow and intentional. A wet, deliberate stroke from base to tip that made his whole body jolt.

Max's fingers tangled in my hair. Tight, but not forceful. Just there. Grounding him while I dragged my tongue along his cock again, tasting the salt and heat of him.

"Jesus Christ," he rasped, his voice wrecked.

I hummed in approval, and he groaned again at the vibration. I wrapped my lips around him and sucked, slow and deep, hollowing my cheeks as I took him into my mouth. Pulled back. Did it again.

His hands tightened, hips twitching as I set a rhythm: slick, hungry strokes paired with a twist of my wrist and the occasional flick of my tongue right under the head. I knew exactly what I was doing, and he knew exactly how fucked he was.

"Rayann—baby, I'm not gonna last if you keep—"

I pulled off just enough to look up at him, my mouth slick, my smile dangerous.

"Then don't."

His breath caught.

"You first," he rasped.

The words had barely landed before he surged up, caught me around the waist like I weighed nothing, and flipped me onto my back. My hair spilled across the rug in a messy halo of chaos and heat.

His mouth crashed into mine, hot and messy and claiming. I didn't care that my lips were still wet with him. In fact,

I liked it. I liked that he tasted himself when he kissed me. I liked that he didn't hesitate.

God, I'm gone for him. And he knows it.

His hand slid between my thighs, fingers finding me soaked and aching through the fabric of his shirt.

"You're fucking drenched," he muttered against my mouth, his voice rough silk. "How long have you been this wet for me?"

"Since you opened that goddamn champagne," I breathed.

He let out a laugh that sounded more like a groan. "Jesus, Rayann."

He pushed the shirt up, exposing me fully, then dragged his fingers through my slick folds like he was mapping me. I moaned, hips lifting, needy and shameless.

When his thumb found my clit and circled, slow and devastating, I nearly came right then.

"Max—holy hell—"

"Not yet," he whispered, kissing down my neck as his fingers slid lower. "I want to feel you fall apart first."

And then he sank two fingers inside me.

Deep. Curling. Just right.

I gasped, grabbing at his shoulders, riding the rhythm of his hand as he thrust slow and steady, his palm never once leaving my clit.

My orgasm built fast, hot and sharp, cresting with every stroke. When it hit, I shattered beneath him, my body seizing around his fingers, my cry muffled against his throat.

"Fuck," he gritted, pulling his hand free just long enough to guide himself to my entrance, thick and flushed and ready. "You feel that?"

I was still pulsing when he thrust his cock inside me.

All the way.

Deep and rough and perfect.

I cried out, arching into him, and he moaned like he'd lost his mind.

"You're mine," he told me, low and rough, driving into me again.

I dragged his mouth to mine, tasting myself on his tongue, clinging to him as he fucked me with the kind of hunger that didn't ask permission. It just took.

And I let him.

And he did.

I was still trembling from the first orgasm when Max pulled out slowly, dragging a groan from both of us. My body clenched at the loss, left empty and aching, until I saw the look in his eyes.

Focused. Feral. Fucking lethal.

He wasn't done. Not even close.

Max sat back on his heels, grabbed the bottle of champagne off the table, and twisted off what was left of the foil with that calm, precise ease that made my thighs twitch.

"What are you doing?" I breathed, chest still heaving.

His gaze flicked to mine as he held the bottle by the neck, the cold condensation trailing over his fingers. "Told you earlier," he said. "Depends where you want it."

This beautiful man. Fucking unreal.

"Max."

"Shh." He shifted closer and tipped the bottle just slightly, letting the coldest goddamn drizzle hit my stomach.

And then his mouth was on me.

Hot. Open. Wet.

He licked a path through the champagne, trailing it lower, lower, his tongue chasing the icy streaks in slow, sinful strokes.

Oh my fucking God. Arrogant, talented asshole.

This man's every move oozed calculated, alpha-level sin.

"You taste fucking incredible," he muttered, kissing the inside of my thigh like a man making promises with his mouth.

I couldn't think. Couldn't breathe. Especially not when he slid his hands beneath my ass and pulled me toward the edge of the rug like he owned me.

And then?

Then he buried his face between my legs.

His tongue was everywhere, slick and purposeful, teasing my clit with slow flicks before sucking me into his mouth with ruthless precision.

I cried out, fingers tunneling through his hair, hips jerking against his face, but Max didn't stop.

He gripped my thighs, kept me open, kept me still, and kept fucking worshipping me with that devastating mouth.

When he slid two fingers back inside me, crooked just right, and added a slow grind of his tongue against my clit, I saw stars.

I bucked beneath him, moaning his name, barely holding on as the second orgasm built hard and fast, riding the edge with every slick swipe of his tongue.

"Come on," he growled against me, voice low and dark and fucking filthy. "Give me another."

I shattered.

Again.

This time harder. Deeper. With a full-body tremble that left me sobbing his name like it was the only word left in my body.

Max kissed my inner thigh, licking me clean like he wasn't done tasting me.

"Goddamn it," I gasped, breath wrecked, eyes still unfocused. "What the amazing hell just happened?"

He grinned like a man who knew exactly what he'd done.

"My turn," he growled, then slid back inside me with one hard, perfect thrust that knocked the breath from my lungs.

I saw stars. I gasped, nails dragging down his back as he bottomed out, staying there for a heartbeat, deep, thick, like he wanted me to feel every fucking inch of him before he moved.

And then he did.

Slow at first. Deep, dragging thrusts that rubbed everywhere I needed, hitting that perfect spot with maddening precision. Each one more deliberate than the last, his hips rolling like he knew my body better than I did.

"Look at me," he commanded, voice raw.

I did.

Eyes locked, breath tangled, bodies straining.

His pace quickened, each thrust harder, deeper, filthier.

"I want you to feel me for days," he rasped against my mouth. "I want every part of you sore and dripping and thinking about this."

My body responded like it belonged to him. In this moment, it did.

He drove into me, one hand fisted in my hair, the other gripping my thigh, pinning it up around his waist. The angle sent shockwaves of pleasure spiraling through me.

"You feel that?" he ground out.

"God, yes—Max—"

"Clenching around me like you're trying to keep me."

"I fucking am."

Something snapped in him.

He bit my shoulder, not hard enough to hurt, just enough to make me arch. Then he fucked me harder. Wilder. Hungrier.

My orgasm built like a freight train.

Unstoppable. Desperate.

"Touch yourself," he ordered, breath ragged. "Rub yourself for me, Rayann. Let me watch you come."

Sweet mother of dirty talk, Max Harrington just got ten times hotter. Sign me the fuck up.

I didn't hesitate.

My hand slid between us, fingers finding my swollen clit and circling fast, messy, frantic. I was so close I could taste it.

"That's it," he moaned. "Jesus Christ, you're so goddamn hot when you fall apart."

I came with a scream, head thrown back, body seizing around him as I shattered, light bursting behind my eyes, thighs trembling, gripping him like I never wanted to let go.

"Fucking hell—Rayann—" Max's voice cracked as he snapped his hips one final time and came hard, deep inside me, his body jerking against mine with every pulse of release.

He groaned against my throat, one long, wrecked sound, his arms tightening around me like he didn't trust himself to stay upright.

We stayed like that.

Breathless. Slick. Twined together in a tangle of limbs and sweat and sex and too many emotions neither of us had the strength to name yet.

Eventually, his hand brushed my cheek.

"You okay?" he asked, voice low and gravel-rough.

I laughed, soft and shaken. Totally ruined.

"I think you just ruined my pelvic floor."

He smiled, kissed my temple, and muttered, "Worth it."

Max didn't move for a long time.

Just hovered over me, breath ghosting across my neck, heart pounding against mine like he wasn't entirely sure we were done.

Honestly? I wasn't sure either.

His body was still inside me, softening now, but his hands were everywhere. One on my thigh. The other in my hair. Holding. Stroking. Not possessive anymore. Just... there. Real.

Real.

"I should move," he said eventually, voice a low scrape against my throat.

"You move, I bite."

He huffed out something between a laugh and a groan. "Noted."

We stayed like that, tangled and sticky and wrecked, for another stretch of silence that somehow felt louder than anything we'd just done.

His breath slowed. So did mine.

It was quiet. Too quiet.

I should've said something snarky. Something safe. Something Rayann.

Instead, I turned my head and let my lips brush the corner of his jaw. "That was..."

"Yeah," he murmured.

"I mean, I've had good sex."

Max lifted a brow.

"But that was... next-level. Like, if this were a video game, I'd need an achievement badge and a post-coital hydration warning."

His mouth curved. "Pretty sure I just leveled up too."

He shifted then, gently pulling out, and I hissed at the overstimulation. He paused, murmured something under his breath that might've been "sorry" or "holy shit," and grabbed the throw blanket off the couch.

Then he wrapped it around both of us and pulled me into his chest like it wasn't a question.

I didn't resist.

Which was... new.

He kissed the top of my head. "You're alright?"

I nodded against his shoulder.

"Sure?"

"No," I admitted. "But I will be."

He was quiet for a beat. Then: "You wreck me, you know."

I smiled. "Right back at you."

His arms tightened around me.

And for the first time in forever, I didn't want to run. Not from him. Not from this.

Chapter 25

All the Parts I Tried to Hide

WE STAYED THERE FOR a while, curled up on the rug, our skin cooling while the fire crackled low beside us. Eventually, my back started to ache from the hard floor, but I didn't want to be the one to break the spell. Moving felt like it might shatter something delicate.

Max moved first. "C'mon," he murmured, brushing his lips against my temple. "You're shivering."

I hadn't even realized it. But the chill had crept in, curling around my spine, and I didn't protest when he pulled me to my feet and guided us toward the couch.

Or maybe I was in shock because I'd crossed some invisible line between fun and feelings and my brain hadn't caught up yet.

He sank into the cushions, tugging me with him like it was the most natural thing in the world. Then he wrapped the throw around my shoulders and pulled me into his chest. His body radiated warmth. Solid. Grounding. Impossibly steady.

Neither of us spoke. We just listened. The fire. The wind. The way the old cottage seemed to settle around us like it approved.

That's when I felt it. Not silence, exactly. More like stillness. The kind that only shows up after something big.

Something in me had softened. Everything felt exposed.

A soft rain tapped at the windows, no louder than a breath, like the whole world was exhaling with us.

I let my eyes linger too long.

Yeah. Big mistake.

Because of course he caught me.

"What?" he asked, voice rough with satisfaction, like he hadn't just wrecked my nervous system and was now casually basking in the afterglow like some smug sex sorcerer.

He lifted one brow, like he already knew exactly what I'd been thinking.

I looked away too fast, yanking the blanket higher like it could shield me from how absolutely unhinged I felt. "Didn't peg you for the type who sticks around after the fireworks, Harrington."

Low blow. I knew it the second it slipped out.

I was spiraling, okay?

Max didn't flinch. Didn't blink. Just hit me with that maddeningly calm gaze, like he was some kind of human lie detector.

"Why do you think I'd want to leave you?"

Oh, no. We are not doing this.

I laughed. Sharp. Defensive. The verbal equivalent of flinging glitter and sprinting for the exit. "Come on. Let's be real, Max. Guys like you don't stick around for girls like me."

His brow creased. He tilted his head, gaze locked. He wasn't letting it slide.

"Explain."

Nope. No. Abort mission.

But I was already unraveling. My fingers found a loose thread on the blanket and picked at it like it held the damn answers.

"I'm a hot mess," I said, trying to keep it breezy, like I wasn't peeling back my entire operating system in real time. "Impulsive. Brain runs like a Maserati with no brakes. A million ideas a minute, no landing gear. I'm... a lot."

God. That last word landed too soft. So soft it made my stomach twist.

Shit. I didn't mean to say that out loud.

Bury it, Rayann. Joke over it. Smother it in sass.

Max didn't blink. Didn't look away. Just pushed up onto one elbow and locked in like I was the only thing that mattered.

"You're not a lot," he said, voice low. Steady.

"You're more."

I braced for a full-blown rom-com monologue. My eyes were primed and ready.

But then he hit me with it.

"You're fire," he said. "You're momentum. The spark boring people spend their whole lives chasing. You don't just dream. You pull people in. You give them the adventure they didn't even know they needed."

I just... stared.

Because seriously, what the hell do you even say to that?

Run? Laugh? Set myself on fire and launch into orbit?

And of course, Max wasn't done.

"Swear to God," he said, full grin in place. "You, on your toes, calling me a coward for skipping the kilt race? Sexiest ambush of my life."

My jaw actually dropped.

Words? Gone. Evaporated. Replaced by emotional static loud enough to fry circuits.

Max leaned in like he was engraving the whole damn moment onto stone. "Or the tug-of-war. You, flat on your back, furious and speechless? I'll be riding that high for months."

I narrowed my eyes and yanked the blanket up, like it could somehow shield me from his ridiculous grin. "Wow. The humility? Impressive. Be sure to log that under 'personal achievements' on your spreadsheet."

He chuckled, low and warm, infuriatingly pleased with himself. His fingers found the edge of the blanket, trailing a slow line along my calf where it had slipped.

"Wouldn't miss it for the world."

The silence that followed wasn't awkward. Or empty. It was full. Saturated. Like the room itself had stopped to hold its breath.

Then Max spoke again, quieter now.

"I *see* you, Ray."

My head snapped up. "Okay. That sounds... vaguely serial killer-ish."

But he wasn't smiling.

His eyes held that maddening calm, steady and soul-deep, the kind that made me want to bolt and melt at the same time.

"*All* of you," he said. "Not just the charming, flashy parts you toss like confetti. The chaos too. The overthinking. The messy stuff you think you're supposed to hide."

Goddamn it. That one got through.

My throat tightened around a swallow I wasn't ready for. "Careful, Harrington. You're making me like you."

His grin spread, slow and unapologetic. "Yeah. I'm really hoping that's the problem."

I figured that was it. A cheeky one-liner. Perfectly timed smirk. Curtain closed.

But then something shifted. The grin faded. The air between us turned heavier.

"The chaos," he said, voice lower now. "It's kind of a family thing."

I blinked, caught off guard by the sudden shift.

"My sister's the wild one," he said, gaze fixed on the fire. "Brilliant. Kind. Total tornado energy."

His eyes flicked back to me. "You'd love her. My little brother's been through it—anxiety, addiction. Some good days. A lot of hard ones. And me?"

He laughed softly. "I pulled the OCD card. Alphabetized the cereal boxes. Sorted my Star Wars action figures by category and release year. Drove them both insane."

My chest squeezed, even as he tried to keep it light.

"Guess we're all wired a little sideways. My parents too. The whole damn tree leans left."

He laughed again, but softer now. It still didn't reach his eyes. "Apparently the well-adjusted gene gave our branch a hard pass."

"I think I'd like your sister." I hesitated. "Maybe I'll meet her someday."

"Oh, you will," he murmured.

Then, softer. "That's a promise."

But inside? I was spiraling.

Oh my god. Did he just say I'm going to meet his family? Like... his actual family? Rayann, what did you just do?

And then—on top of that—

Holy shit.

Everything he just said. The chaos. The rewiring. The way he described his sister. That wasn't just about them.

That was me.

He sees it. All of it. And he's still here.

It was the way I interrupted people mid-sentence because my brain always outran my mouth. The way I forgot what I was doing halfway through doing it. The way my thoughts never shut up—not even when I begged them to. Not even when I was kissing him.

I'd spent most of my life treating it like a personality quirk. A lovable mess. Something to joke about before anyone looked too close.

But Max hadn't flinched.

Hadn't tried to fix it.

Or explain it.

Or joke it away.

He just made space for it.

For me.

And suddenly, breathing felt impossible.

Max didn't say another word.

He didn't need to.

He stayed beside me, fingers trailing across my skin like he didn't know how to stop—and I didn't want him to. Not tonight.

Not when everything suddenly felt different.

"Max?"

"Hmm?"

"You know, you could've just told me she wasn't your secret Scottish lover."

Max blinked. "Who?"

I gave him a look. "Annabelle Sinclair. Silk slip. Tuscany. Ring any bells?"

He stared at me—then barked out a laugh. "Jesus. That's what this has been about?"

"What? No. Maybe. Shut up."

His smirk deepened. "So the whole time, you thought I was into Annabelle?"

I folded my arms, defensive and mildly mortified. "She touched your arm like it came monogrammed. And you let her."

He cocked a brow. "She's married."

I blinked. "What?"

"Yeah. Some McIvey cousin. Twice removed, I think. Why?"

"Then why the hell did you drop me like a hot coal the second she appeared during the ceilidh dance?"

He leaned in, mouth brushing mine. "She waved. Figured she needed something. Didn't think twice."

And just like that, every meltdown I'd spiral-scripted came crashing down in one giant flaming heap of *oh-my-God-I'm-an-idiot.*

Eventually, the fire sank low, and a chill crept across the floorboards. My toes curled under the blanket, but Max was already moving. He tugged it tighter around me, then stood and held out a hand like it was the most obvious thing in the world.

"Come to bed with me," he said.

It wasn't a command. Or a tease.

Just an invitation. Quiet. Simple. One I could finally say yes to without losing any part of myself.

So I did.

And for once, I didn't overthink it.

Chapter 26

Synced. It's Fine. I'm Fine.

I WOKE UP TO warmth.

Not sunlight. Scotland didn't do morning light so much as diffused gray ambiance. But warmth. The kind that sank in deep and settled somewhere under your ribs before your brain even caught up.

Max's arm was still draped across my waist, his chest pressed to my back, his breath slow and even against the nape of my neck.

And I didn't move.

Not because I was afraid of waking him up.

Because I didn't want to know if this would break the second I did.

I kept my eyes closed, pretending I wasn't hyperaware of every place our skin touched. My thighs were sore, my muscles wrecked, and my brain still felt like someone had tossed a Molotov cocktail into it sometime around midnight. I should've been panicking.

Instead, I sank into it.

Let it wrap around me like the throw blanket I'd already stolen from Fiona's couch and mentally labeled my emotional support object.

Max shifted slightly, his arm tightening just enough to make it clear he was awake.

"Mornin'," he said, his voice still sleep-rough and unfairly sexy.

My brain short-circuited for half a second.

"Morning," I managed, my voice about twelve octaves lower than usual. I cleared my throat like that might help. "We didn't burn the place down, so I'd call that a win."

He chuckled. Lazy. Content. "Tempting, though."

I bit my lip, then rolled over to face him.

Mistake.

Big, shirtless, tangle-haired mistake.

His eyes were still heavy-lidded, that stupid smirk playing on his mouth like he had every right to look that good while lying in someone else's borrowed bed.

"You okay?" he asked, quieter now.

Sure. Yup. Totally fine. Just had the best sex of my life and caught feelings for the guy I thought I couldn't stand. But yeah, let's roll with 'okay.'

I blinked. "Yeah. I mean... yeah."

Not a lie. Just... not the whole truth either.

He studied me like he could hear the rest of what I wasn't saying. And maybe he could.

He didn't push.

Instead, he leaned in and kissed my forehead like it was the most natural thing in the world. Like I hadn't emotionally undressed in front of him last night and was still sorting through what parts of me were safe to show.

"Hungry?" he asked.

"Yes," I said, entirely too fast.

He laughed again, then peeled himself out of bed with the ease of someone who hadn't just destroyed a woman's entire worldview with one well-timed compliment.

"Stay," he said, already tugging on his shirt. "I'll find something edible."

"Please don't say haggis."

He paused, grinned. "No promises."

I didn't stay.

Not right away, anyway.

I lasted thirty seconds before the smell of coffee started drifting through the cottage like a damn siren call. I splashed cold water on my face, stared at my reflection like maybe she had answers, then threw my hair into the world's most chaotic bun and gave up on emotionally recovering today.

By the time I made it to the kitchen, Max had somehow found eggs, toast, and jam, and managed to wrangle coffee into two mugs without destroying Fiona's absurdly clean kitchen.

I climbed onto a stool near the counter, still wrapped in the blanket, and perched there like some kind of feral goblin who'd stumbled into domestic bliss and didn't trust it.

He set a mug down in front of me and leaned a hip against the counter.

"See? No haggis."

"Heroic restraint," I said, then took a sip. The coffee was hot, strong, and almost made me emotional.

We ate quietly for a bit, but the silence wasn't awkward.

It was easy.

Comfortable.

Which only made it worse, actually.

Because comfortable meant familiar. Familiar meant safe. And safe meant—

Nope. Shut it down.

"Don't look at me like that," I said without glancing up.

"I didn't say anything."

"Your face did."

He nudged his plate aside and crossed his arms, still watching me. "You thinking again?"

"Always," I muttered. "It's a curse."

He leaned in slightly, his voice dropping just enough to make it a problem. "It's one of my favorite things about you."

God. Help.

"You've got issues," I mumbled.

"You're not wrong."

We didn't rush to leave the cottage.

In fact, we didn't really leave at all. Max found a trail behind the cottage, a narrow path that led straight down to the shore. The wind was sharp and salty, strong enough to whip my hair into my face every few seconds. I didn't care.

I was holding Max's hand.

And somehow, I wasn't freaking out about that yet.

The beach stretched in both directions. Rocky and wild, scattered with driftwood and seaweed and things I couldn't name but felt weirdly enchanted by.

Max walked beside me in silence, his fingers occasionally brushing mine like he didn't want to let go. I didn't pull away. Not even when I probably should have.

I stopped when something caught my eye. A small, round object half-buried in the sand near a tide pool.

"Ooh. Fossil." I crouched down, brushing sand away like I was unveiling some kind of ancient treasure.

Max leaned over my shoulder, squinting. "That's a potato."

I turned my head slowly. "Excuse me?"

He shrugged. "It's round, dirty, vaguely suspicious. Definitely a potato."

"It's not a potato."

He crouched beside me, plucked it from the sand, turned it over in his hand. "Nope. Potato."

"You're infuriating."

"I'm right."

"It's prehistoric."

"Looks like lunch to me."

I snatched it from him, held it up like a relic. "This is history."

"It's starch."

We stared at each other. Neither one of us blinked.

Then I laughed. The kind that started in my chest and spilled out in a breath I didn't know I'd been holding for two whole days. Max grinned like he'd won something.

"God, you're smug," I said, brushing sand off my knees.

He offered a hand, tugged me up, and didn't let go once I was standing.

"You're beautiful when you're wrong," he said, voice low.

"Funny. You're beautiful when you shut up."

He stepped closer. The wind caught his hair, and the salt clung to his skin, and I felt it hit me. Right there in the middle of nowhere, holding a fake fossil with bare feet in cold sand.

I kissed him.

I didn't think. Didn't plan it. Just reached up and curled my fingers into the front of his shirt and pulled him down to me.

He didn't hesitate. Didn't ask. Just kissed me like he already knew what I needed and had no intention of giving me anything less.

The kiss turned hot fast. Heat bloomed in my chest, low in my stomach, and settled between my legs like we'd lit a match and tossed it into kindling.

Max backed me toward the nearest flat stretch of driftwood without breaking contact, his hands slipping beneath my sweater, spreading over my ribs like he needed to map me all over again.

I gasped against his mouth, fingers tangling in his hair. "Here?"

His mouth brushed my jaw. "Tell me to stop."

I didn't.

Not even when he lowered me onto the driftwood, not even when his hands slid beneath the waistband of my leggings, not even when the cold air hit my thighs and I shivered.

Because his mouth was on mine.

Because the wind howled behind us, and the sea kept rolling in, and Max made me feel steady even when I wasn't.

His body covered mine, skin warm, hands sure, gaze locked on me like I was the only thing in the world that made sense.

We didn't rush.

There was nothing frantic about it. Just heat and pressure and the kind of need that felt like it had roots.

He sank into me slowly, and I forgot how to breathe.

My nails dug into his back. He groaned against my throat, whispering my name like it was a secret.

And when I came—slow, deep, eyes wide open—I saw him.

All of him.

And he saw me.

Chapter 27

Low Tide

DRIVING INTO TOWN FELT like stepping out of a story I hadn't finished reading.

Sand lingered in places that shouldn't have names. My legs ached in the best possible way. Max's hand rested on my thigh like it belonged there. And maybe it did. Maybe everything had shifted just enough in the past two days to make room for the idea that Max Harrington belonged in my life.

Which—obviously—was terrifying.

Whitewashed cottages came into view. The thatched-roof bakery—with its cheeky chalkboard sign reading *Hot buns, even hotter gossip*—waited at the corner of the square like it always had. Kids darted around a produce stall. A woman sold bouquets from a converted baby carriage. Real life. Bright, ordinary, and ready to swallow us whole.

Max eased the rental toward the market, his hand tightening slightly on mine.

"That was nice," he said, like we'd just wrapped a scenic stroll instead of redefining the laws of sexual physics.

Nice? Like the part where I screamed his name loud enough to traumatize nesting seabirds.

I cocked a brow. "Nice? That's what you're going with?"

He smirked. "You want a PowerPoint breakdown?"

"Obviously. On a secure server, of course."

His thumb traced lazy circles over my knuckles, warm and grounding.

Neither of us said what we meant.

We parked and wandered toward the fishmonger—mostly so I could pretend we were just two people trying to decide what to make for dinner. I reached for a basket. So did Max. Our fingers brushed.

Cue Murdo, emerging from between two vendor tents with the kind of suspicious timing that suggested he'd conjured himself from the sea mist.

Holy hell. What the fuck's sake?

The only thing missing is a puff of smoke and a tartan wand.

He took one look at us, noting our linked hands, wind-tangled hair, and the lingering scent of ocean salt and delicious wreckage of what he did to me on the sand. Then he grinned like a wolf in tweed.

"Well now," he said, eyes twinkling over a half-eaten meat pie. "Didn't expect to see ye two surface so soon."

Max gave a casual nod. "Market called."

Murdo's grin widened. "Uh-huh. Lookin' well-rested, the both of ye."

I picked up a jar of marmalade I had zero intention of buying and winked, "Is there a neighborhood watch I can report this to?"

He chuckled, clearly enjoying himself far too much. "Just glad to see two people returning to town looking like love's in the air."

Love? Oh cool, emotional landmines. Right here in the farmer's market.

Max, the traitor, had the nerve to smile. "Fresh air's good for the soul."

I grabbed a basket with the casual aggression of someone barely resisting the urge to hurl fruit. "I liked it better when you glared and grunted."

Max, infuriatingly composed, picked up a tomato and bit into it like this was just another grocery run.

I briefly considered drowning him in the nearest lobster tank.

"Anyway," Murdo said, flicking his pie crust to a nearby seagull. "It's good to see ye both. I mean it. Ye look lighter. That's worth a lot."

Max gave him a small nod. "Appreciate that."

Murdo's gaze moved between us, far too knowing. "You'll be needing that peace. Storm's on the horizon."

I blinked. "Like... weather?"

He shrugged and walked off without another word.

Cryptic bastard.

We didn't talk much on the drive back—to what turned out to be our last day at the cottage. I blamed the fog. Or maybe it was the emotional whiplash of toe-curling beach sex... followed by Murdo's unsolicited soul reading... followed by the cruel slap of work emails and pants with actual zippers.

By the time we got inside, the silence had settled into something almost comfortable. Max disappeared into the bathroom. I curled onto the couch with my phone—just to check in.

Big mistake. Rookie-level mistake.

Summer: Where the hell are you?

Summer: Change of plans. Clients bumped their time-line. Deveraux party's been moved up. I need you back TO-MORROW.

Summer: And tell Max I said thanks for not letting you fall off a cliff or into a loch or whatever heroic nonsense he probably had to pull off.

I stared at the screen and let out a groan loud enough to summon Max from the shower.

"Trouble?" Max asked, towel slung low around his hips. Distracting. Completely unfair.

Does he seriously expect me to form full sentences while standing there dripping wet and half-naked like it's his God-given right to star in my next orgasm?

I flipped the phone in the air and caught it again. "Just the usual love letter from my boss-slash-sister. Surprise—I'm back on duty tomorrow."

His jaw ticked. Just barely. But I caught it.

"Max... you okay?" I asked.

He nodded once. "Fine. Just—got a call."

I waited. He didn't say more.

"You gonna mysterious-SEAL me again or actually tell me something this time?"

His mouth twitched. "It's... a follow-up. From something I looked into a while back."

I waited.

He finally looked up. "Embassy security. They want to interview me."

Interview? Like the kind that ends with a job? In another country? With him gone and me pretending I'm fine?

That landed harder than I wanted to admit.

"Oh." I turned to my suitcase and pretended to care deeply about the state of my underwear. "That's... huge."

He didn't answer right away. The silence stretched—long, heavy, scraping against something tender I wasn't ready to name.

"It's been months," he said finally. "Didn't think the timing was right. But they followed up. Head of Security. In Italy."

My nod came too fast. "You'd crush that. It's very you. Order. Protocol. Bulletproof glass."

"Right."

My hands trembled as I folded a shirt that didn't need folding. He watched me the whole time.

But he didn't press.

And somehow, that was worse.

I tucked the shirt into my suitcase like it mattered. Like any of this mattered.

Behind me, he shifted. The towel hit the floor with a soft thump. The bed creaked as he sat down.

"Summer needs me. I leave tomorrow," I said, still not facing him.

"I know."

Another beat. Another silence. Another second I couldn't bring myself to break.

I turned.

He sat at the edge of the bed, bare and waiting, elbows on his knees like he didn't trust himself to move. His eyes met mine.

Steady. Quiet. Raw.

I crossed the room and climbed into his lap without asking. He stayed silent, sliding his hands up my thighs—slow, warm—like he needed to prove I was real.

I kissed him, tentative and soft. His mouth opened under mine like a confession.

He eased me onto the bed like he was setting something down he didn't want to break. His body came over mine with that same maddening, Max-level control—measured, focused, like he'd mapped this out and didn't want to skip a single step. Every shift pressed some new part of him into me, warm and steady and terrifying in the way it made me want things I wasn't ready to say out loud.

"Rayann..." His voice cracked.

"I know," I whispered, pulling him closer. "Just don't stop."

When he slid inside me—God, the beauty of it—it felt like the kind of thing you only get once and never really get over.

I wrapped my legs around his waist and held him there, hips lifting to meet every slow, deliberate thrust. His forehead pressed to mine, our breath mingling—shallow, shaky, like we were both on the verge of breaking.

I didn't beg. But I wanted to.

His lips traced my cheek, my throat, the hollow between my breasts—telling me everything he didn't have words for. I arched into him, nails dragging down his back, my body clenching around his with every slow, deliberate build of pressure.

When I came, it wasn't loud. Just a quiet unraveling. A silent plea he answered with a groan against my neck and a shudder that wrecked him.

He stayed inside me. Stayed *with* me.

For a little while, we didn't say anything at all.

We stayed like that—bodies tangled, skin damp with sweat, the room quiet except for the sound of our breathing trying to settle into something steady.

His hand drifted across my back in slow, absent strokes. My cheek pressed to his chest, where his heart beat like it didn't quite trust this peace to last.

Neither did mine.

I wanted to believe this was enough. That our bodies could bridge the space between all the things we didn't say. But the ache in my chest said otherwise.

This wasn't the frantic, clothes-still-on kind of sex.

This was the kind that whispered *please stay* without either of us being brave enough to say it out loud.

He kissed the top of my head.

"You okay?" he asked, voice low and rough around the edges.

I nodded against his skin. "Yeah."

"You sure?"

No. God, no.

But I said, "Mmhmm."

His arms tightened around me like he didn't believe me—but wasn't ready to push.

We lay there, quiet again.

And the silence?

It wasn't soft anymore.

Chapter 28

Boarding Group: Departures Only

THE FIRE BURNED LOW, casting flickering shadows across the stone hearth. Neither of us moved to feed it. Max moved to the couch, elbows braced on his knees, gaze fixed on some middle distance like it owed him answers. I curled on the floor with a throw pillow and a growing sense of dread I couldn't quite smother. I pulled the wool blanket off the couch and wrapped it around my shoulders like armor I'd waited too long to wear.

We hadn't said much since the bedroom.

Not because everything was fine.

Because if we said anything, we might say *too much*.

His phone buzzed on the table. He didn't check it. Just let it hum like it had all the time in the world to ruin what was left of us.

Don't ask. Don't start it. Just sit here and let him go quietly.

Eventually, he picked it up and stared at the screen.

"That the embassy?" I asked, even though I already knew.

He nodded. "Yeah. They confirmed. Interview's locked with the Department of State in D.C. More of a formality."

There it was.

My chest tightened, but my face didn't flinch.

Rayann Wilder: Professional Deflector. Emotional Acrobat. Clown Mask Extraordinaire.

"Congrats," I said with a smile that didn't make it past my teeth. "I hope they're ready for you."

He didn't answer at first. Then, quieter: "I haven't said yes yet."

But his voice didn't sound undecided. It sounded like someone already halfway out the door.

Tell him you want him to stay.

Tell him it's not just sex anymore, not for you—not since the beach, not since this morning, not since five minutes ago when he looked at you like he might already miss you.

Say something, Rayann.

My mouth opened.

Closed.

Max looked at me. Really looked. His brow pinched like he could hear the scream I was swallowing. His lips parted—

"Rayann—"

I blinked. "Summer confirmed my flight."

He leaned back slowly and nodded. "Tomorrow?"

"Yeah. She wants me back for... you know. Stuff."

I couldn't even think straight. Couldn't name the client. The project. Anything. Just sat there in his shirt, clutching that blanket like it could anchor me while the tide kept rising.

The silence dragged, thick and unfinished.

Max rubbed the back of his neck, then started to speak. "I was going to say—"

I turned away before he could finish. Like the topic bored me. Like my heart wasn't already pounding hard enough to bruise me from the inside out.

He didn't move. Just leaned back into the couch, head tilted toward the cushion, eyes closed like he could still feel me on his skin and didn't know what to do with that.

I didn't know what to do about it either.

God, just say it. Tell me you want me. Tell me to stay one more day.

Say something.

But he didn't. We didn't.

We didn't eat.

Didn't talk about the flight. The interview. What the hell we even were.

Just didn't talk.

When he kissed me again, it was careful. Too careful. Like he was afraid I'd break.

Like he already had.

Like we both had.

We didn't fall asleep touching.

When I woke hours later, my back to his chest, his hand so close but not touching me... he didn't reach.

And that?

That was the part that really hurt.

Max loaded both suitcases into the trunk without a word. Dawn was just breaking, the sky smeared with that soft, pale light that made everything feel too fragile to touch. He didn't have to leave today. Not really. But he'd bumped up his flight anyway. Said it made sense. Said he had things to do in D.C. before the meeting.

But I knew better.

He didn't want to stay in the cottage without me.

And I couldn't stay—even if part of me desperately wanted to.

I stood on the porch with my travel mug and the world's tightest smile.

He opened the passenger door. I slid in without meeting his eyes.

The ride to the airport was quiet. Not strained, just full of things we weren't brave enough to say out loud.

I wanted to reach for him, but if I did, I'd never let go.

My coffee had gone cold by the time we hit the main road.

I held it anyway. Like it was a lifeline.

He asked if I had my boarding pass. I said yes.

He offered me the aux cord. I shook my head.

Somewhere between the cottage and the airport, I stopped pretending this didn't hurt.

Don't cry, Rayann. Don't you fucking cry.

Just before we pulled into the lot, he cleared his throat.

"Rayann, I—"

I cut him off. Too fast.

"It's okay," I said, forcing a smile that felt like glass in my mouth. "Really."

He didn't look convinced. Just quiet. Still deciding whether to push.

Didn't speak.

"You're going to do important work at the embassy," I said. "More important than anything you do for us at Horizons. You should go. You should take it. I wouldn't want to be the reason you didn't."

He pulled into a space but didn't move.

"That's not what I was going to say."

"I know," I said. "But some things are better left unsaid."

Max stayed quiet.

"What we had here?" I said, smiling like it didn't hurt. "It was a perfect little bubble. But bubbles don't last."

That was the story I was sticking to. It was clean. Harmless. Almost fucking poetic.

He stared at the dash for a second, then got out and pulled my suitcase from the trunk with a kind of gentleness that made my throat close up.

"You're wrong, you know."

"About what?"

"All of it."

I didn't answer.

We walked inside together. Side by side, but not close enough to brush shoulders.

Not anymore.

The Inverness airport was small. Quiet. One of those regional hubs with slow TSA lines and gate agents too sleepy to care about your emotional baggage.

Of course we were on the same first flight.

Of course we weren't sitting together.

I dropped into my seat near the front like it might catch me.

Out of the corner of my eye, I watched Max head toward the back—where the airline had parked him beside a woman who clearly hadn't been emotionally gutted before breakfast. She smiled. Said something flirty. Tucked her hair behind her ear like she thought he might care.

Max didn't flirt back.

Didn't smile either.

Just nodded once, polite, eyes somewhere far away.

Still, jealousy curled hot and mean beneath my ribs.

When we landed in Glasgow for our connecting flights, I waited outside the gate.

No plan.

No speech.

Just a heart that didn't know how to stop needing him.

My thighs still ached from our days together. My skin still hummed with the memory of his touch.

My heart—

Get it the fuck together, Rayann. Let him go.

He caught up to me, almost surprised I'd waited.

"Ray..."

I almost touched him.

Almost reached for his hand.

Almost told him I didn't want this to be goodbye.

Instead, I smiled like it didn't hurt.

"I just wanted to wish you luck. That's all."

"Safe flight."

Then I turned and walked to my next gate.

And didn't look back.

Chapter 29

The Armor Still Fits

JET LAG AND HEARTBREAK mugged me at 30,000 feet. I stepped off the escalator at baggage claim still carrying the evidence.

Hair scraped into a half-assed bun. Oversized hoodie. Sunglasses that did nothing to hide the 24-hour insomnia stamped across my face. Coffee-stained leggings. No heels, no lipstick, no fucks left to give.

Not exactly the triumphant return Summer was probably hoping for.

Annie was waiting at the curb, sipping a Diet Dr Pepper like she hadn't been an emotional support menace since the moment she could walk. Baby of the family or not, she had a sixth sense for emotional carnage. And apparently, I was waving a flag.

"You look like you lost a fight with a mascara wand and a bottle of dry shampoo."

"Hello to you too," I muttered.

She gave me one slow, appraising blink. "Leggings? On a day flight?"

I shoved my suitcase into the back of her Jeep Wrangler and said nothing.

"Do you want to talk about it now, or should I cue up three hours of true crime until you do?"

"Jet lag," I said flatly.

"Oh, totally." She opened the passenger door with a suspicious amount of cheer. "You didn't just leave for Scotland looking like a bougie vacation goddess and come back like a rejected Peloton instructor because of jet lag."

Ouch.

I slid into the seat and yanked the hoodie tighter around me.

"Annie."

"Fine. No questions." She climbed in, popped the Jeep into drive. "But just so we're clear—" sip, casual flick of her sunglasses "—I'm texting Brynn before we hit the interstate."

I closed my eyes.

"I hate how fast your fingers are."

"You should've packed concealer. Rookie move."

By the time I stepped into the Maris Key office the next morning, I had become myself again.

Flawless hair. Fresh lipstick. Crisp linen pants that didn't dare wrinkle. The exact version of me Summer expected when she pulled me back early. The version I knew how to weaponize.

The lobby smelled like jasmine and ambition. Someone had refreshed the flower arrangements. Emme's voice drifted through the back hallway, sharp and charming, mid-call with a vendor. Our new intern, Daisy, smiled nervously when I passed her desk.

I smiled back.

Big. Bright. Bulletproof.

See? Not wrecked. Not ruined. Not undone. Just fine.

So fucking fine it should've been illegal.

Summer met me outside the conference room, tablet in hand, brows arched like they'd been judging people since dawn.

"Welcome back. You ready to charm the hell out of the Deveraux group?"

"Please. They won't know what hit them."

She gave me a once-over. Not just a glance. One of those managerial sweeps that always felt a little too clinical for a sister.

"You're sure you're good?"

Summer wasn't the sister I usually spiraled with. We didn't do heart-to-hearts. We did calendars. Contracts. Crisis management. Our relationship was built on high expectations and mutual efficiency. Not emotional autopsies.

So there it was.

A little too direct.

A little too knowing.

Did she know something?

God. Did Annie tell her?

Or worse, was it Brynn?

"Never better," I said with a smile polished enough to win an Academy Award.

Lie number one of the day.

I stepped into my office and shut the door like it might actually hold the rest of the world at bay.

It was small but beautiful. Like everything at Wilder, every detail had been curated within an inch of its life. Clean lines. Pale wood. A soft leather chair that hugged just right. The watercolor of the Amalfi Coast behind my desk came from a grateful client who once described me as "relentlessly effective with a charming streak of terror."

I dropped my bag, kicked off my heels, and stood barefoot in the center of the room. Just breathing. Just trying to remember how to feel like myself again.

A knock.

"Come in."

Daisy peeked in with wide eyes and a to-go tray. "Um, oat milk triple shot latte?"

I blinked. "Oh my God. You're an angel in platform sandals."

She beamed. "Welcome back."

"Thanks, Daisy," I said, already making a mental note to learn her coffee order and keep her forever.

When the door clicked shut, I sank into my chair and pulled out my phone like I hadn't been waiting to do it all morning.

Max's contact photo lit up the screen like it had something to say.

I stared at it for three long, ridiculous minutes.

Typed: *How did it go?*

Deleted.

Typed: *Are you back yet?*

Deleted.

Typed: *I miss you.*

Deleted so hard I nearly cracked the screen.

Instead, I sent Brynn a meme about spreadsheets and filed it under *normal behavior*.

I set the phone down like it weighed more than it should have.

That's when I saw it.

A sticky note, slightly crooked on my monitor, scribbled in my own handwriting from a lifetime ago.

Check in w/ Harrington re: Galapagos logistics.□

My chest cracked so fast it felt like I'd heard it happen.

Just a note. Just a line in my day. But it belonged to *before*.

Before the castle.

Before the cottage.

Before he looked at me like I was something worth staying for. And then didn't.

I stared at it like it might change. Like maybe it would rewrite itself to say something useful.

Check in with Harrington about what the hell we were.

But it didn't.

It just sat there, smug and yellow and stuck in time.

I peeled it off and folded it in half. Then again. Then again, until it was a tight little square of denial in the palm of my hand.

The intercom buzzed. Daisy's voice followed.

"Deveraux clients have arrived. I've escorted them to the conference room."

I didn't move.

Then I slid the note into the drawer, reapplied my lipstick like armor, and stood.

Time to play the part.

Chapter 30

Please Mistake Me for Fine

THE CLICK OF MY heels echoed louder than it should as I crossed the foyer to the conference room. Maybe it was just me. Maybe everything felt too loud. My thoughts. My pulse. The quiet absence of Max.

Snap out of it, Rayann.

This meeting wasn't going to charm itself.

I took one last breath, smoothed my blazer, and nudged the door open.

The Devereauxs were already seated: husband, wife, and a personal assistant who radiated the kind of calm efficiency that said she'd already solved three emergencies before breakfast. I respected that. I liked walking into a room and not needing to explain the basics.

"Good morning, I'm Rayann Wilder, Sales Director here at Wilder Horizons," I said, sliding into my chair with the kind of easy confidence you fake after getting gutted by a sticky note and a bitch slap of reality.

"Thank you for coming in. I hope you had no trouble finding the place?"

Mrs. Devereaux looked up, all understated elegance and thin-lipped expectations. "The valet was a bit slow."

"Apologies," I replied smoothly. "We'll be sure to address that. Let's make sure the rest of your visit is seamless."

Cue the gracious host routine.

I smiled. Polished. Practiced. The same one I'd worn on four continents and in more hotel lobbies than I could count.

But inside?

Oh, I was sparkling with exactly zero fucks to give.

I almost left Max in that cottage with a half-zipped duffel bag and something damn close to heartbreak in his eyes. If Summer hadn't called me back early, I wouldn't be here. And if I hadn't been the one leaving, Max wouldn't have said a damn word about his call from the embassy. He would've waited, gathered details, weighed options. Played it cool. But the second I said I had to catch a flight?

He shifted his plans to match mine. Quietly. Casually. Like it wasn't a big deal.

Like leaving me was just a logistical detail.

Now I was back in a conference room pretending to care about the Devereauxs' destination budget, when all I really wanted was to crawl back into that cottage bed and rewrite the ending.

So yeah. I'd smile. I'd sparkle. I'd sell the dream like it didn't cost me a damn thing.

But this pitch? It better be flawless.

Because I'm done performing for people who don't know what it costs to stay.

So go ahead, Mrs. Devereaux.

Test my patience today. I fucking dare you.

The meeting ended with a handshake, a signature, and the faint whiff of designer cologne clinging to the contract. Mrs. Devereaux didn't smile. She wasn't the type. But her assistant did—a subtle nod that said, *You passed the test*. And that was enough.

"Welcome to the Wilder Horizons family," I said, rising as Daisy swept in with gift bags like a perfectly timed encore.

The Devereauxs exited with all the warmth of a tax audit, but I didn't care. The deal was done. Another win on the board. Another reason for Summer to sleep easier tonight.

Speak of the devil.

Summer appeared in the doorway, her expression unreadable in that COO way she'd mastered. Polished. Composed. Impenetrable. But something flickered as she scanned my face. Maybe concern. Maybe suspicion. Expertly disguised behind her signature approval.

"Nice work," she said. "That was a tough sell. I know they asked for this last minute, and I appreciate you adjusting your schedule."

"No problem," I said. "Happy to make it happen."

She nodded once, then hesitated. "Everything okay?"

Just two words. Simple. Neutral. But Summer's version of an emotional check-in was rare enough to catch in my throat.

"Yeah," I lied. "Just tired."

She didn't push. She never did.

She gave a small nod, already pivoting toward her next task. "You're prepped for the Baxter presentation. Get some rest. You've earned it."

And just like that, she was gone.

I lasted thirty-two minutes and one cup of breakroom coffee before my office door swung shut and Brynn locked it behind her.

"Oh, good," I said, deadpan. "Because nothing says privacy like a twin interrogation in a fishbowl made of glass."

"Spare me," she said, flopping into the chair across from my desk. "You dodged my calls. You ghosted my texts. You flew home early and acted like a zombie bride on Benadryl, and now Max is mysteriously MIA."

She leaned in, expression flat. "What happened?"

I sighed and let my head fall back against the chair.

"I didn't mean to bail on you," I said. "I just... couldn't talk about it yet."

Brynn stayed quiet. She waited. Because she *knew*.

So I told her. Not everything, but enough. About the call. About the goodbye that wasn't really one. About Max shifting his flight just so we'd leave together, like it meant nothing. Like I wasn't already falling apart at the seams.

"And now?" she asked gently.

I shook my head. "I don't know. He said he was focused on the interview in D.C. At least that's what he called it. It sounded more like a formality. He didn't ask me to wait. Didn't make promises. Just... left."

"Jesus," she muttered. "Ray."

"Don't say anything to Summer," I said quickly. "Please. It's not my place to share his business. He reports to her, but as far as she knows, he's just taking a couple extra days for personal stuff."

"And you're okay with that?"

"No," I admitted. "But it's not about what I want. He needs space. And I'm trying to respect that, even if it's killing me."

Brynn reached across the desk and squeezed my hand.

She squeezed once, then said, "You're a better woman than me. I'd've driven to his apartment with a bat and a bottle of whiskey."

I smiled, small but real. "I'll keep that in my back pocket."

I was halfway through typing up notes from the Devereaux meeting when my phone buzzed with a text.

Max: *I'm back in town. Have dinner with me tonight?*

Just that. No preamble. No emojis. No *hope you're well* or *thinking of you.* Just cool, calm, completely Max.

And it wrecked me.

My fingers hovered over the screen, useless. I didn't know what to say. I didn't even know what I wanted. One part of me screamed yes; the other slammed on the brakes like I'd just spotted emotional carnage on the road ahead.

I set the phone face-down. Picked it up again.

Then flipped it again and muttered, "You have got to be fucking kidding me."

After six full minutes of internal ping-pong, I typed:

Me: *Sure.*

Yep. That was all I had in me. One-word brilliance. Pulitzer-worthy emotional insight.

Max: *How's 7:30 at Mar Azul?*

Fancy. Waterfront. Candlelight optional but highly likely. The kind of place with a wine list the size of a novella and waiters who say *infused foam reduction* without irony.

I sent it before I could overthink it.

That bought me about fifteen minutes. Then I had to get up and stretch my legs.

I was walking past Annie's office when Daisy's voice floated out from the breakroom.

"Yeah, I just saw him."

"Who?" someone asked.

"That security guy Rayann traveled with. Max Harrington. The *I'll protect billionaires and somehow make security escort sound like a fantasy trope* guy. He's here. And he's meeting with Juliette and Summer behind closed doors."

A collective pause. A soft gasp. The unmistakable squeak of a boba straw sliding through plastic in reverent awe.

Someone sighed like they'd just seen the face of Adonis.

"God, he's so unfairly hot," someone whispered.

"Like, weaponized. Does he even know?"

"Not a clue," Daisy said. "He just walks around radiating *thou shalt not touch*, and we're all over here trying to remember how to spell our own names."

Cue internal screaming.

My feet stopped. My brain, however, did not.

Max. Meeting. With *Juliette and Summer.*

Behind closed doors. Without *me.*

What the hell was going on?

I spun on my heel, power-walked back to my office, flung the door shut, and stared at my reflection in the dark monitor like it had answers. It did not.

What was this? An evaluation? A reassignment? Was he resigning? Was he telling them I was unfit for field assignments due to vibrator-related misconduct and excessive emotional damage in the presence of tactical hotness?

Oh my God.

Was he ratting me out for mixing business with orgasms?

I dropped into my chair and immediately regretted it when the impact knocked my monitor askew. I fixed it. Then fixed it again. Then realized I was still gripping the mouse like I was preparing to launch a nuke.

Breathe, Rayann.

You are a professional. Capable. Composed.

What if he's asking for a transfer?

What if he doesn't want to work with me anymore?

What if this is a "we need to maintain professionalism, and this has been fun, but…" kind of dinner?

I slammed the lid on my laptop like that could shut down the existential crisis crawling under my skin.

Max Harrington was in the building.

Meeting with the CEO and the COO.

Right before our first dinner since everything.

There was a non-zero chance this wasn't just dinner.

This was the last supper.

Chapter 31

Right on Time

MAX HARRINGTON WAS IN the building. Somewhere behind a closed door with Juliette and Summer, talking about God knows what, while I sat in my office pretending not to be one exhale away from spontaneous combustion.

Emails blurred. My coffee cooled. I reread the same line in a contract three times and still couldn't tell if I was finalizing a seven-figure itinerary or planning a summit in the Azores.

I glanced at the hallway.

Just a peek.

Nothing.

I looked again, casually, like I was absolutely not checking whether Max had stepped out of the meeting and was headed my way.

Still nothing.

He knew where my office was. He could walk in. Say hi. Flash that smile that made my ovaries file HR complaints. But he didn't.

Of course he didn't.

Because I was an idiot. A sweaty-palmed, emotionally un-well, dignity-on-clearance idiot.

I shoved back from my desk and stood up.

Daisy glanced up from her screen like she was about to ask if I needed anything, but I waved her off with a vague hand flick and a half-muttered, "Running errands. Back later. Or not. I don't know."

I didn't wait for her to respond.

I just needed air. And space. And possibly a ritual cleansing.

The parking garage was blessedly empty. My heels echoed off the concrete as I made a beeline for my Audi like it was a bomb shelter.

I climbed in, shut the door, and turned the A/C on full blast. It was 72 degrees outside, but I was sweating like someone had dared me to emotionally regulate and then filmed the aftermath.

I sat there.

Breathing.

Trying.

Failing.

What if he was quitting? What if he was meeting with my sisters to tell them this whole thing was a mistake? What if this dinner wasn't a dinner, it was a professionally-worded goodbye and a quick slide of a company NDA across the table?

My breath went shallow.

No. Nope. Not doing this.

I popped open the center console and found a half-crushed protein bar, an expired pack of gum, and a very stale biscotti from that client gift basket full of artisanal coffee and pretentious cookies. I held it like a relic.

"This is fine," I muttered, tearing it open with my teeth like a feral raccoon in lipstick.

It tasted like drywall and sand, but I kept chewing.

Pressure clamped down on my ribs.

I grabbed a paper bag from the passenger seat—the one from a client gift I never delivered because life imploded—and started breathing into it like I was about to pass out mid-hike through my own neuroses.

Inhale. Exhale. Mild whimper.

The paper crinkled with every breath. Somewhere, a valet was probably watching security footage and placing bets on my collapse.

I looked down. My hands were shaking.

"Rayann, you're such a chicken shit," I hissed at myself, voice muffled by the bag.

Just two days ago, we devoured each other like dinner, drinks, and dessert, and we licked the plate clean. We'd played naked champagne splash pad like it was an X-rated, resort-sponsored fantasy ad, and now I was hiding from an innocent dinner. In public. With witnesses.

Grow up.

I tossed the bag into the back seat and grabbed my phone to text Summer.

Leaving early. Need rest. Per your rec.

She'd told me to rest after the Devereaux meeting anyway. It wouldn't raise any flags.

But if Max walked by my office later and found it empty?

Good. Let him wonder how it felt. Let him hear what absence sounds like. Let him choke on the silence I've been swallowing all day.

I pulled out of the spot with more throttle than necessary.

My Audi purred like it didn't know I was using it as a getaway vehicle from a man who made me feel things I had no training to process.

Three hours before dinner

I was fine.

Totally fine.

Just a grown-ass woman in a very expensive condo, one uncharacteristically organized closet, and absolutely nothing to wear to what might be a relationship post-mortem with the man who dismantled every defense I didn't even know I had.

I threw another dress onto the bed.

Too sexy. He'd think I was trying too hard.

Grabbed a pencil skirt.

Too corporate. He'd think I was pitching a merger.

I held up a breezy linen jumpsuit.

Too... *I'm spiritually detached and thriving.*

I wasn't thriving. I was spiraling. And I didn't want to look detached—I wanted him to choke on how good I looked.

I needed a dog.

Or a cat. Something soft and judgment-free that would look into my eyes and whisper, "Yes, you are emotionally competent enough to attend dinner without losing your dignity in front of a charcuterie board."

I grabbed my phone instead.

Me: Are you home?

Brynn: Alive and lounging. You?

Me: Standing in a pile of rejected outfits. Having a full personality crisis.

Brynn: Oh good. Tuesday.

She called before I could answer.

"You sound like you're about to enter your 'I need a lobotomy or a large cheese plate' mode," she said.

"I'm trying to figure out what to wear."

"To dinner with Max?"

"No, to my emotional fucking execution. Of course it's Max."

Brynn didn't miss a beat. "Okay, hear me out. Understated sexy. Like, your dress says *I'm over it,* but your legs say *psych.*"

I blinked at the closet. "So slinky murder vibes with a smile?"

"Exactly."

Then my phone rang again.

Emme.

Jesus Christ.

I answered anyway.

"Hey, sis!" she chirped. "I heard Scotland was a wild success! Minus the whole castle fire thing."

"It was something," I managed.

"I meant to pop over today, but meetings. How was it, though? I haven't even had a proper debrief. Max was with you, right?"

My throat tried to close.

"Yep. Super fun. Tons of rain. Gotta go. My shoe just ate a toenail."

I hung up.

Two hours before dinner

I poured myself a glass of wine like it was a sedative and collapsed onto the couch.

One sip turned into three, and then I opened BuzzVid.

Just a few dumb videos to pass the time.

Two golden retrievers danced to Taylor Swift in a synchronized routine. Cute. Scroll.

A woman was reviewing airport carpet designs with the intensity of a crime scene analyst. Scroll.

A woman was breaking down the stock market using shrimp cocktail and a corkboard. Respect. Scroll.

And then I found her.

Linda.

The haunted doll restoration lady.

She had a buzz cut, talon nails, and a slow, hypnotic voice as she glued eyelashes onto a porcelain face that looked like it whispered threats in the dark. "

This one's name is Mabel," Linda cooed. *"Mabel was burned in a storage unit fire but told me she still wants to love again."*

Same, Mabel. Same.

Forty-five minutes vanished in a puff of glue fumes and emotional avoidance.

Then I glanced at the time.

6:45

"Oh. Fuck. Me."

One hour before dinner

I launched off the couch like I'd been shot from a cannon, bolted to the shower, and came out dripping, swearing, and knocking over a shampoo bottle that moaned like Max on a good day.

Three outfit changes. Three different hairstyles. Zero clarity.

By outfit five, I just stood there, staring into the mirror like she might have an answer.

I finally landed on a soft pink slip dress. Feminine, curve-hugging, not too revealing. Strappy wedge heels. Hair down and curled like I'm pretending it'll last more than five minutes in Florida humidity.

In Scotland, I wore flannel. Sometimes, I was literally naked under Max's shirts. And he still looked at me like I was the sexiest woman in the castle.

And now? I was five bobby pins from cardiac arrest because I couldn't decide between low-cut and low-risk.

"This is stupid," I told my reflection. "You're stupid."

She didn't argue.

Thirty minutes before dinner

I slid into the godblessed luxury of my Audi, freshly dressed and flushed with wine and setting spray. The restaurant was only ten minutes away, but I left early on purpose. I needed a drink. I needed air. I needed to pull myself together somewhere other than my own damn bathroom.

The hostess barely looked up when I walked in.

"Just me," I said. "I'll be meeting someone. I'll wait at the bar."

The martini menu was its own kind of therapy.

The Dirty Dirty: vodka, extra olive brine, three blue-cheese stuffed olives, □

served with the emotional satisfaction of flipping someone off in slow motion.

Sold.

I slipped onto a stool at the end of the bar, one ankle tucked behind the other, my strappy wedge dangling like I hadn't had a full mental breakdown an hour ago.

And then:

Max.

At the far end of the bar.

Rolled sleeves. Jacket off. Elbows on the counter like he'd been there for a while. His drink already half-finished. He looked calm. Collected. Annoyingly sexy.

I blinked.

He spotted me. Eyes caught mine across the row of barstools. No smile. Just a quiet pause, like he was reading the weather before stepping into a storm.

Then he stood and walked over. No rush. No theatrics. Just Max, closing the space like it belonged to him.

He slid into the seat beside me.

"You're early," I said.

"So are you."

I arched a brow. "Had to make sure the martini wasn't poisonous."

He nodded toward mine. "I'll let you know in ten minutes."

And then, God help me, we both laughed.

Real laughs.

Easy, light, un-fucked-up laughter.

The kind that didn't need to be dissected or defined.

Just like that, for one minute, we weren't spiraling.

We were just Rayann and Max.

And somehow, we were right on time.

Chapter 32

The Reverse Uno Card

THE WAITER HAD BARELY poured my wine when Max hit me with it.

"I took the job."

No warm-up. No starter flirt. Just that. Rich baritone, casual confidence, like he was ordering a second round instead of detonating my frontal lobe.

I blinked. "Rome?"

He nodded once. "Four-year tour. Head of Security at the embassy. I head to D.C. in two weeks. Rome a month after."

My hand did not tremble as I lifted my wine glass, thank you very much. Internally, my soul hit a full-screen buffering error.

"That's…" I took a sip and prayed my voice wouldn't betray the scream I swallowed. "Big."

Max studied me over his glass like he already knew what was unraveling inside my head.

You wanna join my private meltdown... or just stare while I combust?

Pause.

"I want you to come with me," he said.

Calm. Casual. Like he hadn't just invited me to pack up my entire life and move across the Atlantic. Like he hadn't once licked champagne off my belly button and made me forget my own name.

I froze with my glass mid-air. "You want me to...?"

"Come with me," he repeated. "To Rome."

My brain snapped into a full slide show titled: *Top Ten Reasons Why This Is Definitely a Trap.*

- I have a life here.

- I don't even speak Italian.

- I get lost in IKEA.

- What if this is just sex brain pretending to be love?

"You don't have to decide right now," he said.

Adorable. As if I hadn't already blacked out and started free-falling through a void made of pasta, panic, and his stupidly perfect jawline.

I cleared my throat. "That's a long time."

"It is."

"That's...a lot."

"It is."

I set my glass down. It had officially become a weapon. "Max, I—"

He leaned in. Not rushed. Not pushy. Just Max. Steady. Focused. Eyes locked on mine like I was the only thing in the room that mattered.

"I'll give you a week to freak out about it," he said. "Then I'm coming back for you."

Breathing? Not happening.

Max didn't raise his voice. Didn't smirk. Didn't flirt. He just laid it down like a blueprint, like he'd already built the house and I was the only one who hadn't walked through the front damn door.

"You're not a backup plan, Rayann," he said. "You *are* the plan. So take the week. Spiral. Shout. Make a pro-con list and light it on fire. I don't care. But don't pretend you don't feel it too."

My heartbeat pounded like a rave inside a jewelry box.

"And if I say no?" I asked, because apparently I'm contractually obligated to self-sabotage during emotionally significant moments.

He didn't flinch. "You won't."

Oh.

No.

My stomach dropped. My thighs clenched. My frontal lobe opened a chat support ticket.

This man just Reverse Uno Carded my entire emotional wiring. And I'd never been more turned on in my life.

I excused myself like a polite, composed human woman.

"I'm just going to the ladies room."

It came out one octave too high and ten degrees too fast.

Max nodded, cool as sin. Like he hadn't just verbally undressed me at the dinner table and set my life on fire using nothing but eye contact and a casually delivered *You're mine.*

I made a beeline for the bathroom like it had air-conditioning, life advice, and a priest with a vodka tonic.

Inside, I locked the stall door. Not for privacy—just symbolism. Then I stared at the coat hook like it had the answers.

"He said he's coming back for me," I whispered.

Louder: "He said he's coming back for me."

One more time: "He said—"

I had to sit down. Not on the toilet—please. I still had my dignity. But the closed lid worked fine as a panic perch.

My reflection in the paper towel dispenser was no help.

Flushed. Wide-eyed. Like someone who'd just been told *You're the plan* by a man with no business being that hot *and* that sincere at the same time.

"You cannot ugly cry in a Michelin-star restaurant," I muttered, digging through my purse for lip gloss, breath spray, and whatever emotional stability might be wedged behind my travel-sized dry shampoo.

One deep breath.

One tissue dab.

One last mental slap.

And then I walked out of the bathroom like I hadn't just practiced rejecting him in three different languages.

He stood when I returned.

Of course he did. Polite. Gentlemanly. Probably trained in some secret SEAL protocol for destroying emotional defenses and pulling out chairs at the same time.

"Everything okay?" he asked as I sat.

"Oh, totally," I said, unfolding my napkin like it owed me money. "I just had to go hyperventilate into a very expensive hand towel."

He didn't blink. Just grinned, the corner of his mouth twitching like he enjoyed watching my slow implosion in real time.

"So..." I stabbed my fork into my risotto. "Four years in Rome."

"Technically three years and ten months now."

"Oh, good. That makes it way less terrifying."

His smile widened. He didn't say a word.

Because he *knew*.

And I *knew* he knew.

So I chewed, stared at my wine, and tried very hard not to fall in love with a man who already had a plan with my name in it.

I got through four bites of risotto before the panic came back.

Perfectly cooked. Creamy. Earthy. Topped with something that looked suspiciously like gold leaf and existential seasoning. I chewed, nodded, pretended this was a normal dinner and not a soul-crushing audition for the rest of my life.

Max didn't press. Just ate. Calm. Methodical. Like a man without a single worry.

Which, naturally, made me even more unhinged.

"So…" I said, because silence was dangerous and I was one spiral away from crawling under the table. "You'll be doing what, exactly?"

"Security. Embassy operations. Protocol enforcement. A lot of logistics."

"Sounds thrilling."

He smiled into his wine glass. "It will be."

I took another sip. A big one.

He didn't fill the silence. Didn't push. Just waited. Watched.

Max fucking Harrington. Head of Quiet Confidence. Destroyer of Denial. Sitting across from me like a patient predator in a tailored shirt.

"Do you always do that?" I asked.

He looked up. "Do what?"

"That thing. The waiting thing. Like you're giving me space while secretly betting against me."

His fork stilled. "Rayann, I'm not betting against you."

Oh no.

Here it comes.

He set down his silverware and leaned in. Elbows braced. Voice low. Unshakably calm.

"I'm betting *on* you."

Boom.

That was it. That was the line. The slow-motion emotional sniper shot that landed between my perfectly mascara'd lashes and made me forget how forks worked.

I dropped my gaze to my plate. Swirled my wine. Focused on breathing like I wasn't seconds away from jumping into his lap and proposing in Latin.

But I didn't say yes.

I didn't say no, either.

Because I was Rayann Wilder. The reason seven-figure clients sleep at night. Chaos queen. Full-time snark goblin with commitment issues and a Prime subscription for emotional avoidance.

I just picked up my fork again and said, "This risotto's pretty good."

Max nodded once.

"It is."

No pressure. No ultimatum. Just heat. Presence. Certainty.

He already knew.

And he'd wait.

We didn't talk about Rome again.

Not during the rest of the risotto. Not during the silky chocolate mousse that arrived like a truce offering between two people emotionally unraveling beneath dimmed lights and $30 cocktails.

I wanted to bring it up. I could feel the words stuck between my third bite and my fourth glass of wine, but they wouldn't come. Because if I said anything—anything at all—it wouldn't come out wrong.

It would come out *true*.

So instead, I laughed at his joke about the waiter's mustache. Licked mousse off my spoon like it wasn't a full-body religious experience. Watched his hands, his lips, the way he sipped his drink without breaking eye contact.

And Max?

Max just *waited.*

Not in the way that says *please like me.* In the way that says *you will.* Calm. Certain. Goddamn lethal in his patience.

By the time we finished dessert, I was in full-blown emotional denial—whipped cream on the side and zero grip on reality.

He paid. Of course he did. With one of those black cards that probably opened doors to secret airports and presidential wine cellars. I didn't even argue.

Outside, the air was warm and still—the kind of night that begged for clarity I absolutely didn't have.

He took my keys without asking, steering me toward his Land Cruiser. "I'll take you home." Max opened the passenger door, and I slid in like a woman who had not, moments ago, imagined crawling into his lap and whispering *take me to Rome, you emotionally terrifying masterpiece."*

He didn't play music.

He didn't talk.

Just drove. Steady hands. Steady heart. The kind of man who didn't chase. He let you come undone, then met you there without judgment.

When we reached my condo, he walked me to the door. I fumbled with my keys like a woman being haunted by her own ovaries.

At the door, I turned. Ready to say *thank you for dinner* or *have a good night* or *please ruin me gently for four years and maybe forever.*

But then he brushed his hand down my arm. Just fingertips. Just a touch.

And I leaned in.

No thinking. No planning.

I kissed him.

Slow. Soft. Full of things I couldn't say yet and wasn't ready to admit.

He kissed me back like he had all the time in the world. No urgency. No pressure. Just warmth. Heat. A promise baked into every slow drag of his mouth on mine.

When we pulled apart, I was dizzy.

"Good night," I whispered.

He didn't move. Just looked at me like he already knew how this ended.

"One week," he said.

Then he turned, walked to his Land Cruiser, and left me standing there—mid-cuddlefuck with my own decision fatigue.

I didn't go inside right away.

I just stood there, keys in hand, heart in throat, wondering how the hell I was supposed to sleep knowing that the one man who saw through all my bullshit wasn't going to wait forever.

But for now?

He was giving me time.

Just one week.

Before he came back for me.

Chapter 33

I Might Be in Love...
Or I Just Need
Electrolytes

I DIDN'T EVEN TAKE off my heels.

Just kicked the door shut, dumped my purse on the floor, and stumbled directly to the couch like it owed me therapy and a Xanax. The martini and four glasses of wine tap danced through my bloodstream, which obviously meant it was the perfect time to call Brynn.

I flopped back against a throw pillow and stabbed at my phone screen with the urgency of a woman ready to emotionally self-destruct. Then I hit video call.

She answered on the third ring with her hair in a bun, sheet mask on, wine in hand, and popcorn straight from the bag.

"You're calling me with heels on, makeup still flawless, and a look in your eye that says you either just got proposed to or ran someone over with your car," she said. "What the hell happened?"

I blinked. "He kissed me."

Brynn froze mid-chew. "Max?"

"No, Brynn. The valet. *Yes, Max.*"

She peeled her face mask off with one dramatic swipe and tossed it over her shoulder like a cape. "Oh my god. Did you faint? Did you combust? Did he lift you onto a grand piano and whisper operatic promises into your bra strap?"

"Worse."

She leaned in. "Worse than piano sex?"

I nodded, dead serious. "He told me... *I'm* the plan."

There. I said it. And now it was real, hanging in the air between us like a confetti cannon of commitment.

Brynn made a noise that was part gasp, part wheeze. "Like... *the* plan?"

I threw my arm across my eyes like I was starring in a 1950s drama about fainting disorders. "The plan. As in, no backup, no alternate ending, no casual maybe-we'll-see. Just—*you're it.*"

"Holy shit," she whispered. "He reverse Uno Carded your ass right into your own feelings."

"I *hate* how accurate that is."

She grinned like the smug gremlin she was. "And let me guess. You told him you care, expressed your fears calmly and vulnerably, then made a totally rational decision about your future?"

"I said the risotto was good."

Brynn nearly choked. "You WHAT?"

"I panicked!" I said, pacing now, heels clicking like a stress metronome. "He kissed me at the door and said I had one week, then walked away like a goddamn romance novel come to life. I've been standing here ever since, debating whether to text him 'I'd move to Rome for your face' or just eat a sleeve of Oreos and cry into my throw blanket."

"You're so in love, it's physically offensive."

"I'm not in love," I snapped. "I'm in a state. There's wine. There are hormones. I probably still have mousse on my teeth. And this man? This completely unreasonable man with his tailored shirt and quiet confidence and his fucking blueprint for our entire future? He just left like I'm supposed to sleep after that."

Brynn took a sip of her wine, calm as ever. "So. Just to recap. He told you you're the plan. Kissed you like a man with GPS for your soul. Gave you time. And you're mad because... what? He didn't wrestle you onto the welcome mat and make you scream *Ti amo*?"

I narrowed my eyes. "I don't need lip from a woman who once said almond milk was a lifestyle."

She laughed. "You need to breathe. Maybe sleep. Definitely don't text him tonight."

I stared at my phone.

"Rayann."

"What if I just send a sexy, emotionally vulnerable meme? Something like... 'I miss you even when I'm not horny.'"

"I swear to God, Rayann, if you send Max a cartoon e-card full of emotional nudity, I will drive over there and physically remove your phone."

"Or that one that says, 'I wish I could copy and paste you into my bed.' It's romantic. It's tech-savvy. It's got layers."

"It's got *desperation*."

"Oh, oh, wait! What about the one with the girl holding up a meme sign instead of confessing her feelings? That one feels *deep*."

"You are *unwell*."

I sank to the floor, like emotional gravity finally hit. "I don't know what to do, Brynn."

She softened. "I know. You don't have to figure it out tonight. Just let it be real for a second."

I pressed my cheek into the couch cushion. "What if I say yes and ruin it?"

"And what if you don't say yes and miss the best damn thing that's ever happened to you?"

My eyes stung. "I hate how smart you are when I'm drunk."

"You'll figure it out," she said softly. "One week isn't a deadline. It's a lifeline. You just have to decide if you're brave enough to take it."

I stayed quiet.

I closed my eyes, heels still on, and let myself picture it.

Rome.

Max.

Us.

And for the first time, I didn't want to run.

Holy hell, I was possessed.

I woke up sideways on the couch.

One heel still on. One eye glued shut with last night's mascara. My dress bunched under one hip, and I clutched an empty wine glass like it was emotional support. My phone buzzed under my thigh.

I groaned.

Correction. I whimpered like a Victorian orphan denied soup and tried to sit up.

Everything hurt.

My head. My back. My dignity.

Also, I was ninety percent sure I'd sweated through my nicest lacy bra while dreaming about Max whispering "You're the plan" straight into my uterus.

Because nothing screams emotionally stable adult like heat rash and nipple chafing.

"Kill me," I muttered to the empty room, dragging myself upright. My phone slipped off the couch cushion and thunked to the floor with a sound that could only be described as regretful.

I didn't reach for it yet.

First, I needed water. And coffee. And probably legal representation.

I staggered into the kitchen, pulled my hair into a lopsided bun that screamed emotional damage with a side of dehydration, and tried to remember how many drinks I'd had last night.

Martini.

Wine.

More wine.

Then Brynn.

Then maybe tequila?

Did I text Max?

Oh God.

DID I SEXT MAX?

I spun back toward the couch like it owed me answers. Snatched up my phone and opened my messages with the kind of panic reserved for checking a pregnancy test in a Taco Bell parking lot.

Nothing.

No texts sent. No embarrassing gifs. No eggplant emojis with Italian flags.

Thank Christ.

I exhaled, walked into the bathroom, and caught sight of myself in the mirror.

Mascara like war paint. Lipstick smudged halfway to my ear. One blue cheese-stuffed olive stuck to my collarbone like it was trying to flee the scene of the crime.

"Classy," I muttered, dabbing at the damage with a towel that smelled vaguely like anxiety and setting spray.

I made it halfway through brushing my teeth before the dread hit.

Max.

One week.

He said it like a promise. A dare. Like he'd already built the life and was just waiting for me to decide if I was brave enough to show up.

And what if I said yes, only to make him regret choosing me?
My chest clenched.

I leaned against the sink and stared at my reflection like she might have answers.

"What if I'm not enough?" I whispered.

My reflection, unhelpful bitch that she was, said nothing.

Back in the kitchen, I poured coffee with shaking hands and finally checked my phone again. I hadn't missed any texts.

Wait.

One new one.

From Max.

Sent at 7:14 a.m.

I froze.

My thumb hovered over the message like opening it might explode my entire nervous system.

Then I read it.

Morning. Hope the risotto was worth the spiral. Let me know when you're ready to talk. I'll be here.

I sank to the floor.

Not in a cute, graceful way. In a full-body collapse where my ass hit the tile and I just stared at the screen like it was trying to resurrect my soul through gentle male competence.

He wasn't pushing. He wasn't baiting me.

He was just steady.

And he was still here.

Giving me time.

One week.

I pressed the phone to my chest and let myself breathe for the first time since I kissed him.

And for a second, I let myself believe I might actually be brave enough to say yes.

The answer was easy. The fear was whether he'd still want it once the shine wore off.

Chapter 34

All In

9:oo A.M.

Opened my inbox.

Closed it immediately.

Reopened it like a masochist.

Started crying over an Amazon order confirmation for olive oil—because Max likes olive oil.

Because I like Max.

Considered therapy.

Took a mint. Choked on it. Honestly? Fair.

10:00 A.M.

Attended the weekly check-in with Summer and the rest of my sisters—except Juliette, who had already jetted off on her luxe safari trip. She was probably sipping champagne beside a giraffe while I sat here crying like a baby warthog who imprinted on a house cat.

Said the word "Rome" out loud and immediately pretended to cough for seventeen full seconds just to drown out the sound of my own heartbreak.

Summer looked concerned. Annie offered me a lozenge. I said no, then opened my slide deck and realized I had accidentally renamed our Q2 strategy file *MaxPlsJustLoveMe.xlsx*. The Wi-Fi went out before I could delete it. I consider this divine intervention.

I stared at it in silence. Annie slowly slid the lozenge toward me again like it was a tranquilizer.

Summer didn't say a word.

She just turned her head, locked eyes with me across the table, and tilted one perfectly arched eyebrow like she was calculating how many minutes of my meltdown she could legally ignore before calling in a wellness check.

"Rayann," she said finally, her voice sharp enough to cut granite, "is there something you'd like to share with the team?"

"No," I said, clutching my water bottle like it was filled with emotional support vodka. "Just... really passionate about quarterly data."

Summer blinked slowly. The kind of blink that said *you're lucky I love you and also I will murder you after this meeting.*

11:00 A.M.

Attempted to focus by creating a detailed itinerary for the Deveraux package.

Typed "Max" instead of "Malta" three separate times, then gave up entirely and labeled it *Hot Man Island* in the shared drive.

Cried.

Briefly Googled *"can heartache cause dehydration."*

Switched to decaf in a wild act of self-sabotage. Immediately regretted it—and started shaking anyway, which felt like a personal attack from the universe.

Renamed a folder *Emotional Collapse: The Trilogy.*

Drafted a text that said, *"I like your face. That's all. Okay bye."*

Added a heart emoji. Then a fire emoji. Then deleted the heart. Put it back.

Hovered over Send.

Deleted the entire thing.

Threw my phone across the desk like it was haunted and buried my face in my hands so dramatically Annie asked if I was praying.

I told her yes.

Technically, not a lie.

12:00 P.M.

Not "a little flustered." Not "mildly distracted by sexy man thoughts."

I was in full-blown, espresso-fueled, emotionally Scotch-taped, *feral* heart-splintering chaos. I'd opened and closed Max's text so many times my phone was showing signs of trauma.

I'd reapplied lip gloss three times, even though I hadn't spoken to another human since the morning meeting.

And I was sweating through my underwear like I was being questioned by the CIA.

The sticky note was still there.

Smug. Yellow. Centered just off-kilter like it was trying to gaslight me.

Check in w/ Harrington re: Galapagos logistics.□

God, I hated it.

And yet somehow, I couldn't stop staring at it. My emotional support Post-it.

I leaned in, elbows on my desk, voice barely above a whisper.

"You're the plan," I murmured to it. "You absolute bastard."

"...Should I come back?"

I jumped like I'd been caught sexting a printer.

Daisy stood in the doorway, holding a stack of vendor contracts and looking like she'd just caught me whispering sweet nothings to office supplies.

"You're not... talking to your sticky notes again, are you?"

"No," I said, way too fast.

We both looked at the Post-it.

Then at each other.

"Okay," she said slowly, setting the papers down. "Do you want tea? Chocolate? Therapy?"

"Do you have therapy?"

"No, but I could probably Google a hotline."

"I'll take a Twix."

By late afternoon, I'd survived a Zoom call, two passive-aggressive Slack threads, and one very entertaining story about Annie's date who tried to pay for dinner with airline miles.

Which is why, by the time I made it home, I wasn't just tired—I was emotionally jet-lagged from a full day of pretending I was fine.

When in reality, I'd spent the morning crying over a man who texted like a responsible adult and made risotto look like foreplay.

I dropped my bag, kicked off my heels, and stared at the ceiling like it might beam divine wisdom directly into my eyeballs.

It did not.

It did, however, make me realize I didn't want to go to sleep with his message still sitting there. Quiet. Steady. Waiting for me to decide what the hell to do with it.

So I picked up my phone and did what any mature, emotionally stable woman would do:

I called him.

Max answered on the third ring—unfairly composed and sounding suspiciously like a man folding a T-shirt with military precision.

"Wilder," he said, his voice low and solid. "Wasn't expecting you."

"Well, I wasn't expecting to wake up with a stuffed olive on my collarbone and a new fear of commitment. So we're both having a week."

He chuckled. "You okay?"

"No," I said, sinking into the couch. "But I might be getting there."

A pause. The kind where everything unsaid buzzed between us.

"What are you doing right now?" I asked.

"Packing," he said. "Just put the house on the market. Trying not to overthink it."

"Oh." I picked at a thread on my throw pillow. "Are you, um... packing alone? Or are you one of those psychos who hires a team and labels things like *entryway drawer chaos* and *cords from 2008*?"

"I'm not a monster," he deadpanned. "And yes. Alone. Unless you count a playlist that keeps suggesting '80s breakup songs, which I do not appreciate."

I smiled.

And then I said it.

"Come over."

He went quiet.

Then: "Now?"

"I mean, not unless you're currently in hand-to-hand combat with a junk drawer full of batteries, bungee cords, and miscellaneous dude stuff. But... yeah. Now."

Another beat of silence. Then I heard the unmistakable clink of something being set down—keys, maybe. Or his resolve.

"I'll be there in fifteen," he said.

And true to form, he was.

No dramatic entrance.

No violin swell.

No cinematic pan or sweeping strings to catch the moment I lost all grip on composure.

Just one knock. And then Max—walking in like he'd done it a hundred times before.

And then he *looked* at me.

Not like I'd ghosted his text.

Not like I'd whispered "you're the plan" to a Post-it note before lunch.

Not even like I'd spent the past two days trying to prove to myself it was just a fantasy, only to realize I'd built my entire mental resistance on the crumbling foundation of *total bullshit*.

Nope.

He just looked at me like I was still it—like he'd just been waiting for me to catch up.

It was unsettling.

It was grounding.

And it was very hard to maintain eye contact while holding a half-eaten block of cheese like it was a coping mechanism.

Which I was.

So I cleared my throat and said the first thing that came to mind.

"Hi. Um. I didn't have time to cook anything, so I stress-bought three kinds of fancy crackers and ate half a block of sharp cheddar straight from the wrapper. If you're hungry, I have... guilt hummus?"

Max didn't laugh. Not at first.

He just took one slow step toward me, his gaze never leaving mine.

And then another.

Until he was close enough that I could smell him—clean soap, warm skin, and the faintest trace of laundry detergent that somehow made me want to cry.

"I didn't come here for snacks, Rayann," he said quietly.

Cue full internal system crash.

"Right," I managed. "Of course not. That would be... absurd. Ha. Obviously."

His brow lifted slightly, amused. "You okay?"

"No," I said, my voice barely above a whisper. "But I might be getting there."

He didn't move.

He just waited.

So I gave him what he came for.

"I don't need the week," I said. "I don't need more time—I just needed to believe you meant it."

A pause. A heartbeat. The kind that said everything.

Then: "I meant it."

"I'm a mess, Max."

"I know."

"I don't organize my socks. I buy groceries based on cravings and coupon placement. Sometimes I talk to myself in the shampoo aisle."

His voice dropped, warm and wrecked and just a little teasing. "Rayann—"

"And I might panic again. Or cry. Or try to run. But if you want me—"

He didn't let me finish.

Because suddenly he was on me.

Hands in my hair. Mouth on mine. Body pressed against me with zero hesitation and absolutely no room for interpretation.

He kissed me like he was *done waiting.*

Like there was no maybe, no pause, no holding back.

Like he knew exactly what he wanted—and it was *me.*

"There's no *if* about me wanting you," he growled against my lips—low, rough—before dragging his mouth back down like he'd been starving for this. For me.

I whimpered. Actually whimpered.

Which only made him curse softly and kiss me harder.

His tongue swept into my mouth with slow, devastating precision, one hand sliding around my waist, the other gripping the back of my neck as if to say, *I'm right here. And I'm not letting go.*

And just when he started to pull back. Just when he thought he was done...

I snapped.

I grabbed the front of his shirt, yanked him back down, and kissed him like he'd *pissed me off* by stopping.

Because he had.

I bit his bottom lip—not enough to hurt, just enough to make him groan into my mouth and grip my hips like he was bracing for impact.

"Don't you dare give me the soft version," I whispered, breathless and wild. "You lit the match, Harrington. Burn with me."

He didn't need to be told twice.

We collided again, harder this time, mouths crashing together like we'd both been starving and stupid for days. It wasn't graceful. It wasn't careful. It was teeth and hands and breathless, clumsy desperation.

I clawed at his back like I could memorize him with my fingertips.

He pressed me against the wall like he wanted to leave an imprint.

We were a goddamn natural disaster—and I'd never felt more alive.

When we finally slowed, chests heaving, bodies still pressed tight, I rested my forehead against his and whispered—

"Now *that* was a welcome back."

Max smiled—wrecked and reverent.

"You have no idea," he murmured.

He exhaled like he'd been holding that breath since the night I walked away.

Then he reached up, brushed a strand of hair from my face, and said—

"Let's build the damn plan, love. I'm all in."

Chapter 35

Epilogue: Benvenuto a Roma

SIX MONTHS LATER — **Rome, Italy**

Living in Rome *seems* glamorous on paper.

Until you have to explain to your Italian neighbor that your internet bill is overdue because you Venmo'd your esthetician instead of the utility company.

Twice.

"I'm adjusting," I said brightly, fanning myself with a crumpled trattoria receipt while Max handles the damage control paperwork for the fifth time this month.

To be fair, Max knew exactly what he was getting into.

Especially once I started running Wilder Horizons' first international office out of a shared co-working space that smelled like burnt espresso and Amalfi lemon oil diffusers trying too hard to justify the rent.

The Rome expansion had been Summer's idea.

Or Juliette's.

Or Emme's, technically.

But the second I touched down and opened my laptop from our little apartment with antique tile, a terrace that groans when you lean on it, and more charm than structural integrity, it became mine.

I was the woman in charge of Europe now.

Which mostly meant I logged into video calls at ungodly hours, sold rich people on "authentic Mediterranean experiences," and yelled *questa è una situazione di capra!* during tech meltdowns because I'd learned how to say "this is a goat situation" in Italian and immediately weaponized it.

Max was *thrilled*.

Especially when I started learning all the *wrong* Italian words.

We tried Duolingo.

We tried flashcards.

Then Max made the mistake of buying me a slang-heavy phrasebook from a market stall where I immediately fell in love with the phrase *scopami come se fossi l'ultima mozzarella sulla Terra.*

He asked what it meant.

I told him: "Make love to me like I'm the last mozzarella on Earth."

He choked on his espresso.

Two minutes later, I was pinned to the kitchen counter while the moka pot hissed on the stove like it was judging us.

We didn't *actually* do it with the gas on. We're not savages. We're just... emotionally fluent in cheese metaphors now.

Honestly? It works for us.

Some couples go wine tasting. We go vocab testing—with *incentives.*

I get a kiss for every verb I conjugate correctly.

A full-body kiss if I use it in a flirty sentence.

If I manage an entire conversation without calling someone's dog a sandwich? I get to be on top.

Max had just returned from a weeklong assignment down in Naples—still sexy, still steady, still built like the architectural love child of a gladiator and the Roman goddess Venus—when he walked in and found me shouting *testicoli!* into my phone.

"Do I want to know?" he asked, setting down his briefcase like a man used to emotional turbulence.

"It's for work," I lied.

It was not for work.

It was for Carla, our new neighbor. A forty-five-year-old firecracker in three-inch heels and a Versace knockoff who had a little Pomeranian named Vito and absolutely zero regard for noise ordinances.

We'd met when I accidentally knocked over her herb planter with a rogue baguette and apologized in such horrifyingly broken Italian that she decided I was a national treasure and should be included in all future gossip.

Including, but not limited to:

- Her suspicion that the guy in 3B was secretly a German pop star

- Her declaration that Max had "shoulders like a Roman god and the aura of a man who needs lasagna"

- And her insistence that I start learning *real* Italian, not "bedroom dictionary trash."

"Signorina Wilder," she'd scolded, while handing me a tray of pistachio biscotti. "If you're going to yell about mozzarella during sex, you should at least be able to order proper cheese at the market."

Fair.

So now we meet every Wednesday in the courtyard for Espresso and Embarrassment, where she quizzes me on phrases, corrects my accent, and occasionally asks if Max has any single brothers with similarly "robust forearms."

"Do you know what *stuzzicadenti* means?" Carla asked, cocking one expertly arched brow over the rim of her espresso.

"Yes," I lied.

She narrowed her eyes like she could smell my bullshit through my bronzer. "Then why did you just tell the cheese guy at the market your boyfriend has a toothpick?"

Max, who had shown up halfway through my panic-ordering, smiled like the smug bastard he is. "Maybe I should come with you next time. Help out with translation."

"Absolutely not," I snapped. "Last time you went, you almost got us adopted by the butcher."

"That's because I said we were newlyweds," he said, tucking a strand of hair behind my ear with maddening precision. "In my defense, it felt accurate."

Carla snorted. "You two are like a telenovela I never want to turn off."

She took another sip of espresso, then stood. "Alright, amore. I'll let you get back to whatever sweaty, pasta-fueled sin you're planning next."

"Thank you for your blessing," I deadpanned.

She blew a kiss and disappeared into her apartment with a rustle of chiffon and threat-level-high perfume. Vito the Pomeranian barked once in approval.

Max found the whole thing wildly entertaining. Especially when I told him last week's vocab word was *cannone.*

"Means cannon," I said proudly.

He raised an eyebrow. "And how exactly did that come up in conversation?"

"Let's just say Carla is a nosy legend and may or may not have asked if you had any... tools of proportion."

I told her, "'It's what happens when God gives one man too much and expects the rest of us to keep our composure.'"

Now he can't walk past her balcony without her giving him a thumbs-up and shouting *complimenti!*"

Which I've been told means "congratulations," but Max insists it's code for "Your girlfriend is very lucky and I think you could bench press a Vespa."

She's not wrong.

I was still smiling when it hit me—

the way he was looking at me.

Max, my terrifyingly composed, maddeningly beautiful, infuriatingly steady man, was suddenly looking at me like I was the only thing in Rome worth seeing.

"You okay?" he asked softly.

"Yeah," I whispered. "I really am."

That made him smile.

He stepped in close, pressed a kiss to the corner of my mouth. "I've been thinking," he murmured.

"Uh-oh."

"Don't worry. No PowerPoint this time."

I froze. "Wait. Last time you said that, you kissed me like the world was ending and then told me I was 'the plan.' So what exactly are we topping that with today?"

He didn't answer. Not with words.

Instead, he pulled something from his back pocket—a small black box. No theatrics. No down-on-one-knee. Just Max. Standing there. Steady. Certain. Eyes locked on mine like this wasn't a question, but an anchor.

"You're still the plan," he said, voice low and wrecked. "You've been it since the second I stopped pretending you weren't."

Then he opened the box.

Inside was the most beautiful, completely impractical ring I'd ever seen. Like someone had turned passion and chaos and the color of my favorite lipstick into jewelry.

"Rayann Wilder," he said. "Say yes."

And just like that, I was gone.

Emotionally. Physically. Spiritually. Gone.

I launched myself at him.

The ring box went flying. Vito barked somewhere in the distance. Carla definitely gasped through her window.

And Max?

He caught me.

Held me.

Kissed me like Rome was burning and I was the only thing he'd save.

"Yes," I whispered against his lips. "Yes. Yes. Yes."

Because holy hell.

I'd finally said it.

And this time, I meant it.

Every syllable. Every breath.

And every dirty Italian word I'd scream into his pillow later.

Craving just *One*. *More*. sinfully steamy, can't-look-away proposal night scene?

Yeah, you do.

Grab your exclusive BONUS CHAPTER right here → https://shorturl.at/Ehtto

Hey. Max here.

I don't usually do this sort of thing. But then again... I didn't plan on Rayann either.

If you made it to the end of our story—and you're still thinking about it—do us a favor and leave Kate Sweden a review.

She's the reason we ended up in the same damn castle. The same suite. The same bed.

And yeah, she'd probably call it some bullshit like "fate" or "story magic."

But I know better.

She made it happen. Every look. Every fight. Every time I nearly lost my mind and kissed her anyway.

So if you laughed, cursed, blushed, or screamed into a pillow—**let her know**. Reviews keep stories like ours alive.

Drop your review here. It matters more than you think.

I'll leave you with this: Kate's not done.
Rayann's sister Brynn is up next.

She's headed to Costa Rica. There's a rival. A pitch battle. And wild animals.

And rumor has it... someone's getting tied to a hammock.
You didn't hear it from me.

Tell Rayann I said hi.

And if she blushes?

She's lying.

Oh my God, Max.

You're seriously ending this with "Tell Rayann I said hi"? What is this—*The Notebook: Tactical Edition*?

Hi. Brynn here.

I'm the twin with better instincts, better legs, and *no patience* for fake emotional depth.

But... I will say this.

If Kate Sweden gave you even one moment of chaos-induced happiness, steamy distraction, or the urge to text your ex—**leave the woman a review**. She thrives on that kind of emotional damage.

You know what to do. Right here.

Also? I'm up next. Costa Rica. Rival. Pitch battle. Possibly a jaguar. And one seriously annoying hot guy that is determined to piss me off.

I'm bringing the sass. He's bringing the heat.

Buckle up.

Afterglow, Extras, and Contacts

Come Kick Off Your Heels in the Lounge

Looking for sassy sneak peeks, steamy reader chaos, and wildly inappropriate group chat energy?

You belong in Kate Sweden's Reader Lounge.

I've got spoilers. I've got smut. I've got memes that will spiritually wound you (in the best way).

Basically, it's book club—but with less wine and more fictional orgasms.

    Come hang out: → https://shorturl.at/qW1Sj.

Wanna Stay in the Wilder Loop?

Spoiler alerts, spicy extras, behind-the-scenes chaos, and the kind of newsletter that'll make your inbox blush?

Sign up for my newsletter here and let the Wilder shenanigans begin" → https://kateswedenromance.com/mailing-list

Craving More Chaos, Spice & Sneak Peeks?

Explore exclusive bonus scenes, upcoming release goodies, and the kind of behind-the-scenes extras that should probably come with a warning label—

Right this way, babe:

www.KateSwedenRomance.com.

Let's Get Social (Yo Know You Wanna)

Come for the chaos. Stay for the thirst traps, TikToks, unhinged reader theories, and late-night overshares.

Follow me here:

Tik Tok – @kateswedenromance

Instagram – @katesweden_author.

Goodreads – Kate_Sweden

Link Tree – https://linktr.ee/kateswedenromance

Your Review = Our Happy Ending

Your reviews? *They have superpowers.*

They help new readers find their next favorite spicy escape—and keep authors like me doing the happy ugly cry in public.

If Max and Rayann wrecked you (in the best way), I'd be wildly grateful if you'd drop a quick, honest review on **Amazon** or **Goodreads**.

You rock. You're hot. I adore you.

Amazon→ https://www.amazon.com/dp/B0F2GRPB-MX

Goodreads → https://shorturl.at/XEfQl

Max & Rayann's Afterparty

Finished the book and still emotionally compromised?
Same.

So I made you things.

Want to *see* Max's bedroom, Rayann's chaos-core aesthetic, or that kilt situation in full visual glory?

There's a whole Pinterest mood board waiting for your un-hinged deep-dive:

Pinterest Mood Board→ https://shorturl.at/q8VcQ

Want to *feel* every stolen glance, every slow burn, and every spicy disaster all over again?

The official Max & Rayann Spotify playlist is basically a rollercoaster of tension, yearning, and sin:

Playlist → https://shorturl.at/6DCWc

Turn it on. Fall apart. Repeat.

Acknowledgements

To my Wild Magnolias team—thank you for championing this book, the very first in the *Wilder Horizons* series, with tireless pep talks, bags of salted milk chocolate caramels (bless you), and a suspiciously bottomless supply of pinot grigio. You believed in this story long before it was wearing pants.

To my son, who sat across from me during homeschool hours, solving for x and y while I was over here trying to solve the romantic calculations between two fictional people—thank you for being blissfully unaware of the completely inappropriate chaos unfolding on my screen. Stay innocent, sweet boy. Forever, if possible.

To my incredible beta readers—you were such an essential part of this journey. Your sharp eyes, big hearts, and endless encouragement made this book shine brighter than I ever could have on my own. I have had so much fun working with you! Carol Lopez, Cassie Springer, Chelsey Kraft, Cheryl

Thigpen, Conceição Cardoso, Daniela Schrenk, Frances Mackay, Gracelyn Footit, Hilary Litzinger, Jessica Aranda, Kelly Montgomery, Skye O'Connell, Vanessa Mata, and Veronika Dopitová. Thank you!

To my ride-or-die street team: thank you for shouting about this book from the rooftops (and TikTok, and Instagram, and probably to random strangers in Target). Your passion, hustle, and hilarious messages kept me going. I couldn't have done this without you.

And to my family. Thank you for your boundless love and support. Always. There are never enough words.

About the author

Kate Sweden is a romance author with a flair for funny, a soft spot for slow burns, and a love of happily ever afters with heat. A former Air Force officer, educator, and lifelong book nerd, she traded briefing rooms and lesson plans for plot twists and first kisses. These days, she lives in Northeast Florida with her husband, their teenage son, and a very opinionated dog named Sailor—plus a pantry that's suspiciously short on chocolate.

Wrecked by You: Book Club & Reader Guide

Drink + Snack Pairings

Buckle up! Make your book club spicy *and* delicious:

- **Champagne & Closet Debrief Cocktails** – A splash of Prosecco, a hint of elderflower liqueur, and a rim you'll want to lick

- **One-Bed Nachos** – Messy. Overloaded. Impossible to share without accidental touching

- **Scottish Highland Mule** – Ginger beer, whisky, lime... best served with a smug man in a kilt

- **Freckled Blondies** – Salted caramel bars with a dusting of cinnamon freckles (a tribute to Rayann's sexiest insecurity)

Tropes Checklist

Check off your favorite romance tropes featured in *Wrecked by You*:

Enemies-to-Lovers

Forced Proximity

Opposites Attract

Grumpy/Sunshine

Office Romance

Broody Hot Guy

Competition

Secret Past

Miscommunication

Comical Sidekick

Family Dynamics

Spice Scale: How Hot Are We Talking?

Total Heat Rating: out of 5
(Your Kindle might need a fire extinguisher.)

Scene Breakdown:

- **Chapter 17** – *The Only Easy Day Was Yesterday*
Location: Bedroom. Vibe: Tender, hungry, wreck-me-now energy. Max. Goes. Down.

- **Chapter 20** – *The Evening Briefing*
Location: Linen closet. Vibe: Fast, filthy, hands-over-mouth steam with an aftershock kiss.

- **Chapter 23** – *Climbing the Tree*
Location: Cottage fireplace. Vibe: Slow-burn turned inferno. Her freckles don't stand a chance.

- **Chapter 26** – *Synched. It's Fine. I'm Fine.*
Location: Beach. Vibe: Wild, salty, full-body worship. Max gets feral.

- **Chapter 35 (Epilogue)** – *Benvenuto a Roma*
Location: Rome. Vibe: When Max drops the box, Rome itself holds its breath.

Book Club Discussion Questions

Pour the wine. Grab the dark chocolate. Let's talk.
Bonus points if you share in our Link Reader's Group: Kate Sweden's Reader Lounge (yes, please!)

1. Rayann hides behind humor. Max hides behind control. How do they chip away at each other's defenses?

2. Whose emotional journey changed the most by the end of the book—Rayann or Max?

3. Rayann has a lot of internal spirals and "what-if" moments. Did any of her thoughts hit close to home for you?

4. If you had to describe Rayann in three words, what would they be? What about Max? What would *they* say about each other?

5. How does Rayann's relationship with her sisters shape her decisions, especially with Max?

6. Did Rayann and Max's dynamic ever remind you of a past relationship—either in the best way or a "yeah, we needed therapy" kind of way?

7. Did you catch the moment Max *chose* Rayann emotionally before she caught up? What tipped you off?

8. What moment made you want to *shove them together* already?

9. What scene made you laugh-snort the hardest?

10. What advice would you give Rayann before her dinner date with Max in Rome? And what would you *warn* Max about?

11. Let's talk favorite tropes: Which one in this story hit the hardest for you? Why do you think those tropes work so well together here?

12. What's one line or moment you had to reread because it was too spicy, too funny, or too swoony to move on from immediately?

13. If *Wrecked by You* was a movie, who would you cast as Max and Rayann?

14. If this book had a Spotify playlist, what song would you put on repeat during the cottage fireplace scene? Or the beach scene? Or that *proposal*?

15. What do you want to see next from the Wilder sisters?

Author's Note from Kate Sweden

This story was inspired by one too many *what-if* conversations, a lingering crush on alpha men, and the delicious idea of what might happen if a control freak fell for a walking disaster with a heart of gold. (Also: my husband *really* didn't expect to be quizzed on vibrator logistics over dinner. Sorry, babe.)

Max and Rayann are fictional.
But the need to feel loved just as you are? That part's very real.
Thanks for reading. Thanks for swooning.
And if someone makes you feel seen, safe, and maybe just a little wrecked... hold on tight.
That's where the magic begins.

KATE SWEDEN

A Rivals to Lovers
Romantic Comedy

Wilder Horizons Series

Preview of Challenged By You (Wilder Horizons, Book 2) - Brynn's Story

glass had eyes, it would've looked concerned. Possibly judgy. Maybe even preparing to stage an intervention.

I took another sip—salt rim, top shelf, exactly the way I liked it—and narrowed my gaze at the glowing laptop screen in front of me.

The screen's light caught my hazel eyes, probably amplifying the unholy rage behind them. My dark brown hair was twisted into a topknot, and my sun-kissed skin—freckles thriving despite my twin's campaign for daily SPF—was already plotting revenge.

There he was.

Jerrick Thorne.

Chief Marketing Officer of Adventura Luxe, based in Austin, Texas, where stress is a flex and people pay ninety bucks for bottled air.

And the smug bastard had done it again.

Unveiling the Future of Elite Travel: Elevation. Curation. Obsession.

I slammed my laptop shut. The pen cup rattled. The margarita sloshed. Wilder Horizons wasn't a travel agency. We curated chaos for billionaires—honeymoons, retreats, events. My scoreboard wasn't bookings—it was repeat contracts and referral deals. Which meant this panel wasn't just PR. It was currency.

"You've got to be fucking kidding me," I muttered, sinking into my chair, the picture of a villain who'd upgraded to Manolo Blahniks. "Obsession? That was my line, you tan, expensive-looking thief."

Across the room, Bali, my long-limbed tabby with an attitude problem, lifted her head, blinked, yawned—her version of flipping me off—and resumed her coma.

I flipped my laptop back open. The press release was still there—cocky little shit.

That pitch? I tested it on Daisy—our chaos-qualified intern—at last month's strategy roundtable. She squinted, chewed her pen cap, and called it "expensive cult energy." I told her that was the point.

As Chief Marketing Officer of Wilder Horizons, the luxury adventure travel company I run with my five sisters, I don't sell high-end vacations. I sell escape. Fantasy. Bucket-list dreams, gift-wrapped in glitter and just enough danger to keep your therapist employed.

Cue the Oscar-worthy sigh.

Right as I launched into a very professional, extremely justified rant—to Bali, obviously— Rayann's face lit up my screen, mid-eye roll, already judging.

"Babe. You spiraling again?"

Rayann. My mirror image. The slightly less unhinged one. She knows every thought I have before I've even cursed it into existence.

"Define spiraling."

Rayann snorted. "You're drinking at your desk. Alone. Murder-vibe playlist. Skulls and crossbones all over your pitch notes. That's a yes."

"I'm not spiraling. I'm spiraling *strategically*. There's a difference."

"Right. Please don't set anything on fire. Again."

"That one time was a *birthday candle malfunction*."

Rayann laughed, equal parts comfort and chaos, the human version of my favorite dirty latte.

"So what'd he do this time?"

"He hijacked my launch language. The 'obsession' angle we ran in last quarter's Mirage package? He dropped a campaign teaser that reads as if my PowerPoint presentation had a baby with his jawline."

There was a pause. "Okay, gross, but also impressive."

"I hate him," I growled. "We're talking tropical parasites and papaya-in-a-salad level hate. I hope a howler monkey pegs him with a rotten mango mid-press conference."

Rayann cackled. "You've been working too hard. When's the conference?"

"Next week. Osa Peninsula, Costa Rica." I jabbed at the screen, unapologetically hostile. "And guess who they announced as my co-host?"

I swiveled toward the giant whiteboard on the far wall of my Maris Key condo, the Florida sunlight still blazing like a spotlight through my floor-to-ceiling windows. My condo was the ultimate paradox: sleek white walls and minimalist furniture paired with shelves crammed with tropical trinkets and gold pineapple sculptures that collect dust I pretend not to see, color-coded binders, and no fewer than four aggressively scented candles. I think of it as "Tropical CEO Chic." As though I led a silent retreat for Type-A control freaks who flowchart their inner peace.

I was curled up barefoot in my lemon-yellow silk pajama set—a tank top and matching shorts I justified as office attire because from the Zoom frame up, I looked like I might invoice you for something expensive.

The laptop blinked back to life. Right there, beneath the words **Luxury Travel in the Social Age**—our names. Together. **Wilder & Thorne**. Wild ambition. Thorny history. What could possibly go wrong?

"He's not just attending," I said. "He's co-presenting. With me."

Rayann let out a low whistle. "Want me to come? I can pack a taser and an emotional support bottle of tequila."

"Tempting, but no. I've got this."

Because I did. I always do.

Some days I was two clicks from madness—but I'd still set the whole game aflame before anyone clocked the fractures.

I wasn't just the *spirited* Wilder twin. I was the deal closer. The mind behind every viral campaign Wilder Horizons had launched in the last three years. I played dirty with guerrilla charm, and I sealed deals in heels that could double as weapons.

Thorne might've stolen a few words—but I had ideas. Big ones.

And maybe—maybe—a prank or two up my sleeve.

I grabbed my Santorini pen—dark green, gold logo, stolen with flair from a cliffside resort that charged extra for sunshine, and faced the blank whiteboard.

"Oh, Jerrick Thorne, you son of a bitch," I whispered, lips curving into a smile that would've terrified my therapist. "You made this personal."

By midmorning, I'd traded my silk pajamas for wide-leg white linen pants (still warm from the dryer), a silky halter top, and enough dry shampoo to constitute a federal offense.

The Wilder Horizons office shimmered as always—perched on the sun-drenched Gulf Coast of Maris Key, Florida. Coastal views. Glass everything. And enough tropical greenery to suggest our CFO might secretly be a houseplant.

The scent of lemongrass diffusers, high-achieving humidity, and sister-induced anxiety hit me the second I stepped inside.

"Brynn," my sister, Emme, called, catching me outside the break room with a folder in one hand and a green smoothie that resembled something you'd cleanse a colon with in the other.

She was all crisp lines and early morning efficiency, with her black hair slicked into a no-nonsense ponytail and her phone already buzzing. *Vendor Relations Barbie*, if Barbie carried a stun gun for delayed shipments.

"Don't touch the frogs in Costa Rica," she said.

I blinked. "That's... oddly specific."

"They look cute. They are not. They're wet demons in disguise."

"Noted," I said. "Have a magical day, sunshine."

"Don't get arrested," she called over her shoulder.

"I said magical, not criminal."

Summer's door was already open. Of course it was.

I stepped in and found her seated behind her desk, posture straight, laptop open, a single pen aligned with military precision on her legal pad. Her blazer was beige. Her soul—laminated.

"You're late," she said without looking up.

"I'm exactly four minutes early."

"Exactly four minutes behind *me*."

God, I loved her.

"Relax," I said, sliding into the chair across from her. "I'm not going to light anything on fire before the Costa Rica trip. Probably."

She looked up. Summer Wilder, our oldest sister, Chief Operating Officer and wielder of the sacred highlighter system, had the kind of stare that could freeze a volcano mid-eruption.

"This isn't a vacation," she said. "The conference is a high-stakes PR opportunity. We'll be in front of our competitors, clients, and possibly international royalty. Please don't embarrass us."

I smiled. "I never embarrass us. I make us memorable."

"You are a one-woman crisis management department, Brynn."

"Flattering."

She clicked something on her screen with extra aggression. "I need your deck finalized by tomorrow. You'll be co-presenting with Jerrick Thorne. And before you ask, yes—I approved it. He's already confirmed."

"Oh, I know," I said sweetly. "We've been emailing."

"Brynn..."

"Strategically spiraling," I said, holding up a finger. "Not emotionally combusting."

Summer closed her laptop like she was resisting the urge to throw it at me. "Remember, you're representing the brand. Not one of your Instagram reels gone rogue."

I stood, already halfway out the door. "What if I represent both?"

She didn't answer. She was already typing.

The air shifted the second I crossed into our end of the hall—Rayann's office directly ahead, mine tucked to the left, and Summer's command center looming diagonally behind me like a boardroom Bat-Signal, ready to summon doom. Focused. The kind of energy that said someone was about to lose it—and odds were good it'd be me.

Daisy, stationed at the floating desk just outside our offices, popped up like a meerkat who'd sensed a disturbance in the Force. I gave her a breezy wave and kept moving.

Straight into my office.

Glass door.

Controlled slam.

Instant relief.

I dropped into my chair, flicked open my laptop, and clicked on the blinking icon of doom: Email (17 Unread).

Jerrick fucking Thorne.

There he was again—smug, sharp, and lurking beneath a subject line that practically smirked: **"Panel Content Framework – Updated Flow Suggestions"**

I opened it. Read. Stared. Rage stretched, cracked its knuckles, rolled its neck.

FROM: Jerrick Thorne

SUBJECT: Panel Content Framework – Updated Flow Suggestions

Brynn,

Attached is my proposed structure for our segment next week. It aligns with the original event goals but streamlines the talking points for clarity and cohesion. Happy to discuss adjustments if needed.

– JT

I massaged my neck. Picked a pen. Clicked it twice, purely for effect.

Then I replied:

FROM: Brynn Wilder

SUBJECT: Re: Panel Content Framework – Updated Flow Suggestions

Hi Jerrick,

Thanks for the reminder about structure. Your version is … admirably safe. I'll be revising on my end to add back some of the actual excitement people came for.

Warmly,

Brynn

He replied three minutes later—three.

FROM: Jerrick Thorne

SUBJECT: RE: Re: Panel Content Framework – Updated Flow Suggestions

Brynn,

Noted. Let me know when to duck and when to smile. Shall we keep the word *obsession* off the table?

–JT

I stared at his bullshit PowerPoint foreplay. Bali's judgmental spirit echoed in my mind. I flexed my fingers, took a steadying sip of cold coffee, and fired back:

FROM: Brynn Wilder

SUBJECT: Re: Re: Re: Panel Content Framework – Updated Flow Suggestions

Only if you promise to keep your ego in a carry-on. Excited to collaborate.

Truly.

BW

When I hit send, my lips curled as if I was about to sell him a dream and shove him off a cliff.

Wilder Horizons wasn't just a travel company—it was our father's masterpiece. He built it from nothing but charm, grit, and a refusal to settle for ordinary. When he died, the six of us stood in his office staring at the contracts and the chaos, and we had two choices: take it on together or walk away. Nothing halfway. We chose together. Our name. Our lifeline. Dad's legacy to protect—or torch.

As Chief Marketing Officer, my job was to make sure the world still believed in Wilder magic. That meant dazzling new clients, locking down the ones who already loved us, and making damn sure no rival agency stole what was ours. This Costa Rica conference wasn't just a networking event—it was open season. Competitors like Adventura Luxe—and every other high-end agency—would be circling, hungry for any slip. If we lost ground here, it wouldn't just bruise my pride. It would tarnish Dad's legacy.

Which meant babysitting Jerrick Thorne wasn't just a punishment—it was a test. And if he thought I'd roll over while he flexed his spreadsheets, he'd seriously underestimated how feral I could play.

Rayann and I were twins, but somehow she'd become "the strategist" while I was branded "the sparkler"—the one guaranteed to light things up and maybe set the curtains on fire in the process. People remembered my chaos, my jokes, the bad-timing pranks...not the planning that went into them. Sitting in my office, staring at the Costa Rica briefing packet, I couldn't shake the worry that I was more mascot than mastermind. The Wilder twin you invite to the party—then hire someone else to clean up after.

My pen tapped an uneven rhythm against the desk, undecided between building a strategy and starting a fire.

Across the glass, Daisy clocked the look and immediately busied herself with her keyboard.

Smart girl.

Hey loves —

Think that first chapter was fun? Oh honey, that was foreplay. Grab your margarita, pack your sunscreen, and dive in ***Challenged By You***—where rivals get reckless, rules go missing, and the jungle turns up the heat.

Grab your copy here!

XO Kate